I08192̸32

ALSO BY RAY NAYLER

Where the Axe Is Buried

The Tusks of Extinction

The Mountain in the Sea

PALACES OF THE CROW

PALACES OF THE CROW

A NOVEL

RAY NAYLER

MCD  FARRAR, STRAUS AND GIROUX NEW YORK

MCD
Farrar, Straus and Giroux
120 Broadway, New York 10271

EU Representative: Macmillan Publishers Ireland Ltd, 1st Floor, The Liffey Trust Centre, 117–126 Sheriff Street Upper, Dublin 1, D01 YC43

Copyright © 2026 by Ray Nayler
All rights reserved
Printed in the United States of America
First edition, 2026

Tree art on case cover by YIK2007 / Shutterstock.com; photograph of bird silhouettes on case cover, title-page spread, and verso of part openers by JakubD / Shutterstock.com; Part One opener photograph by Tom McPherson / Shutterstock .com; Part Two opener photograph by DeepSkyMotion / Shutterstock.com; Part Three opener photograph by Sokolov Alexey / Shutterstock.com; Part Four opener photograph by Roland IJdema / Shutterstock.com.

Library of Congress Control Number: 2026004696
ISBN: 978-0-374-62075-2

Designed by Abby Kagan

The publisher of this book does not authorize the use or reproduction of any part of this book in any manner for the purpose of training artificial intelligence technologies or systems. The publisher of this book expressly reserves this book from the Text and Data Mining exception in accordance with Article 4(3) of the European Union Digital Single Market Directive 2019/790.

Our books may be purchased in bulk for specialty retail/wholesale, literacy, corporate/premium, educational, and subscription box use. Please contact MacmillanSpecialMarkets@macmillan.com.

www.mcdbooks.com • www.fsgbooks.com
Follow us on social media at @mcdbooks and @fsgbooks

10 9 8 7 6 5 4 3 2 1

This is a work of fiction. All of the names, characters, organizations, places, and events portrayed in this work are either products of the author's imagination or used fictitiously.

For Anya and Lydia

Thus, from the war of nature, from famine and death, the most exalted object which we are capable of conceiving, namely, the production of the higher animals, directly follows. There is grandeur in this view of life, with its several powers, having been originally breathed into a few forms or into one; and that, whilst this planet has gone cycling on according to the fixed law of gravity, from so simple a beginning endless forms most beautiful and most wonderful have been, and are being, evolved.

—Charles Darwin, *The Origin of Species*

The war of each against all is not *the* law of nature. Mutual aid is as much a law of nature as mutual struggle.

—Pyotr Kropotkin, *Mutual Aid: A Factor of Evolution*

CONTENTS

ONE

Zoological Philosophy

We become real only at the moment of our ruin. Our shtetl takes form at dusk, as the Cossacks ride into its outskirts.

We become solid as the shutters slam, as our shaking hands extinguish candles and the pogrom begins.

All between is shadow. The silversmith taps at his mold, a sound as spectral as the finger of a séance ghost behind a wall. Grain is bought and sold by spirits. Tinsmiths guide their shears through metal as frail as cobwebs.

From Tu B'Shevat through Yom Kippur and Hanukkah the holidays cycle, year after orbiting, insubstantial year. A dream of home and safety.

We wake to reality and the reek of fire.

—from *The Autobiography of a Burned Village*
(found manuscript, author unknown)

1
NERIYA

June 1941

BUSTER STOOD AT THE OPEN GATE, his head cocked, watching Neriya with a black and glossy eye.

He was waiting for her to follow. He turned and walked several steps, then stopped and looked over his shoulder at her again.

Neriya hesitated.

Buster walked back to the gate and cawed. It was a loud caw, his whole body bent over, his throat and head spiked with ruffled feathers.

"All right, all right." Neriya went to the gate.

Buster began walking along the road that curved away from the shtetl and through the fields.

Neriya glanced back at her quiet house, the dark windows with her parents asleep behind them. The morning dew was still on everything, the wood of the fence and the gate wet with it.

Later, Neriya would remember every detail of that humble, mended gate. The way it sagged on its hinges, dragging in the dirt so that it had to be lifted a bit and set on its old latch. How many times her father had fixed that latch. How he nailed it back into place after it worked loose. How he finally wrapped it with wire in a failed attempt to hold it in place . . .

Neriya's mother loved to say that, for a man so good at fixing people, Neriya's father was terrible at fixing things.

But it was a back gate, her father had always replied. The family gate, leading through the rear yard and into the kitchen. It didn't need to be fancy.

Buster cawed at her again, so loudly he might wake her parents.

"Shh. Okay. I'm coming." Neriya closed the gate carefully behind her.

Buster was a large, handsome hooded crow. When he visited Neriya in her yard he strutted around, looking under the old table and the benches, accepting her gifts of walnuts and other treats. He always hopped up on the table to pace back and forth in front of her, demonstrating what a good-looking bird he was, black wings folded over his pearl-gray back, his black tail swishing from side to side like the coattails of a Vilnius gentleman with arms folded behind him, out for a stroll in his new frock coat.

Neriya had named him Buster in honor of Buster Keaton. During her summers in the shtetl, the movie theaters of Vilnius were what she missed most. But one summer, a traveling movie company had visited. They set up a rattling projector in the shtetl's meeting hall and showed old silent films projected on a sheet, the image juddering as a woman in a leather jacket and beret, a cigarette in her mouth, banged away at the old town piano, an instrument never played for comedy before—at least, not intentionally. They showed *The General*, *Steamboat Bill, Jr.*, *The Navigator*.

Buster Keaton's serious, impenetrable dignity in the face of everything had reminded Neriya immediately of the cleverest of all the crows who visited her. Of the dignity in his swaying little gentleman's walk.

Buster never lost that dignity, even when he played games with her, or solved the little puzzles she built for him. He never got frustrated: he just cocked his head, contemplating, until he understood what to do next.

Now the bird flew twenty meters or so, landed, and looked back at Neriya again.

She, in turn, looked at the shtetl where her family spent their summers. At its crooked roofs wet and glistening in the early morning.

In front of the house that the communists had commandeered from the former village head, the red flag of the Soviet Union hung limp in the still air.

The communists had turned the house into what they called a "library." Her father called it (but only in the privacy of their own kitchen) the "nonsense house."

The village head they had taken the house from was gone. Some said that he had fled into the forest. Others, that he was in prison somewhere in Russia.

Once, Neriya had passed a group of men talking on the corner and heard one of them whisper that he had been shot.

This year, when Neriya's family had arrived in the shtetl, it had been filled with new people. Many people had fled the Bolsheviks. They were replaced by people who, even if they spoke Yiddish, were not the same. People who spoke of collectivization of labor. Who spoke of "kulaks"—mythical rich peasants who gobbled up the resources of shtetl and farm for themselves, leaving nothing for the poor.

The new people hung Stalin's mustached face everywhere, like an Orthodox icon and just as unwelcome.

They claimed they were bringing liberation, but Neriya's father crossed the street when he saw them coming.

"If you think you can trust the Russians," he said, brooding over his tea one evening with her mother in the kitchen, "just ask anyone who had to live under them. My father knew the Russians. He was educated in Moscow. Nobody spoke Russian better than him. But he joined the Lithuanians and Germans to help push them out after the Great War. Anything to save us from returning to Russian rule. And now they walk in and take over, just like that. Call them communists or Bolsheviks or Soviets or anything you like. They are Russians, and we have known them for a long time."

But now, just one summer after they had come, the Bolsheviks were on the run. Now it was the Germans who were coming. They were already across the border. In a few weeks, at most, they would be here. There were worries about that too.

Here and there in the shtetl, a chimney released a vertical streak of soot, dividing the endless sky. Later Neriya would remember that as well: The still threads of smoke that rose into the air. Breakfast being cooked. Bread being baked. The quiet, almost invisible life of early morning.

With all its worries, old and new, the town still felt whole. Her father had his practice, in the room that had once been the family parlor, its walls painted white, the inherited china cupboard repurposed as a medical cabinet.

In the evenings, while Neriya listened and pretended to read, her father and mother talked through medical cases, drifting between Yiddish and the Königsberg-inflected German Neriya's mother had grown up speaking. Her father's German was halting, dotted with Yiddishisms. He had learned it as a quota student at the medical school in Warsaw—German was the only way, he said, to read the best medical texts.

These evening discussions of goiters, abscesses, fractures, arrhythmias, and sepsis were, besides Neriya's time with her crows in the morning, some of her only entertainment here.

In the summer, Neriya missed Vilnius. She missed the cold stone city, heavy with age, full of wonders. She missed the movie theaters with the newest films. She missed huddling down in that velvet dark.

She even missed school, and the meager warmth of the classroom's coal stove.

But leaving for the village in the early summer, she was excited to see her crows. She was excited for the walks in the fields, and grateful to finally be out of the oppressive classroom and away from uniforms, starch, chalk, the rest of it.

In the city, she longed for the shtetl, and in the shtetl, she was homesick for Vilnius.

"Always where she is not," her mother would say.

"Like a young woman I once knew," her father would reply.

Buster cawed again, so loudly she was afraid everyone in the shtetl would wake up.

"Okay, okay. I'm coming."

She quickened her step.

After the war, some returned home to the shtetlach to make revolution. To destroy the old world and clear a way for the new.

I came here searching for the past. For Judith's chestnut-colored eyes. For my *bubbeh* and *zaydeh*, if they could take me in and cook me a meal that healed me.

But Judith died of a fever—the same fever that took my bubbeh away. And my zaydeh no longer knew me.

—from *The Autobiography of a Burned Village*

2
CZESŁAW

June 1941

THE MAN WRITHED ON THE GROUND. His pistol was in the grass. His hands were smeared with his own blood, and blood was spattered across his pallid face. He clawed at his chest, searching for the hole Czesław had put in him.

"What have you done?" Andrei screamed at Czesław.

"He was going to kill us!" Czesław screamed back.

Andrei was the only other person in Czesław's unit who was still alive.

The rest were dead. Or scattered.

Maybe all of them were dead.

There was another man with them. Kolya, a *tankíst* from another unit.

Kolya was deaf. Dried blood streaked down from his ears to his collar. Andrei and Czesław had found him lying in a ditch, unarmed, clutching at his charred cloth helmet, rocking back and forth and screaming.

They had dragged Kolya with them as they fled. They had asked him several times what formation he was with, but all he could do was point at himself and yell, "Kolya!"

"He was going to kill us," Czesław repeated.

They had been running when this man, this Bolshevik *politruk* whose own unit must have been destroyed, burst out from behind a smashed staff car, waving the pistol and screaming, "No retreat! We have orders! We will hold this position to the last man!"

"Our unit is *gone*!" Czesław had screamed back at him. "Our unit is *gone*, and we are surrounded! We need to break out of this pocket, any of us who are still alive, and find the new front line. We need to regroup!"

"You are trying to surrender to the enemy!"

"The Germans are killing men who surrender! We are trying to break out of encirclement! We need to form a new line of defense!"

"We have orders! We will hold this position to the last man!" the politruk screamed, in exactly the same tone as before.

He has a recording inside him. If you opened his head you would see it, the tape going from one reel to the other.

Dead men were scattered all around the smashed staff car the politruk had been hiding behind. The parts of dead men. A headless torso in its finest parade uniform lay in the middle of the road.

Something had come loose in the politruk's mind. And

Czesław knew how dangerous these Bolshevik enforcers were. How many men they had shot in Finland when they were trying to retreat, regroup.

He tried to speak calmly to the politruk. "Comrade, the men who gave those orders are all dead or captured. The ones who are captured are probably dead as well. We saw the Germans shooting a line of prisoners just up the road."

"I saw this as well," said Andrei to the politruk.

That was when the politruk swung his pistol toward Andrei.

And that was when Czesław shot the man.

Now the politruk lay on the ground, tearing at his uniform to find the hole in his chest, bright blood pouring from his mouth in the morning light.

"He was going to kill *you*!" Czesław said to Andrei.

"He was just frightened! What you've done is treason!"

"He was going to kill *you*!" Czesław repeated. "I saved your life!"

Andrei began to turn toward Czesław, raising his rifle.

Kolya dropped to his knees on the ground, scrambling for the politruk's pistol.

Czesław ran. He ran for a line of trees, expecting at any moment the bullet's impact in his back, knocking him flat before he even heard it, laying his body out in the summer grass.

He ran with all he could muster, the rifle in his hands, his pack clanking, the shuddering line of trees growing closer.

He imagined the bullet hitting him. He imagined himself falling and lying there. Turning over with his face to the sun and lying there, and thinking, *At least I am intact.* A whole body. Not the *thing* so many of the others became. The shapeless, torn *gore*—the ripped and burned bodies of his unit, the pieces of them scattered in the grass, flung across the road, shapeless muck flopped over the lip of a ditch, meat with burning uniform lodged in it, smeared like a bloody rag across the door of an armored car.

He saw himself dying, but whole. His face intact, his limbs whole, dying in the sunshine. There was a triumph in that. In dying whole, at least.

Then he was in the trees. He skidded on leaves, fell to his knees.

He expected, when he turned, to see Kolya and Andrei still standing there, their guns aimed at him.

But their backs were to him. Their hands were over their heads.

Several German soldiers in *feldgrau* stood in a loose half circle around them.

One of the soldiers pointed a rifle at the politruk on the ground.

When Andrei raised a hand to stop him, the Germans shot Andrei. Then Kolya. Then the politruk.

When my parents left here and took me to the city, I was little more than a child. The shtetl seemed complete to me, tightly binding me within its reality.

It bound all of us then.

—from *The Autobiography of a Burned Village*

3
NERIYA

June 1941

LATER SHE WOULD REMEMBER this exact moment. The forest beyond the town—the verge of trees so dark in the early morning it looked black. Turning and seeing, for the last time, the streaks the shtetl chimneys sketched on the sky. And that alien flag of scarlet hanging from the shuttered synagogue.

Looking at her family home with its carved and painted gables and windows, their house the farthest from the center, out where the edge of the inhabited world gave way to a ring of fields and then to the forest.

The roofs of the shtetl stacked in layers. The jutting, ornate brick chimney of the *beit midrash* at the center of it all, the whitewashed bell tower of the church where the goyim came to worship on Sundays.

Buster hopped back toward Neriya, looked up at her, cawed again, and flew a little farther up the road.

"And where are we going?"

At the edge of the forest, he settled on a low branch.

"In there?"

But then, why not? She had been to the forest for mushrooms and berries with her parents often. Not too deep in, but she knew the first half kilometer or so well enough.

Her parents would be unhappy about her going into the forest alone. If they found out. But they would never find out. It would be hours before they were up. It was Shabbat, and they had no patients.

Though her parents were not very observant, they kept the Sabbath as a day of rest. "One of God's better ideas," as her father put it. On the Sabbath, they only saw patients in emergencies.

The road skirted the trees, undulating past farther fields. A footpath branched off and led between the columns of the forest trunks.

The path here was wide, worn deep by woodcutters and foragers. It was cooler here, under the trees. Neriya wore her father's quilted coat. The sleeves were rolled up and pinned, showing the purple lining her mother had sewn into the coat to make it warmer. Lately, the days were already hot. But the mornings were still cool, so she wore the coat during her "crow time" in the yard, early in the morning when the rest of the family slept. She was glad to be wearing it now. She tied the belt of the coat and buttoned it up to the collar.

Buster flew farther in. He stood on a stone where Neriya had once rested with her father and mother after gathering berries, and called to her.

She heard, deeper in the forest, other crows calling.

Answering Buster? The sound was faint. The forest was filled with the sounds of birds beginning their day of mating, foraging, nest repairs, territorial battles, caring for their young.

"Do you want to show me where you live, Buster? Since you've come to visit me so many times? What is crow hospitality like? Do you have tea and cookies?"

Buster flew still farther in.

For half an hour or more she followed him. The path forked several times, shrinking each time until it was nothing more than a narrow track lost in fallen needles.

It was damp here, and dark, and cold.

She began to feel afraid.

It had been fine at first, following Buster. He was a friend, after all.

Was that the right word for it? *Friend?*

It seemed right. He had begun visiting her when she was only seven years old. She trusted him.

And she trusted the other crows who came to her in the yard. Some would perch on the padded sleeves of her quilted jacket, their dangerous beaks close enough to her face to put out an eye if they had ever wanted to.

She had never feared them. Why would she? They came to her of their own accord. They had come since she was small. Since they had seemed huge, the size of storks. They *chose* to spend time with her.

She trusted all of them, but she trusted Buster most of all.

Buster had come to her first, gobbling up a pile of shelled walnuts she had set out on the old table in the yard, then cawing and flying back into the forest.

That had gone on for most of the summer—she put the nuts out for Buster, and he took them. She watched him eat. Sometimes he stopped and watched her watching. Then he began to bring other crows along.

She had named each of them in turn. She had quickly learned to tell them apart, noting small differences in their plumage, the skin of their legs and feet, the shape of their beaks, their size and behavior. Until they were as easy to tell apart as people were. Or easier.

One day she came out to the yard and found a medal on the table. An old thing, smeared with dirt.

When she brought it to her father, he told her it was an Order of Saint Anna medal, 4th Class. A relic from the World War.

"It must be Buster who brought it. He must have stolen it," Neriya said. "But whose can it be?"

"I do not think," her father had answered, "that whoever once wore it needs it anymore."

Neriya had stopped reading children's books early. Instead, she began taking books from the small library of biology and medical texts her father kept in his study in Vilnius. Some were in Russian, and many were in German.

Her Polish and even her Russian were better than her German—she got more practice in them—but she had been tutored in German twice a week since she was five. At seven she read Darwin's *Über die Entstehung der Arten—On the Origin of Species*, in its German translation by Bronn.

Much of that book had been over her head. There were so

many unknown words and concepts. What she got out of it was little more than a sense of the vastness of life, a love for the study of animals.

But she memorized a passage from it so she could carry the words with her everywhere:

> *Thus, from the war of nature, from famine and death, the most exalted object which we are capable of conceiving, namely, the production of the higher animals, directly follows. There is grandeur in this view of life, with its several powers, having been originally breathed into a few forms or into one; and that, whilst this planet has gone cycling on according to the fixed law of gravity, from so simple a beginning endless forms most beautiful and most wonderful have been, and are being, evolved.*

She had carried that memorized passage with her for years, like a song from the Torah or a passage of Goethe assigned by her German tutor. She had stumbled over the difficult words until she mastered them.

Endless forms most beautiful . . .

She snatched up new additions to her father's library and read them before he did.

Her father accepted this with a smile. Over breakfast, she would summarize what she had read so far of the latest book she had pilfered from his library. He would listen, sipping his tea and pausing her stream of new knowledge once in a while to ask a clarifying question or to compare the book to something else he or they had read.

She read Kropotkin's Взаимная помощь как фактор

эволюции—*Mutual Aid: A Factor of Evolution*—and it briefly turned her into an anarchist as well as a naturalist.

Her father accepted her political conversion with a smile.

Her mother took part in these discussions as well, when she felt like it.

Her mother had wanted to be a scientist, even a doctor herself. But when her own father died, her family moved to Warsaw to live with distant cousins. Neriya's grandmother worked as a clerk in a grocery store the cousins owned, in exchange for room and board. And Neriya's mother eventually took a clerical job at the university. That was where Neriya's parents had met.

This summer, Neriya was reading the recent Russian translation of *Umwelt und Innenwelt der Tiere* (The environment and inner world of animals), by Jakob von Uexküll, from her father's library.

The slender book was now in the right patch pocket of the quilted coat. She had been intending to read it after her time with Buster. Often, after her crows flew away to go about their day, she sat and read at the table in the yard until she heard the clatter of dishes in the kitchen—the sound of coffee being prepared by her father.

When her father first saw her reading *Umwelt und Innenwelt der Tiere*, he said, "Ah yes, I bought that one on a recommendation from a friend, who knows the Russian translator. It is a private printing. A good translator. It will be excellent for your Russian vocabulary, I think. And it contains many fascinating ideas. The author is another German antisemite, and a Nazi. But his ideas are useful. Take the ideas, and throw the man away. These fools always forget that when they write books their ideas become available to everyone—even to the people they hate, and who may one day use those ideas against them."

The medal of the Order of Saint Anna had been only the beginning of the crows' gifts. Buster and the other crows brought Neriya many other things. They brought her coins, buckles, thread, hairpins, a silk flower she suspected might have been torn from a woman's hat, a bit of lace . . .

She showed some of the gifts to her parents, who were amused (though her mother was a bit appalled by the clearly stolen silk flower). Neriya kept the gifts in a birchwood box in her room in the shtetl.

She took the box with her to Vilnius in the fall. When the winter lay on the city, its pallid white light barely penetrating the fogged glass of her bedroom window, she would open the box. And the crows would be there with her again, bringing the shtetl summer with them.

At nine years old, she began constructing her games for the crows.

Her first games were clumsy. Buster and the others ignored them, cawing at her impatiently until she agreed to hand over their nuts and treats.

The first game that caught Buster's interest was a game in which he could put rocks into a narrow jar until the water level grew high enough to float a walnut within reach of his beak.

At first Buster had played the game without flourishes. Then he began to do a little side-to-side hop before inserting every rock, as if showing off to her.

He didn't simply want to play—he wanted to *perform*. He

wanted her to see what a *smart* crow he was. If she looked away while he was playing, he would immediately stop what he was doing and caw loudly at her until she centered her attention on him again.

Just as he was doing now, from a branch deeper in the forest.

There is no one here but outsiders. There are no more Jews: all go under other names now. Bundists, Bolsheviks, Zionists, territorialists, folkists, Mensheviks, anarchists . . .

We wander among them. We who once were Jews but now are nothing at all. We broken men, back from war, our heads full of slaughter, carrying our stolen rifles, viewing the world through cracked eyeglasses.

—from *The Autobiography of a Burned Village*

4
CZESŁAW

June 1941

CZESŁAW CREPT DEEPER into the trees.

He forced himself not to run.

Had the Germans seen him running away? It was impossible to know.

If they had seen him, would they follow him into the woods?

The Germans had smashed through the Red Army all along the border. They were in territory they did not know.

It was one thing to move through open country, sweeping up the remnants of defeated battalions. It was quite another thing to enter the forest. To hunt for men who might see you long before you saw them. Men who could lie in wait for you.

The Germans would be afraid of the forest.

But Czesław was not afraid of the forest.

He found the moss growing on the north side of the trees. Taking his bearings, he moved east, deeper in.

He breathed in the smell of the place, so similar to the smell of the forest in Siberia. The forest where for his whole short life he had tracked, trapped, and hunted with his father and his grandfather was far away—thousands of miles away—but all forests were related.

His father and grandfather. People had said of them that Czesław, his father, and his grandfather looked like the same man at three different times in his life, all present at the same time, together. Long boned and big through the shoulders, with wide-set eyes. The impression of them all being the same person was increased by the fact that Czesław looked years older than he was, and his grandfather and father both looked younger than they were. They were a man in a rush to reach adulthood but reluctant to grow old. Three times in a man's life, somehow hunting together, bent over bowls of soup together, talking together.

People joked to his mother: "What was your part in this? The boy is not *like* his father—he *is* his father."

"They ran out of molds for Poles," his mother would say. "They had to start using the same ones over and over again."

The Bolshevik authorities had not come for Czesław's father and grandfather at night, the way they had come for some of the others. It was not that stereotype of a Black Maria idling outside the house.

And anyway, out in their part of the forest, deep in the taiga where Czesław's family had been sent into exile, there were no houses. There were only rough barracks, where families lived together among lines of washing and the sounds of crying children through the thin partitions.

They came for Czesław's father and grandfather in broad daylight, at the logging camp.

The men who came were not even wearing uniforms. They were just two friendly looking young men in canvas coveralls, flat caps. Men who smoked the same cheap Belomorkanal cigarettes everyone else at the logging camp smoked.

When Czesław came from school, having run home all the way, he heard one of his mother's friends comforting her. "Who knows why, Marta? These days, it could be for anything at all."

"It is because we are Polish," his mother said in her accented Russian. "We have done everything they asked of us, but we cannot erase who we are. And now who we are is a crime, again."

"You will see your husband soon," the woman said to his mother. "And his father too."

But Czesław heard the hollowness in her voice. He would never see his father or grandfather again.

That evening, Czesław took his birth certificate from the drawer where his mother kept it. He altered the year as best he could. He turned himself from a fourteen-year-old boy into an eighteen-year-old man with a clumsy smear of eraser and a blundering application of ink.

At the recruiting office, they barely glanced at his documents. What they saw in front of them was the tallest man in the logging camp. A young man who knew already how to handle a gun.

Exactly what was needed. And their quotas weren't going to fill themselves.

What he sent home from his pay wasn't enough, he was sure. But it was something, and his mother was thankful for it. And thankful that, for now at least, Czesław was safe. His own Russian was perfectly fluent—better than his Polish, which he only spoke in the kitchen with his parents.

The other men in his unit Russified his name, calling him "Slava." In the Red Army, he became one of them. The same as everyone else.

He fought with them in Finland. And now he was fighting here.

For days, they had fallen back ahead of the German onslaught. Every time they retreated there were fewer and fewer of them left. The retreats became more and more chaotic. Their commanders were dead. They fled carrying what they could, leaving behind their smashed tanks, their bombed-out or disabled trucks.

Soon, they abandoned equipment that was still whole. Trucks bogged down on the roads. Artillery pieces that could not be moved fast enough. Also abandoned were the bodies of their men, unburied.

By yesterday, there was no front line anymore. There was nothing more than the remnants of shattered Red Army units, straggling in from all sides. Many men no longer carried rifles, or any weapons at all. Nearly everyone was wounded.

It was like when they fought the Finns, but worse. Everything happened at a terrible speed. Death came from everywhere. The Germans were a few small shapes on the horizon, a massing of armor climbing over a hill. Never close enough to fight. There was just the glint of sunlight on a scope or on field glasses. Then came the scream of a shell or the crack of rifles, and more of the Red Army torn to pieces.

There was nothing to fight against. The rifles that Czesław

and a few others had managed to preserve were useless against an enemy they could barely see before it destroyed them. All they could do was run, hide, and die.

Czesław had stopped thinking of survival days ago. He had stopped being able to imagine it. Now all he was able to imagine was making a good corpse. Being whole when he died. Not some bloody rag. Not some shapeless thing dripping gore from where it hung in the splintered branches of a tree. Not some *it*.

Survival was impossible, so let him simply *die*, and not be humiliated by death—let him not be reduced by death to something monstrous, like so many of his friends had been.

He stopped moving and listened to the forest. He was deep inside it now.

He had been walking for nearly an hour. Overhead, the canopy had grown thicker. It was dark and cool here, fragrant with summer herbs in the undergrowth. There was none of the dust and heat of the open spaces.

Birds called—some alien to him, others he recognized. Above it all was the racket of crows, close to him and farther away.

He heard a crashing in a thicket. The deer was not visible to him, but he knew it by its sound.

At a small stream, he washed his hands and face, then sat down to eat crackers and a can of *tushonka*, stewed meat.

He had no shortage of food. Czesław and the others had been practical—always stripping the dead they came across of the food in their packs. Czesław's pack was full of cans of condensed milk, crackers, tushonka.

When a large crow landed near him, tilted its head, and cawed, Czesław tossed it half a cracker.

"They aren't very good," he said to the bird as it picked the cracker up in its beak. "But they'll keep you alive. Here . . ." He dug into his pack and came out with a loaf of bread, salvaged from the burning remnants of a mobile bakery yesterday. "Have a piece of this. It's better." He tore a chunk off and tossed it to the crow.

The bird dropped the cracker and edged toward the more appetizing bread cautiously. It was just over an arm's length from Czesław. It looked at him with one eye, and then the other.

A bold one. Or tame?

It snatched the bread up in its beak and flew away.

Czesław walked farther into the forest.

Now that he was alone, with the sturdy Mosin-Nagant rifle and several days of food, with the ability to hunt for more, he could survive. At least for a while.

It was easier to think of himself as already dead, as he had for days now. Now that he might live, there were only problems. The problems of finding food, of finding shelter, of hiding and avoiding German patrols.

And it was not only the Germans who were his enemies. There would also be men like the mad politruk.

And men who were much worse. Men like the Red Army stragglers and deserters scattered in the woods of Finland during the Winter War. Ghouls wrapped in rags, driven mad by cold and starvation, who would kill anyone they came across. Not only kill them—*eat* them as well.

And there would be local partisans and police, aligned with the Germans or aligned with no one at all. There would be hungry peasants, fleeing the violence of both sides.

And it would go on for as long as the war went on.

How long could the war continue? It was impossible to say.

If the Germans kept coming like this, Moscow would fall in months.

Let it fall. Then, at least, there might be a surrender. A return to his mother, their village . . .

Was such a thing possible?

Yes. At the rate of the German advance, at the rate they had torn through the Red Army's lines, it was possible.

But could the Germans continue that way? All he had seen was chaos. The Germans overwhelming them. Men dead and dying, men fighting for the last foothold, men breaking and running, men shot from behind by politruks from their own units when they tried to surrender.

Were his father and grandfather dead already? Or in a camp somewhere, starving?

He could not wish for a German victory—but how could he want the country that had taken his father and grandfather away to win the war either? The country that had taken them for no crime at all, no crime but being Polish?

He had not joined the Red Army out of patriotism. He had joined so that he could disappear. So that he could hide inside its mass. That was all. He had understood that if the secret police took him as well, it would kill his mother. So he had to stop being himself. Become no one.

"Well," Czesław said to himself out loud, "now you are no one, all right. Now you will really disappear. They won't even find your bones."

He was deep in the woods now. He had walked quickly, and for hours, skirting a bog, tireless and driven. Ignoring fatigue, or made immune to it.

It was the last hour of light in the forest now, and objects had begun to lose their color, taking on the blue shift of approaching night.

The sound of crows was louder here.

A stream had cut deeply into the earth. It flowed loudly over stones in its trench.

On the other side, the bank was nearly vertical—eroded, as steep as a cliff, its sides matted with the roots of trees clinging to soil being slowly cut out from under them. Here and there the roots wound around a boulder, as if seeking a safe anchor to hold fast to.

Go around? But how long did this barrier continue for? He walked a few hundred meters in each direction. It remained the same. Who knew how long he would have to walk to bypass it?

He scrambled down the bank. He picked his way over the rocks, then across a fallen log that bridged the stream.

On the far side a narrow foothold jutted from the base of an eroded wall of earth. Several large stones formed a loose ladder. He could scramble up here, holding on to tree roots for support. He pulled himself up, slipping several times, struggling to keep his grip and balance.

Finally, he was over the top.

The sound of crows was louder now.

Looking up into the branches, Czesław saw hundreds of them. Then thousands. Tens of thousands?

Rank on rank extended above him, filling every branch up, from the forest floor to the canopy.

A wall of wings, sharp beaks, black eyes. Broken twigs and feathers littered the ground. And the smell of the forest was overcome, here, with the smell of the birds.

He took a step forward. He expected—he could imagine—a

sudden burst, all of them flying at him at once. They shifted weight, jostled for their places on the branches. One of them, on a low branch, cawed loudly.

Czesław took another step forward.

The avian wall shuddered. Every glossy eye was on him. The whole forest had come alive. Every tree watched him with hundreds of eyes. Every stone had grown a feathered sentinel.

A deep, guttural croak came from a thousand throats. The threat in it was clear.

He heard the distant sounds of gunfire, mixed with the grinding sounds of vehicles and other noises. The familiar sounds of war.

Everything in his body told him to stay away from that sound.

But what if it was a counterattack directed against the German encirclement? What if the Red Army had broken through and there was now a way out? A way back to the anonymous mass of men? And, eventually, back home?

Czesław let himself back down the cliff. Down the ladder of roots and boulders. He paused on the narrow bank.

Although he could not see the crows, he could feel their presence up there. Something gigantic, a collective body of beak, feather, and claw. Crouched up there, filling the forest from its floor to the tops of the trees, listening to him. Waiting to see if he was really leaving.

And if not? What would it do to him then?

Czesław crossed the stream and began moving toward the noise of war. He walked at first, still fighting his body's urge to stay away. Then he began to run.

We thought war was something that ran through the landscape like no-man's-land, limited by our lines of trenches. A gouge of mud and filth, strewn with corpses, its seams filled with the stench of dead horses and wounded, dying men.

But war did not stop there. The front line collapsed, the men poured from their trenches in the chaos of defeat, and the cracks spread with them. The trench-wounds became fissures, cracks that grew the way a crack in glass will lengthen, spiderwebbing the fragile material of everything.

Until they split towns, leaving a rift through the center of a cobblestoned street.

Until they cut through dining rooms, dividing families.

Until finally the entire structure of our world collapsed, and everything it had stood for.

—from *The Autobiography of a Burned Village*

5
KEZIA

June 1941

ONE OF THE GERMANS KEPT CALLING to her, in their language she did not understand.

As if she would come out. As if she would suddenly reveal herself to them. Willingly give herself up to death, and to the prelude to death they had planned for her, worse than death itself.

Kezia was well hidden. She had crawled into the hollow of a rotting log, the corpse of a massive pine. She had plugged the hole behind her with dry branches shaken down by spring storms.

It was dark where she was, her legs pulled up to her stomach, the smell of decay all around her—not an unpleasant smell, the gentle smell of the trees turning into dirt, which, soon enough, would be more trees again.

A few coins of light fell in, like scattered change. She could not see out beyond the branches. But she could hear the Germans calling. Stomping around under the trees. Loud, sure of themselves. And drunk.

She could hear the distressed sounds of the horses. Her family's horses. They reared and pawed at the ground. The horses smelled the blood and the other death smells of their old masters. She could identify the voices of every mare, foal, and stallion.

Kezia's family had abandoned the wagon yesterday, taking what they could with them on the horses. They had tried to sell the wagon. Their home. But there were no takers.

And who would buy such a thing now? Everyone on the road knew that eventually everything would be lost. There was no use in buying anything but what could be carried, worn, or stuffed into your mouth.

They had ridden into the forest with the remnants of their lives packed on their horses. Her older sister, Cosmina, had complained of the forest cold, of the branches pulling at her hair. What was new? Cosmina always complained.

Kezia had stayed silent, riding the mare Georgeta, trailing behind.

"Bad days," their father had said, setting up camp once they were deep enough in the woods. Making a circle of stones for the fire, using the flint he kept on his belt to light the brush and sticks he gathered.

Hobbled, the horses had searched for sustenance, nosing through pine needles for fresh leaves and grasses. The four of them—her father, Grigore, her uncle Luca, and the two sisters—slept in a circle around the fire.

They had agreed to meet up with the others in their band in Vilnius. The four of them had then separated from the larger group, taking their wagon, to see if there was a way to sell the horses in the countryside.

The Germans were coming. War was coming. Better to sell the horses now, her father and uncle had agreed. Once things got worse, they would be stolen.

Once the horses and other valuables were sold, the band would move on. East, most likely—but really on to anywhere there was no fighting.

"It is good the wagon is gone," her uncle Luca had said in the dark, the only light that of a cloud-blotted crescent moon and the fire's embers. "Many of us died trying to keep our wagons or our horses in the last war. And the rest of us ended up on foot anyway. Better to lose everything now but keep our lives."

In the morning, they woke to six Germans, their rifles held loosely, standing in a ring around them.

How had the Germans found them? Had they followed the horse tracks into the forest? Or just stumbled across them?

Her father rubbed the sleep from his eyes and smiled, gestured at the horses. "*Guten Morgen, meine Herren. Möchten Sie gute Pferde kaufen?*"

Her father spoke some German. He had traveled in Prussia, as a boy.

A German submachine gun rattled in answer.

Her uncle Luca died with a smile on his face, rubbing the dark stubble of his chin, the big white teeth he was so proud of gleaming.

Her father, on the other side of the fire, was shot from behind. He died with his destroyed face in the ashes.

The German who fired the gun could not have been more than sixteen. His round face and jug ears made him look younger than that.

Kezia ran.

Cosmina ran as well. But five minutes later, Kezia heard Cosmina screaming. And the men, laughing and calling to one another.

Kezia was glad her mother was dead. Glad her mother did not have to hear those sounds. Glad she did not have to hear when Cosmina stopped screaming, and then stopped making any sound at all. Did not have to hear the second rattle of the submachine gun. Or, afterward, the mocking laughter of the men.

She remembered what her mother had said to her: "Even if a *gadjo* claims to love you. Even then, remember: We are nothing to them. For the gadjo, we are not alive. We sing and dance and are lovely, but we are no more human to them than the mechanical wonders at a fair."

Maybe, as they walked away from Cosmina, that was what they saw: nothing more than the exposed gears and broken springs of an automaton, the puppet pose of a broken and discarded toy.

The men stopped calling for her. Their voices rose in anger as they struggled with the horses, dragging them away.

Kezia's mare Georgeta gave one last equine scream. *Me. She is calling for me.* The clanking of the men's gear faded into the distance.

Kezia waited. She listened. But the only sounds were forest

sounds, and the sounds of her own muffled breaths. Finally, she struggled from her hiding place.

The two dead men lay where they had fallen. Her uncle Luca was still smiling.

The pack Luca's horse had been carrying lay on the ground. The Germans had torn it open and scattered its contents—a camp shovel, a saw, a spoon, a fork, a knife of tarnished silver, a pewter bowl, some clothing.

If they had dug deeper, they would have found the Nagant revolver, with its twine-wrapped handle. And the few dozen bullets, wrapped in a rag.

Her uncle Luca had bragged that he used the revolver in a robbery, years ago. He had bragged, too, that he killed the man he took it from. Snuck up behind him with a knife and cut his throat. Because he wanted it—that was all.

No one believed anything Luca said, though he was certainly cruel enough to kill a man, and certainly mad enough to rob a store with a revolver.

What was true was that last year, a month after Kezia's twelfth birthday, Luca had held this gun to her head, a few hundred meters downstream from camp, where she had been washing herself.

When he was done with her, she had a bruise from the barrel. A crescent moon, staining her temple.

She had told her mother she bumped into a tree.

Kezia began to assemble a pack for herself. She took her bedroll, the revolver, her bowl and utensils, the shovel and the saw from Luca's pack. She took her father's axe and the food he had been carrying.

She saw a scattering of black and gray feathers near the camp. Then the bird, dead, a hole through its breast. A crow. It must have been hit by a bullet when the Germans killed Luca and her father.

Not knowing why, she dug a small hole in the soft earth, and laid the crow down in the hole. She gathered its scattered feathers and laid them in the hole as well, then carefully covered the bird with earth.

She heard the sounds of other crows in the trees, calling to one another.

She tamped the earth flat.

When she stood up from the burial, she saw crows in the trees around her. A hundred of them, at least.

When had they come?

They watched her in silence. She should be afraid . . . but there was nothing threatening about them. And she had run out of fear for today.

"I am sorry," she said to the crows, using the same voice she used to speak to horses, or to a deer glimpsed in the forest. A voice similar to the one she also used when speaking with children she cared for.

One of the crows opened its beak and made a sound. An animal word, but Kezia did not know what it was.

Sometimes, when the horses spoke to her, she felt she could understand them.

This crow seemed to be saying, *Such is life.*

The crow bobbed its head, stroked its beak on the branch, and blinked at her.

"Yes," Kezia said, and heard the echo of her mother's voice, because her mother had said the words to her so many times.

"Such is life. But it ought not to be this way. It ought to be better."

With the shovel still in her hand, she walked past her father and Luca. "Face down in the ashes is where you belong."

A few paces away, she stopped. She went back, kicked a bootful of ash and cinders onto Luca's corpse as well.

"That's all the burial you will get from me."

Kezia walked for an hour around the trampled, defiled area near the camp.

She never found Cosmina's body.

Had the Germans hidden it so well? Had they taken it away? Slung her corpse over one of the horses? Was Cosmina somehow alive? Kezia had heard the gun.

But had they been killing her? Or simply firing it at something else, or into the air?

She circled and circled, searching for her sister. But Cosmina was gone, as completely as if she had never existed at all.

Kezia had an image of Cosmina being taken up to heaven, bodily, her palms raised, her face upturned as she rode a gold-leaf beam into the sky, like a saint in a church fresco.

Could something so terrible happen to you that you not only died but disappeared forever? Something so terrible that it erased you, as if you never had existed at all?

She put a hand over her mouth to stifle a mad laugh.

Returning to the bodies by the fire, she took her father's flint from his belt. She took his knife. She took Luca's good hat, which she had always coveted. A Greek fisherman's hat he had won in a card game and did not deserve.

She found her father's money pouch where it was hidden inside his pants. There were six gold coins inside and several silver.

Gold and silver were all her father had ever trusted. Those metals and his own cunning.

She struggled to untie the strap keeping the money pouch against his leg, but her hands started to shake, and she started to cry a bit, so instead she cut through the leather thong.

Leaning against a tree, Kezia vomited carefully, not getting any of it on her skirts.

She put the hat on, adjusted the pack, and started walking.

Her family had been headed deeper into the forest, away from the road and due east. That seemed as good a direction to continue in as any.

"Thank you for giving me a bed, Grandfather," I say. "I won't stay long."

"You are a good boy. But I can't give you any more than that until the goyim bring in the harvest," my zaydeh says. "Then I can sell a kettle or two." He stares out the window. "After the harvest there will be jam and fiddling."

He says the same thing a hundred times a day. *After the harvest there will be jam and fiddling.*

—from *The Autobiography of a Burned Village*

6
NERIYA

June 1941

NERIYA STOPPED and looked at the samelike columns of trees, the repetitive features of these woods.

They were alien to her now. She was deeper inside them than she had ever been.

Would she be able to find her way back along the branchings of the paths she had taken? Not if she went much farther.

Buster was quiet, waiting, regarding her crookedly.

A sound broke the silence. An inarticulate rumble. A sound like thunder, when the storm is distant.

But the sky was cloudless.

There were other sounds mixed in, too far off or jumbled

together to fully discern. They raised the hairs on the back of her neck.

For a few days now, they had heard in the shtetl of ragged, defeated bands of Red Army soldiers coming down the roads, headed east.

Their own family did not have a radio, but a few others did, and shared what they heard on forbidden foreign broadcasts: The alliance between the Soviet Union and Nazi Germany was broken. The Germans were on the offensive. The Soviet armies were falling back in disorder.

Yesterday in the kitchen her father had told her mother, "The Russians will fall like dominoes."

"And what," her mother had countered, "of the rumors from German-occupied Poland? Of the shootings, and the pogroms, worse than anything the Russians ever did?"

"I don't believe it," her father had said. "The Nazis have encouraged the worst of German antisemitism. They will bring it along with them—but we already know German antisemitism well. You lived through it in Königsberg. And we both lived through the Polish and the Russian versions, with their university quotas and their sneers, in Warsaw.

"What is the difference between them? And what is new about antisemitism? The Germans claim to hate us, the Poles claim to hate us, and the Russians claim to hate us. But in the end none of them can live without us. We have been here in the Pale for more than five hundred years! Little will change. The Nazis are barbarians, but the Germans are, in the end, a cultured people. And they are not all Nazis. Things will calm down. Eventually we will be better off under them than under these commissars, these maniacs looking for the next counterrevolutionary or kulak to shoot."

The Germans! Could the sound be the Germans, approaching? But none of the fighting could be anywhere near the shtetl yet, could it?

There was no way the Russians could collapse *this* quickly. There was no way the Germans could already be *here* . . .

But the sound she heard was not thunder. It was a grinding roar composed of many sounds. And one of those sounds was gunfire.

"I have to go back, Buster. I'm so sorry. I would like to have paid a visit to where you live. But not today."

She turned in what she hoped was the direction of the village.

Buster cawed at her.

"Really. I have to go." And now her smile, her half-joking words, seemed false even to her.

She was aware of how small she really was, and how frightened. She looked at her skinny wrists jutting out from the purple lining of her father's jacket, seeing them as if they were someone else's hands. "I would have loved to have tea with you in your little crow house, but I have to get back. Something is happening . . ."

War. War is happening.

". . . and I have to get home."

She turned to go. She was sure of the way. She could trace in her mind the turns she had made.

Buster landed in front of her, right in her path. He cawed up at her, his entire body straining forward, a mass of spiking feathers.

"Tomorrow," she said. She did not like the way her voice sounded. The fear in it. The way it had shrunk, somehow.

She took a step. Buster scrambled forward, the way he did when defending territory from another crow. He came right up to her foot. Hesitating, she took a step back.

It had seemed as if he was going to peck her.

"Really, Buster. That's no way to act."

She tried to go around him.

In a burst of wings, Buster flew directly at her face.

He did not touch her with his claws or beak, but she felt his feathers against her hands as she threw them up to protect herself. She staggered back.

"What are you doing?"

When she finally took her hands from her face, Neriya saw Buster perched on a low branch, not far from her head. He was swollen, ragged, glaring down at her.

For the first time since she had begun feeding him when she was seven years old, she was afraid of Buster. Aware of how large he was. Of how much of him was sharp and capable of hurting her.

And she was alone here, in the forest, with him.

But maybe something had only startled him. She took a step forward.

He came at her again, launching himself from the branch and directly at her face. This time, when she put up her hands to defend herself, Neriya felt a claw across the flesh of her knuckles.

She staggered backward and sat down hard on a fallen log. Her hands were shaking. There was blood on her knuckle, a long scratch.

In all the summers she had been playing her games with the crows, none had ever hurt her.

Now she thought back to the earliest part of the morning,

when she had come out to the table in the backyard and set up her game. When Buster had come flapping in and landed on the table.

He had seemed different, hadn't he?

He had not played the new game she built. Usually he was so curious—but this time he had not even looked at it. He hadn't seemed interested at all. All he had done was caw and hop around the yard, agitated. Impatient with her.

Everything was wrong.

There was a sound, close by.

Not like thunder now. Like an explosion. And something underneath it all that she could not make out but that pulled at her fears. And more gunshots. Those were gunshots, for certain. Gunshots, growing terribly close.

She stood up, took a step.

Buster burst from the ground, again aimed at her face. Although she covered her head with both hands, she felt a claw open a cut in her scalp. She slipped and fell to her knees in the thick mat of needles on the forest floor.

She could find a stick. She could fight him off with that . . .

But she might hurt him. The thought of hurting Buster—of him on the ground, with a broken wing or leg that could not be fixed—terrified her more than anything else.

When she sat up, Buster was close to her—close enough that she could reach out and touch him.

"I have to go back."

She reached out a hand. He shuffled forward in his familiar way.

"See? It's just me. We've been friends for so long. But now you are frightening me, and that's not right."

But the moment she tried to stand up, Buster jabbed hard at her with his beak. Was it on purpose that he struck her wrist where her coat covered? Even through the padded sleeve, rolled up at the wrist, the peck hurt. She sat back down.

She had to think of what to do. How to get past him without hurting him, or being hurt by him.

"I'll stay a few minutes, Buster. But then I have to go."

She needed to run to her mother and her father. She needed to warn them, to pull them away from that sound approaching their shtetl.

Was the sound approaching? Or was it already there?

Buster had retreated to a broken stump several meters away. Neriya tried to drive away panic by breathing more slowly.

Her father had taught her this. Panic was a cycle. It was more in the body than it was in the mind. She could break the cycle. She held her fingers at her wrist, still aching from Buster's peck, and felt her pulse. Willed it to slow.

But sitting there in the dark of the trees on the thick needles, trapped, with Buster's dark eye watching her, Neriya realized that the sound mixed in with the roar and gunshots, the sound that filled her with dread more than the rest of it, was the sound of screams.

And that even if Buster were not keeping her trapped here with him in the forest, she would not be able to find the courage to run toward that sound.

TWO

The Origin of Species

The rabbi walks through the shtetl with his hands clasped behind his back. He crosses the muddy quadrangle of the market square in stained boots. No heads turn in his direction.

He still feels he is the center of a system, revolving eternally around men like him, circling his gravity and the gravity of the Torah scrolls, of holy days and ancient wisdom.

He is not. No longer. But where is the center now? What holds this world together now? That leather-jacketed commissar leaning against a barrel? The anarchists over there, haggling with an old woman over a basket of bruised apples?

There is no common orbit. And the people of the shtetl, pulled away by centrifugal force, will spin off into the cities, into other towns. Or wander roads filled with other people wandering roads, forever.

—from *The Autobiography of a Burned Village*

7
NERIYA

December 1940

NERIYA LOOKED OUT through the kitchen window of her family's Vilnius apartment. In the bleakness of the flagstone-and-whitewash square, a group of crows battled over something, taking flight and circling to get a better position, sparring and jousting with their beaks, batting one another with their wings.

Neriya watched them, her breath near enough to the pane to fog it, and to feel winter bleeding through the thin membrane of glass. In the fogged circumference she wrote out the chemical composition of glass with a fingertip: SiO_2 $CaCO_3$ Na_2CO_3.

Her father sat at the table, lingering over tea and the Yiddish newspaper. He had finished with the Russian one, capped by a hammer and sickle, and had shoved it aside with an exhalation of disgust. He looked over the top of the Yiddish paper at her.

"When we are in the shtetl, you spend every morning with the crows. But here, you hardly have anything to do with them. Do you have a prejudice against city crows? Are they too sophisticated for your tastes?" He had said it in the teasing manner he used when his mood was good, or when he was pretending his mood was good.

"No," Neriya answered. "It's the opposite. It is the crows in the shtetl who are sophisticated. These city crows are smart, but . . . they are just crows."

Now her father had put the paper down. "What do you mean by that? *Just* crows?"

Neriya took the last biscuit from the tray on the table and broke it in half. She put one half of the biscuit back on the tray and crammed the other in her mouth. She chewed for a moment, washed the rest down with a bit of cold tea from her neglected cup, and said, "I used to feed the crows here in the city, remember? And I tried to play the same games with them, but they couldn't play. Not really. They could do a few things, but not much. Not like the crows of the shtetl."

"Did you put the same effort into it? Into befriending them?"

"Maybe more—we are here in Vilnius nine months of the year, and in the shtetl for only three months. I wanted to play the same games with the crows here. And to carry on the same experiments. But the Vilnius crows were never very interested in any of it."

"I suppose," her father said, "they are too urbane. Little city flâneurs with plenty of other distractions."

He may have meant it as a joking aside, but Neriya said, "I don't think so. I mean, what is a city to a crow? It's just another kind of field or forest. No, it's something else. The crows of the shtetl are different."

"A bit smarter."

"Not *a bit* smarter, Papa. It's more than that. It's . . ." She hesitated for a moment. "If I show you something, will you promise not to tell anyone?"

Her father shrugged. "Of course."

"Not even Mama."

They both looked toward the door. A few rooms away, the other third of their family was fast asleep, spending her Shabbat morning in the way she liked best.

"All right," her father said. "Not even Mama. Unless she asks me directly."

"Not for any reason."

"Not unless I am compelled to confess under pain of torture."

Neriya laughed. "Good enough."

In her room, Neriya gathered up the birchwood box in which she kept the gifts given to her by the crows. In the dining room, she set it down on the table.

"Your treasure box," her father said.

She opened it. In the compartments of the box's top tray were the gifts in the order she had been given them, starting with the Order of Saint Anna medal, 4th Class, that Buster had given her. A small paper card accompanying each gift listed the date the gift was given and the name of the crow who had brought it.

Her father nodded. "It's unusual, for certain. I've told you, I think you should document this behavior. You could write a paper, submit it to one of the societies . . ."

He stopped talking when Neriya had removed the top tray and took out the tray underneath.

Her father moved as if to touch one of the objects in the tray but withdrew his hand. He looked into Neriya's face.

He's looking for falsehood. He's looking to see if this is some kind of joke. It's not because he does not trust me; it's because he simply cannot believe it. The way I could not when Buster brought me the first one. The way I looked around the yard for the person who was playing the joke. Because the gifts cannot be real—but they are *real.*

"When did the crows begin bringing you these?"

"Two summers ago," Neriya said.

"And you've kept it a secret that long? Why?"

"At first, I wasn't sure of what I was seeing. And then . . . I don't know. I wasn't ready to tell anyone, that's all."

"You wanted to keep the discovery for yourself."

"For just a little longer. And then the Russians came, and the Lithuanians, and the Russians again. And the world is so unstable, Papa. Everything is changing, all at once. If we told someone, what would they do?"

"You are right," her father said. "For now, we'll keep it to ourselves. And the world is changing, Neriya—but I think soon the world will right itself again. There will be a time for exploring things like this, and for sharing them with others. Who knows? Perhaps—in a year or two—you'll be standing up in front of the Linnean Society in London, presenting your work . . ."

"Oh, *Papa*. Stop."

"You'll have to learn English, of course. We should start the tutoring now . . . and it won't be cheap. I'll have to consult the family budget . . ."

"*Papa.*"

Her father was smiling, but when he looked down into the box, the smile went away.

"For now, Neriya . . . tell no one else."

June 1941

Neriya stood in front of what had been her family's home. The walls, consumed by flame, had fallen in on one another. The home was a smoldering pile of blackened beams.

Smoke still rose from the shtetl. She walked the dirt streets through swirling ash, stumbling in wagon ruts left over from the mud of spring. The streets were covered in new tracks: tire tracks that crisscrossed everything.

Neriya had spent the night in the forest, sleeping on the ground on a mound of needles she had scraped together.

The stained whitewash of the church jutted from the smoking piles of the town. It had been spared burning. As Neriya staggered past, she saw a splatter of dried blood across the low white wall that surrounded it. And a handprint, in blood.

She thought of the sound of screaming she had heard, inside that larger sound of war.

Where had everyone been taken?

The synagogue was ash. She found the red Soviet flag that had flown over the house of the former village head. It was torn and charred, smeared with human shit.

She had walked every street of the shtetl, thinking there had to be someone left. Someone to ask where her parents were, where everyone had run away to or was taken. Had they gone to another town? Fled into the forest? How could everyone in the shtetl simply be . . . gone?

The family gate, untouched by fire, stood closed on its bad hinge clumsily wrapped in wire. As if it still led to a house the owners would return to at any moment.

There were tire tracks everywhere. And how was one supposed to tell if they were coming or going? Then she heard a truck. The whine of its engine. A gear grinding. Just around the corner. She moved toward the sound.

A crow cawed. She saw Buster, his feet clamped to a signpost, his beak open, screaming down at her.

A hand clapped over her mouth, from behind. She was lifted off the ground. She lashed out with her elbows at the person who held her, who was carrying her away, out of the street.

She was pulled into the yard of a home—of what had been a home but now was just another rectangle of charred boards. In the yard was a pile of scrap wood. She was forced to the ground behind it, the hand still over her mouth.

The hand moved her head. She found herself looking into the dirty face not of a man but of a boy, hardly older than her. He put a finger to his lips, then pointed to the truck, then sliced that same finger across his own throat.

The boy wore a Red Army uniform. Could you call it a uniform anymore? A torn jacket bleeding cotton batting, its insignia ripped off. A cloth cap with the shadow of a star, just a darker shape on the fabric where the sun had not yet burned the material to a lighter shade. Over his shoulder was a rifle.

He took his hand from her mouth. She did not scream.

The truck engine idled. There were voices, men speaking in Lithuanian. They could not have been more than one village street away.

The men laughed. One of them fired a gun into the air, and Buster took off from his perch and arced away, headed for the forest. Startled? Or had they actually shot at him?

The boy whispered to her, in Russian, "If those men find us, they will kill us. Do you understand?"

"I understand," she answered in Russian.

"Is this your village?"

She nodded. He did not say anything, but he shook his head.

"Where have they taken everyone?" she asked.

"I do not know."

The voices grew closer now.

Could this boy really be a soldier? Was the mighty Red Army just an army of boys, like this one?

"Where are the rest of you? Where is the army?"

"Dead," the boy said. "Or still retreating, far from here."

"Why were you left behind?"

"We were encircled. I was cut off. I am all that remains of my unit."

The Russians will fall like dominoes.

When had her father said that? Just a few days ago. She heard his voice so clearly in her head. Heard it as if he were there with her still.

Where was he now? Her father? Her mother? Where was everyone?

"Can you understand what those men are saying?" the boy asked.

"No," she said. "I don't speak Lithuanian. I speak Polish and Russian, and German. But not Lithuanian."

She did not mention Yiddish. At the last moment she had swallowed the word. What business was it of his?

And now she heard her mother's voice:

And what of the rumors from German-occupied Poland? Of the shootings, and the pogroms, worse than anything the Russians ever did?

That word. *Pogrom*. A word that stank like her burning village. A word as bloody as the handprint smeared on the whitewashed wall of the church.

She would not tell this boy, or anyone, who she was.

"Come out," one of the men said then, in heavily accented Polish. "Come out and join the others. There's no need to hide. They are eating soup at the collection point. We are evacuating the countryside. We will take you to Vilnius to be with your families."

The voice paused, listening for a response.

One of the other men said something in Lithuanian, then said the word in Polish for soup and laughed.

He said it in a way so filled with sarcasm that this one word, *soup*, and the nasty bark of the laugh that followed it, made Neriya fear she would never see her family again.

The bloody handprint on the whitewashed wall.

A few minutes later, the truck engine started again. The gears ground. The sound of the engine faded as the truck moved away down the road, headed east.

"Come with me," the boy said. "I have found a safe place. Safe for now, at least. It is in the forest, not far from here."

"No. I have to find my parents."

"You can't find them now. Not in all of this. What you have to do now is hide. Hide and wait. These men are murderers. If your parents got away, they will be hiding too. Maybe your family is already in the forest. Maybe the rest of the village is with them. There will be many people hiding in the trees."

"I have to find my parents," she repeated. "They will be worried about me."

But the words were weak. All she could think of was the drifting ash, and that word. *Pogrom.*

"Maybe they are in Vilnius . . ." she said.

The boy put his hand on her shoulder. "Just down the road, my whole unit surrendered. The Germans didn't take them prisoner. Instead, they lined them up along the road and shot them. What is happening here is something worse than war."

"They need me, then! I need to find them!"

"Come with me. Just for now. Later, when things are different, I will help you. We can find your people together."

"Why are you helping me?"

He was already on his feet, shouldering his rifle. Now she saw that he was tall, and big—as big as a grown man. But looking at his face, no one would mistake him for a grown man. Except, maybe, around the eyes. Reddened by smoke, they were already the eyes of an adult.

"It is easier if we do things together," he said. "We can watch out for each other." And then, without looking back at her where she stood, hesitating: "I tried to help the others. I tried to help Andrei. Kolya. But they wouldn't listen. And the Germans killed them. Please, come with me."

When the war began, we were all the same. All soldiers. What we risked, we risked equally.

But as the war dragged on, the seams appeared: Suddenly, this uniformed man, identical to any other, was a Pole. That one was a Tatar. This man was a Finn, and that one a Jew. And what *kind* of Jew?

We found ourselves around smaller and smaller fires—not warming our hands with other Jews but only with other Jewish *workers*.

Soon our enemies were not only the soldiers in the trenches across no-man's-land but also our officers. And our sergeants. And the anarchists and the Mensheviks and the bundists and the royalists . . .

And the fabric of empire rotted, and would hold no stitch at all.

—from *The Autobiography of a Burned Village*

8

CZESŁAW

September 1938

CZESŁAW, HIS FATHER, CASIMIR, and his grandfather Maciej had been out hunting roe deer for several days.

It was not good hunting. An early snow had begun on the second day. By the third day, the forest was impassable. Wind tore at the trees. They lay in the guttering lantern light of their hunter's dugout, trapped by a storm that had ended the day early, the dense clouds hiding the sun and bleeding everything of color, the temperature dropping twenty degrees Celsius in an hour.

True night fell. The wind increased. Branches snapped and crashed to the forest floor.

Czesław had started accompanying his father and grandfather on hunting trips when he was ten. By then he already knew how to use the old Mosin-Nagant rifle his father had given him, the rifle they kept hidden in their dugout, a few kilometers from the logging camp.

The hunting they did was poaching, technically—but they paid the authorities off in good venison to keep their mouths shut. And anyway, everyone in Siberia who was capable of hunting or trapping took what they could from the forest, no matter what the Bolsheviks permitted or did not permit.

The storm, the darkness, the snow slashing against the tree trunks. The snow whirling, torn from the ground by wind, into their faces.

In the dugout it was warmer. They made a fire in the leaky handmade stove. Though neither his father nor his grandfather spoke of it, Czesław could sense there was real danger. They gave it away in the way they did things: carefully, talking them through first, planning more than they normally did.

This was how they always were: When things grew more dangerous, they became more cautious. They hid their fear behind preparation, efficiency, attention to detail.

Czesław felt he could not show his fear either. If he said he was afraid, they would be sympathetic. They would reassure him. But he understood, in a way he could not explain, that they would also lose respect for him.

It was acceptable, in their family, to be afraid. It was natural. It was not acceptable to show it.

As they lay there in the light of the fire through the slots in the stove door, Czesław's grandfather told stories of his own boyhood—something he had never spoken of. He talked of his own father's hunting lodge of wood and stone at the foot of the mountains, its dark rafters webbed with the trophy antlers of deer and moose. He talked of how the shadows danced and their curved bones glowed in the orange light pouring hot from the grand fireplace. He spoke of the formal hunting parties that lasted weeks sometimes, the many accompanying relatives and other nobility attended by servants, the hunting itself accompanied—overshadowed, even—by the traditions around it. By barrels of good wine, by feasting, by secretive, passionate affairs.

For the first time, Czesław felt his difference—his Polishness—as something more than just a liability. He saw his grandfather's nobility—it had always been there, hadn't it? It was in the proud way his grandfather carried himself. It was in his silences more than in anything he did.

And that nobility was in his father too. Inherited, however blurred and incoherent it might be here in Siberia, so far from its context, but somehow carrying over from that lost world.

And it was in Czesław as well. Wasn't it? Yes, he felt it now, a connection to these things: the hunting party, the dance of antler shadows on the wooden walls, the venison turning on a spit over the great hearth.

They lay together in the dark, folded in sheepskins, with the forest torn by wind, and the frozen branches cracking, and Czesław felt that they really were the same person, made and made again. That his grandfather's memories were his own.

He had a connection to something else. Something that had to be *carried on*. Some family meaning that lent a glow even to the logging camp and the washing hung between the partitions of the barracks.

The next day they woke to find the forest filled with

blown-down trees. Some were tangled with others, hanging above the ground, their raw roots burst up from the soil. Others lay on the forest floor among the shattered branches they had torn away as they fell.

The men made their way back to the logging camp empty-handed but were greeted almost as heroes. Everyone had believed they were dead. His mother held him. His father placed an iron hand on his shoulder and said: "Marta, if this boy is not already a man, I do not know what a man is. He was never afraid."

He had been terrified, of course. But he had never shown it.

June 1941

After that hunting trip, Czesław had pressed his grandfather for more stories.

He had built a space in his mind, a theater where he could play out scenes. He had needed his grandfather's stories to populate it. And although his grandfather was never voluble, he had given up the stories—not exactly stories but fragments. Winged and helmeted Polish hussars with sabers as bright as mirrors, bejeweled ladies with fans, fatal charges, mustached helmets and banded suits of armor, coats of arms, crystal goblets, doomed men marching into cannon fire, clean-shaven and brightly polished for death.

It all had mixed with that image of fire-shadow dancing among the antlers, the spit turning on the great stone hearth, the watchful head of a buck breathing mist in the cold morning, its crown of bone turned toward the hunting party that had come to claim its life.

These fragments had projected onto Czesław's personality like a magic lantern slide against a wall, had become a wordless code of conduct. He had not broken under fire in Karelia because he was a *szlachcic* with noble blood. He had shot the politruk without thinking, when he threatened a man Czesław considered his friend, because Czesław was the inheritor of what his grandfather had been—someone the world demanded more from than it demanded of others.

He sat cross-legged on the ground of the *zemlyanka*.

The girl was asleep.

She had told him her name was Agata. She had said it with the false note of someone unused to lying. It did not matter: he would have lied in her case as well. Who was he to her? What right did he have, yet, to know her name?

He had heard stories, from other Poles with relatives in the German-controlled General Government, and from refugees, about German atrocities in occupied Poland. He had seen the Germans shooting prisoners of war. He had seen civilians dead along the roads he wandered after his unit was destroyed.

And two days ago, he came across an anti-tank ditch not far from the village where he found the girl. In the ditch, men, women, and children lay machine-gunned to death, half naked, swarmed by summer flies.

The people of the village this girl came from were probably already dead. Her father and her mother were probably dead. It was a Jewish village. He had seen the burned synagogue, the charred mezuzahs on the smoking doorposts. And the girl was a Jew—she did not want to tell him, but he knew.

The men, women, and children dead in that ditch had been Jews.

He would not tell her any of this. He would let her think her parents were still alive. People needed to think these kinds of things. It kept them going. Like the letters filled with nonsense he sent home to his mother from the front. Talismans to make her work bearable. To keep sickness and death from her door.

In the same way, the thought of his mother out there, waiting for him to return, sustained him here. It made him want to live. He was responsible to her—he needed to live for her. He had to survive so she would have a son return to her and would be happy.

This "Agata" who was not Agata would fight harder to live if she believed her parents were alive. If she believed she might find them someday.

It would be hard for her to fight if she knew they were already dead, lying in a ditch somewhere in a tangle of other bodies. What would be left for her then?

Andrei had not listened to him. Kolya had not listened.

He needed to be more careful with how he spoke to people. How he convinced them of what they had to do to live. He would be careful with her, and she would understand. She had to survive. Then they could find others. With a group, it would be easier.

The only light in the zemlyanka came in through a crack in the planks of the low door. He had hidden the door and roof with branches, but some light bled through them. A ray of it bent across Czesław's hands, across the sheepskin he was sitting on, the shelf on the wall spattered with tallow, the paper icon of a saint he did not recognize nailed to the wall.

He could not see the girl's face, but he sensed that she was awake now. He heard her begin to cry, quietly. He sat and listened.

It must feel so good to cry. He had tried to make himself do it, a few days ago. He felt there was something terrible building up inside him. He had thought crying might let it out, the way you bled pressure off with a valve. They did that with the old steam-driven saw in the logging camp.

He had cried before the war, sometimes—off somewhere by himself, where no one had to know.

Now he couldn't think of when the last time was. He couldn't find the way to do it anymore. He hadn't found the way to do it since Finland.

It was good that she still knew how to cry.

"You must be hungry," he said finally.

The girl sat up. "How long did I sleep for?"

"A few hours. I have potatoes, cooked. And fat I saved from some tinned meat. The potatoes are still warm."

He heard her stomach growl. They both laughed.

He gave her two of the potatoes, in a wooden bowl. "Eat."

"It's so dark in here."

Czesław opened the door, pushing aside the branches. Afternoon light flooded into the small space, the one room, maybe three meters by four, dug into the side of a hill and so deep into the ground that only its roof and a few handspans of wall were above the level of the soil, and the doorway was partially tunneled into the earth.

It was a good zemlyanka, built roughly but well. Inside, its axe-cut log walls were fitted neatly against the earth, the chinks between them stuffed with moss. The roof was formed from layers of branches and bark. There were several sheepskin blankets, an old gunpowder horn, a cracked lantern with no fuel, a clay jug, a few wooden bowls, a box bed of sorts filled with grass as a mattress. There was even a stove, piped properly up through the roof, with a pile of paper and splinters of wood near it for kindling.

But the place had the feeling of abandonment. No one had been here for several seasons. Maybe longer. The zemlyanka had mostly withstood the weather, staying dry inside, but it had been a long time since anyone had warmed themselves here. Any human, anyway. When he found it, there was a hedgehog living behind the stove. It had waddled out with a look of annoyance.

Czesław had worked to cover the roof with branches, and even moved a small fallen tree, so that the low hill the zemlyanka was in resembled a snag of storm-felled trees and branches. A sharp eye might spot the chimney with its sooty hat, but he had hidden this under branches as well.

The girl brushed dark hair from a pallid face. Her eyes were red and swollen. She wore a coat that was too big for her, a quilted coat not unlike the *telogreika* he'd worn in Finland. Her sleeves were rolled up, revealing a purple lining.

The coat had been much loved. The girl too.

"These are so good," the girl said. "I swear, they are the best potatoes I have ever eaten."

They were good: he'd eaten a few while she slept.

He did not tell her he'd found them in the ashes of one of the barns of her village, burst from a sack, roasted in the embers near the blackened skeleton of one of her neighbors.

The world has flooded in, finding the places the fabric was weakest, picking at the loosening seams.
Now everyone in the shtetl is a foreigner. Every one of us.

—from *The Autobiography of a Burned Village*

9

KEZIA

November 1940

KEZIA HAD FOUND A PLACE in the branches of a beech tree, where from a distance she could watch the two campfires flickering between the intervening branches.

Around one, the women wailed. Around the other, the men drank.

Hobbled among the trees, the horses snorted and whinnied, sensing the disturbance in the people but not knowing what it was. The wailing, the snatches of song, the rough raised voices of the men, the cries of the horses, drove away the other forest sounds.

For three days, her family's band had been hiding in the

woods. They had left the roads to avoid the Soviet patrol they knew was hunting for them. For the horses, which they would steal from the band, calling their theft "collectivization."

The people were of less importance to the Bolsheviks. But they, too, would be collectivized: forced to stop their wandering, to work on some dismal farm alongside the Polish and Belarusian and Lithuanian peasants who despised them.

Forced to give up their way of life and become gadjo.

The men had sent out lookouts, reporting the location of the Soviet patrols. The camp had been moved twice, deeper into the woods.

There was fear in the band. The swaggering confidence of the men was breaking.

"The Russians are *everywhere*," they muttered around the campfires.

No one had bathed in days. They worried about the wagons, hidden in a dilapidated barn, covered with leaves and branches but unguarded.

On their second day in the woods, Kezia's mother, Tsura, stopped saying anything but "The end. The end. The end," over and over again.

Nothing anyone said to her would stop it. Something had broken loose in her.

For days, Kezia had sensed something was wrong. Her mother had been saying strange things. She had seemed distracted, a lost look on her face as they moved along the roads, searching for a safe place to camp.

Late that night, Kezia's aunt Mala gave Tsura a dose of something she had mixed. Mala treated horses, usually, but she knew the ailments of people as well.

"People are worse than horses," she would say. "Worse, and smaller. But their problems are much the same."

Sitting next to her by the fire, Mala brought the cup to Tsura's mouth again and again. Then, when Tsura grew drowsy, Mala led her to the tent to sleep.

"The end!" Kezia's mother said loudly, one more time, in a slurred voice. "Of all of it!" and then nothing.

Kezia watched it all from her beech tree.

Settling back among the women, her aunt said something to the other women that Kezia could only faintly hear: ". . . like her mother. And I fear it will end the same way."

Like her mother. And I fear it will end the same way.

What did that mean? Kezia's grandmother had died of exposure, during a terrible snowstorm. The band had been running from the Russians then as well. It was after the World War, when the Bolsheviks tried to invade Lithuania and were barely held off. Kezia's grandmother had died of exposure when their wagons were lost, and the band took to the woods. The snow came heavy that year, and . . .

"The Russians are everywhere," her father was saying at the men's campfire. "And the Jews are everywhere, working with them."

"The Russians have promised the Jews an end to the pogroms."

"Ha! The Russians *invented* the pogroms."

"*These* Russians claim they are different. They have come to unite us all. They are Reds, they say, not the tsar's Cossacks."

"The same Reds who burned the Jews out of their shtetlach all over the Pale in 1919. The same Reds who shot our Roma men dead, claiming we were siding with the Whites. The gadjo can fool each other with their stories, but they can't fool us. Let them all kill each other. Then we Roma will finally be left in peace."

"I would miss the gadjo," her uncle Luca said. "If they died out, there would be no one left to swindle."

There was laughter. The bottle went around again.

Kezia waited until both fires died down. Then she went to the women's fire and found a place near Cosmina. Cosmina was like a hot coal when she slept. Kezia unrolled her bedroll next to her and curled into that warmth.

In the middle of the night, something in the forest cried out in a voice like a human voice. Kezia woke up and stared into the darkness. There was nothing to see. The sound had come from far off.

She woke again, to wailing. The women were screaming, everyone was scrambling into boots and shoes, people were crashing through the trees. It was barely after dawn, cold and dark under the trees, the chill of winter coming on.

Kezia tried to stand, and her aunt Mala, wide-eyed, put a hand on her chest. "No, child. Stay."

But she would not stay. When Mala turned to run with the others, Kezia followed, tripping on roots and slipping on the dew-wet needles.

So she saw them drag her mother's body from the bog, naked and white, her mouth open, the black tendrils of her hair masking her face.

One of the men threw a blanket over her. Two women held Cosmina back as she screamed, "Mama! Mama!" over and over again.

Mala stood with her palm pressed against her forehead, saying, "Again. It has happened again."

Luca's daughter Simza said, "Their women are cursed."

Mala glared at her. "It's no *curse*, you superstitious fool." She spat. "It is in the *genes*, as sure as the coloring of a horse or its temperament."

Then she saw Kezia and opened her arms. "Oh, child. Come here. I told you not to follow us . . ."

But Kezia had already turned and was running.

Mist was on the bog and curling around her mother's white, naked body. And in the mist she had seen the yellow-stained tendrils of her mother's madness. The madness was out of her mother now. It could travel wherever it wanted.

June 1941

Her arms and hands wrapped in rags, Kezia slowly raised the lid from the hive.

The bees buzzed around her—not angry, yet. Almost as if asking a question. Carefully, Kezia selected a frame with most of its honeycombs capped. She pried one of the corners up with a piece of bent metal she had found. Holding the frame in one protected hand, she brushed the bees off with the other. Then she put the frame in a sack and closed the hive.

She walked to the edge of the trees, into the shadow of them, and sat down on a flat stone. There, she broke a chunk of comb from the frame. She placed the chunk in her mouth, feeling the texture of the raw honey as it was squeezed out from the cells. Her stomach contracted at the sweetness of it.

For two days, honey was nearly all she had eaten. She had found the hives, their inhabitants going about their business as if nothing had happened to their owners. Near them was a small granary, all that was left of this farm on the shtetl outskirts. Its house, cattle shed, and corn barn were ashes and blackened beams.

A few hundred meters away, smoke still rose from the heaps of the shtetl's collapsed buildings. A white church was left standing, but when she went inside she heard the sound of flies and smelled rot.

The shtetl chickens had all been stolen. A cow had wandered the main square, lowing and looking for someone to relieve its swollen udders. Kezia found a wooden bucket, milked her into that, and drank the milk warm.

But the next day Germans drove in, loaded the cow onto a truck, and took her away.

"*Eins, zwei, drei,*" she had said to herself, hiding in the trees and watching as they shoved the lowing cow up a wooden ramp and into the truck, its bell clattering. Can't let a cow go to waste.

That was what her father always said about the Germans: "It's all *Ordnung* with them. You see it in their farms. Everything *eins, zwei, drei*, everything painted and in its place. That's why they are going to win this war."

Eins, zwei, drei.

There was no place for Roma in a world run that way. Had her father understood that?

Well, he had learned it. He'd gotten that lesson directly from the Germans themselves. Payback, of a kind, for all the lessons he had taught Kezia.

After the cow was gone, there was not much left to take from the town but honey, and some pickles she found in a root cellar that had survived.

But the bees would keep making honey all summer long, at least. All summer and into the fall. Could one live only on honey? She already felt a bit sick at the thought.

She chewed the comb, looking out across the field, watching the bees buzzing over the field of clover. In the distance, a thunderhead gathered, capped violet in the sunlight, darker at its core. A storm was coming. A damp, electric heat built in the air.

What a beautiful world it could be, emptied of people.

Someone was supposed to go and knock on the hives and tell the bees their master was dead. That was the tradition.

But once the bees were told, would they stop making honey? Maybe she would wait and tell the bees tomorrow. Maybe their master was not dead—maybe he had only been taken. Maybe he had run off into the woods and would be back.

But . . . the smell of rot in the church.

And do you burn the houses of people you are only taking away?

And what does any of that have to do with Ordnung?

She could still hear the burst of submachine-gun fire that had killed her father and uncle.

When she began to hear Cosmina's screams, she pinched the inside of her arm, hard, until they went away.

It wasn't Ordnung—it was madness.

"Little girl . . ."

The voice had come from the forest behind her.

A voice in Belarusian. Too close to her.

She had been lost in thought, watching the bees buzzing over the field, watching the crows circling the church, trying maybe to find a way in to the dead there.

The ever-practical crows.

She had been caught by surprise. If the man had not chosen to speak first, if he had managed to come up on her quietly . . .

She could still hear Cosmina's screams.

There were two of them. Peasants, with big sacks hanging from their belts. Peasants, come to loot the burned Jewish houses.

One of them carried an axe. The other had a knife in one hand. When her gaze glanced off the knife, he put it in his belt and smiled.

"What are you doing here, little girl?" knife-man asked. "Are you from this shtetl?"

She shook her head.

"She's lying," axe-man said. "Look how dark she is. She's a Jew. She must have been off in the woods when the Germans came."

Knife-man nudged his partner. "Are you alone, girl? We came to see if anyone survived. It's terrible, what happened here." He took a step toward her, showing her his filthy palms.

Kezia got to her feet. She measured the distance between her and the two men. How much time would she have?

"What are you doing with those sacks?" she asked.

"We're hungry," knife-man said. "The Germans took everything from our village. Every scrap of bread. And all the livestock. They didn't do to us what they did to your people . . . but what they did was enough. If we don't find food, we'll be dead when winter comes."

"What is it they did to my people?" she said.

"She doesn't know," axe-man said. "I told you—she must have been off in the woods. Gathering wildflowers or something."

The way he had said *gathering wildflowers or something* made her ill.

"They do love to gather their wildflowers, these Jewesses," said knife-man. "Sometimes with their boyfriends." But his friend, or brother, gave him a look, and he shut his mouth.

Knife-man tried on another smile. It was a terrible thing, like the bared teeth of a ferret, cornering a chicken.

"We can show you . . . in the sand pit up the road. But maybe your family survived. They may have taken some of the Jews to work. Making shoes for the Germans. Mending their uniforms. Maybe your family aren't there, in the sand pit. We can go and look for them together."

The way he placed his foot, she saw that he was going to take a run for her.

She had cocked the revolver under her shirt. When his shoulder dropped, she drew it and shot him through the head.

He staggered forward in the pink mist of his brains, and fell to the ground.

Axe-man turned to run. She put a bullet between his shoulder blades.

The crows were flying agitatedly over the church and the rest of the village. She stood in the field and called to them.

"Come and eat! These two are fresh."

She took the knife from knife-man's belt. A good knife, with a handle of antler and a well-sharpened blade. You never knew when you might need another knife.

Then she found a new place to sit, farther from the woods. There might be more of them. And she wanted to be in the sunshine.

The crows circled, examining the feast she had provided for them.

The ever-practical crows.

She could hear Mala's voice in her head:

It's no curse, *you superstitious fool. It is in the* genes, *as sure as the coloring of a horse or its temperament.*

Kezia turned her face up to the sun, the last before the thunderstorm blotted out the afternoon.

Well, if she was mad—as mad as her mother and her grandmother before her—then she fit right in with this world. This was the world madness was made for.

The night before the White Russian hordes descended upon us, I had a dream. Old Rabbi Shochet went from place to place, gathering crows.

The crows were calm in the rabbi's hands, their eyes like buttons. In his yard he stacked the birds like bricks into a shape like a man. A giant of black and gray that now began to rustle and flap, a fidgeting wing at an elbow or a knee, his head a spiked ball of beaks and claws and glistening eyes.

Rabbi Shochet sang Torah verses as he worked. When he was finished, he whispered, "*Emet*," and the man rose off the ground. And Rabbi Shochet's golem of crows floated, with a hiss of wings, above the rooftops of the shtetl. Everyone came from their houses and clapped and sang.

The next evening, as the shtetl was settling into sleep, the real crows came. A screaming vortex in the sky above the town. I ran out from my grandfather's house to watch them. And Joseph descended from that whirling coil in the sky, lunging at me again and again, diving at my head.

And I understood. I went from house to house, pounding on doors to deliver Joseph's message.

Fly!

But no one listened.

—from *The Autobiography of a Burned Village*

10
NERIYA

June 1940

NERIYA SAT ON HER THREE-LEGGED STOOL at the table. Three crows had come that day: Buster, Madeleine, and Moses. Neriya had given Madeleine her name because that one had stolen a madeleine from her one morning last spring. She called the third crow Moses because whenever the crows flew in, he was in the lead. And he seemed, somehow, older than the others. More experienced, though she could not exactly say why.

It was hard to tell a bird's age, once they were adults. They did not show their age like people—like all of the adults she was surrounded by. Adults who seemed impossibly old, lined and battered by life.

And how could birds get old like people, after all? They

weren't like Rabbi Shochet, whose only real movement in his old age was to hobble across the square to open the synagogue (and he didn't even have to do that anymore, now that the Russians had shuttered both the synagogue and the church).

No, birds had to fly. If they aged like people did, that would be the end of them. They must stay healthy until one day . . . what? Maybe they simply dropped from the sky.

She imagined Rabbi Shochet heaving his body into the air and taking flight over the shtetl, his beard in the wind, and laughed.

Moses, in the middle of solving a puzzle she had designed featuring different pieces of string that needed to be pulled in a certain order to release a treat, looked at her as if in reproach.

"Sorry, Moses," she said. "Carry on."

She often imagined what the shtetlach must look like to the birds. She even saw them sometimes in her dreams the way the birds might see them—the rectangles and squares of reed or tile roofs, clustered together at the center of the little towns, then giving way to scatter more thinly over the fields.

Like her own little town. "Barely a shtetl," her mother had said of it. "Barely even a village." A nothing place, little more than a smudge among the fields, with the forest pooling nearly to its edges. A place tied only thinly to the rest of the human world, by a few cart tracks.

And if the crows flew high enough, they would see many other places like it. They would see some that were a little larger, or much larger, adrift in the field-seas between the great green continents of forest.

For people, the country consisted of other people. It was doors and windows, roads and taverns, shops and the stone ravines of city streets. But for the crows, it was a forest world. The forest was at the center of everything. The human places were at the outskirts.

And in the early summer, Moses or Madeleine or Buster or the others might be flying over one of those little ribbons of road and see her below, making her way back to their summer home with her family.

In the early summer, her mother and father locked the shutters of the Vilnius house and the family traveled to the shtetl by wagon, stopping overnight at an inn along the road.

In Vilnius there were many cars now, and fewer horses and carts, but on the country roads the horse was still the main engine.

Her father said, "The shtetl and the city exist in separate worlds. Not just separate places but separate times. One cannot cross over into the shtetl's world by motorcar. Those belong to the city world. We must go to the shtetl by horse and wagon."

Along their slow way, as they passed deeper into the world of the countryside, Neriya would look up and see the birds. She would imagine how easy it must be up above the rutted surface, effortlessly drifting from one world to another.

The wagon passed stork nests on the roofs of humble village houses, the impossibly awkward birds standing among the branches and twigs of their homes like people looking for a lost pocket watch. *And every year they come all the way from Africa, and return there, and know two places, much more different from just Vilnius and the shtetl. Lithuania is their shtetl. Africa is their Vilnius.*

Moses solved the puzzle and gave a caw, which Neriya imagined must sound, to the others, like delight.

In her hand, she held the gift Moses had placed at the edge of the table that morning. When she looked at it, her heart beat faster.

At least now she had someone to tell. To show these things to. She had her father, who—true to his word—had not even told her mother about what kinds of things were hidden beneath the top tray of her birchwood box.

July 1941

"And so I understand," Neriya said, "how Buster knew the Germans were coming. It's easy—he *saw* them coming. He saw them from the air. And he saw that wherever they touched, things were burned or people died. People ran in terror. Buster knew the Nazis were something terrible, the way he would know a hawk was a threat, and would warn his flock. He understood, and he decided he would make me understand too."

She and Czesław were in a neighboring shtetl, several kilometers away from her own. They had walked here through the forest—through parts of the forest that were alien to her but that Czesław already seemed to know well. They had skirted bogs and made their way through underbrush of horsetail and stinging nettle. Occasionally Czesław had put up a hand and stopped them and listened. And sometimes he took something from the forest floor and put it into his rucksack, or examined the berries on a bush, tasted one, and spat it out or did not.

"You know the forest so well."

"I am from Siberia," he said. "Our forests are much like these. Though where I come from, the winter is a bit longer."

Siberia for her meant blowing winds, snow piled high, an Arctic wasteland. When she told Czesław this, he just laughed.

"You are thinking of the far north, where the reindeer herders live. Siberia is a forest. The greatest forest in the world. And it can be cold—it *is* cold—and the winter is long, but there are deer and rabbit to hunt, and in the summers you gather berries and swim in the lakes. When it begins to get cool, that is mushroom season, and you eat well. There are cedar nuts, and if you have been smart you have spent the summer making enough jam to last you through the winter, and you have stocked flour, and pickled everything from the garden, and smoked fish from the lakes and rivers. Siberia is only a terrible place for the people who do not know how to live in it. But most people refuse to learn to live there. They can live there all their lives and do nothing but huddle indoors and complain about the weather. My family is different. We are forest people from Poland. We were sent to Siberia decades ago. But because we knew the forest well, we survived there."

They came up on the village along a path that cut through Norwegian maple and silver birch.

They watched the shtetl from the forest's edge for nearly an hour. Nothing moved among the houses.

But although there were no people, nothing had been burned. Even the synagogue and beit midrash were standing. The shuttered church stood at one end of the square, untouched.

The shops and houses had all been looted. Their doors were smashed in, the possessions of the families—what remained of those possessions—scattered on the floors. In many houses, there was no furniture. The local peasants must have come with carts to take what the Germans had left behind. The pantries were bare, but here and there they found things that had been missed: a can of sweetened condensed milk that had rolled into a corner, a leather belt.

It was here that Neriya saw her first corpse. A man, just inside the doorway of a little house attached to a tinker's shop. A house filled with the smell of death and the buzz of flies.

The man had died with his boots on, shot in his own doorway.

On the doorframe, the mezuzah remained exactly as it should have been, tilted inward for luck. How many had touched it and kissed their fingers? How many times had this dead man, his head in a dried pool of blood, his brains picked over by flies, touched that mezuzah, crossing the threshold into the safety of home?

She did not throw up. She backed out of the house and stood breathing deeply in the street, far enough away from the house to escape the smell of the man's death.

Where were the rest of the people who had lived here?

Czesław came and put a hand on her shoulder.

"You do not have to search that house. I will do it. Keep a lookout."

He walked in, stepping over the man as if he were nothing more than a rolled-up carpet.

It was when Czesław emerged from the house, his rifle over his shoulder, putting a jar of pickles in his bag, that she began talking to him about the crows. About how Buster had saved her. It kept her from thinking about the dead man.

"Buster warned me, the way they warn one another."

Czesław nodded.

"You believe me?"

They were crossing the square, headed toward the tailor's.

Neriya had been to this shtetl, once, to have a fur collar put on a dress before her family returned to Vilnius for the winter.

But she could not remember the tailor's face. She remembered only the man's hands—long-fingered hands on the cloth of her dress, measuring the collar. And the sound, from upstairs, of sewing machines.

"Of course I believe you. That crow follows you everywhere. Isn't that him?" Czesław pointed to the roof of the little town's staved-in, looted general store.

"Yes," Neriya said. "That's Buster."

"I think I met him in the forest," Czesław said. "Him or another one like him. I gave him some bread. I thought he might be tame. Someone's pet."

"He's not a pet."

"Someone's friend, then."

Yes, that was it—he was her friend. That was the only word that made sense.

In the tailor's shop, nothing was left. Not a scrap of clothing, not a bolt of cloth. Upstairs, there were holes in the floor where the sewing machines had been torn out.

They were about to go back downstairs and leave the building when they heard Buster cawing outside.

Czesław crept to the window on hands and knees. "There are three men coming into the square," he whispered. "Not Germans. Lithuanians maybe. Or Poles. They look like farmers. And it doesn't look like they have guns." Czesław crawled back across the room. "We'll climb out the back way. Under the back window is a lean-to. We can get down from that into the yard. There is a shed there, and a back gate."

"How do you know what is out the back window?"

"I looked when we came up the stairs. I always look."

"I did not even think of it."

"You will learn to."

Czesław went through the window first, testing the strength of the lean-to, then dropping down from the edge of its roof into the yard behind the shop.

Neriya caught her jacket on the window frame but made it outside without tearing the cloth. The roof was steep. She was afraid to jump but did not show it by hesitating.

Standing next to Czesław in the yard, she waited while she caught her breath.

She could see Buster circling above the village. He was not cawing now. *He is trying not to draw attention to himself. Or to us.*

She thought of the crows she had seen the day before, flying above the forest. They were her flock, she was sure. They had always been noisy when they returned home, before the war, cawing and chattering with one another. They had reminded her of the tired, disgruntled workers who streamed out of the factories in Vilnius every evening.

But no longer. The flock was so silent that she could hear the sound of their wings beating. The sound of the air passing over their feathers.

They knew there was danger. They did not want their home, deeper in the forest, to be discovered.

The voices of the men drew closer. They were speaking Lithuanian—she recognized its cadence, but none of its words. Czesław pulled her into the shed as she heard the latch of the gate click.

There was hay in the shed. Czesław pushed her into it, then climbed in himself, piling it on top of them.

The morning was still cool, but here under the hay and in her jacket it was hot and stuffy. She could feel Czesław's shoulder, pressed against her own.

The men were in the yard now, talking about something. One lifted the latch of the shed and opened the door. They could not be looking for them, could they? No, they could not have seen them. And the way they spoke was casual, loud.

One of them began taking handfuls of hay from the pile where Neriya and Czesław were hiding. One handful after another, digging down to her. His fingertip brushed the tip of her nose. One more handful of hay and he would uncover her face, staring in horror into his own.

And then?

But the men went out, leaving the door of the shed open. Sunlight streamed through the open door of the shed, and through the thin veil of hay still covering her face.

Neriya lay without moving, listening to the sounds the men made, out of the yard, somewhere in the square again. Glass broke. The men called to one another. Then there were no more voices.

Now she could hear the sound of fire, and smell it. Czesław stirred near her, emerged from the hay, and went out into the yard.

Neriya lay where she was, not sure what she wanted to do—to cry, to scream in terror? Finally, Czesław came back into the shed, his shadow across her face.

"They are gone. I think it is safe for us to go now."

In the square, the synagogue burned. She felt its heat on her face, even halfway across the square. The flames poured from its windows like the orange, roaring heat of a blacksmith's furnace, surging out into the square.

The buildings next to the synagogue had already caught fire. And soon enough, the whole town would.

Was this what these men had intended? Or had they thought they could burn only the synagogue and leave the rest standing? But it was impossible to burn one thing and not another. The houses all leaned on one another for support, sharing walls and structure.

The church would burn as well—the flying cinders would alight on its roof. And the fields around the village would catch fire, in the dry summer heat, and the peasant huts that these men's own relatives had lived in would go up in flames, while the looters hid in the forest and waited for safety. And when the war ended, they would have nothing to return to either.

She wanted to be angry, but the feeling was interrupted by a memory of a time when she had been woken early by a knock at the door. Her parents were both deeper sleepers than her, and so it was she who had gotten into her robe and opened the door a crack, to find herself looking into the desperate, red-eyed face of a Lithuanian man.

She woke her father and mother. Without understanding more than a few words of the man's agitated speech, her family dressed quickly, took the bag of tools and medicine, and piled into the back of the man's hay cart.

At the man's poor farmstead, in a one-room house, they found a feverish little girl in bed, her abdomen as hard as a rock.

Neriya's father had operated on the girl then and there. He

etherized her on the family table, made his incision, and removed the appendix that had nearly killed her. Neriya's mother sewed the girl up, with a stitch as neat as the one she used for mending dresses.

The girl's grandmother, who had watched it all from a corner, kissed her father's hands again and again, kissed her mother's hands, kissed Neriya, and wrapped a newly knitted shawl around Neriya's shoulders.

And when the girl's father, banished from the house for the duration of the surgery, found out his daughter would live, he came roaring into the room and lifted Neriya's father up in a bear hug, holding him so high that he knocked his head against the rafters.

The Lithuanian peasant family stuffed them with food, stuffed their cart with jars and sacks of more food, and drove Neriya's family back to the shtetl singing.

Where was that family now?

Where was anyone?

I feel as unable to speak as these homes put to the torch. It is too much to ask. I am nothing but a mute fragment, as incapable of speech as these charred beams.

The crows in the trees call to one another. Their calls, at least, have meaning. They still have their tribe to call to. I have no one at all.

—from *The Autobiography of a Burned Village*

11
CZESŁAW

January 1940

"P*o-mo-gi-tye!*" The man called for help again.

In his trench, Czesław shifted his head, trying to identify the exact spot the voice was coming from.

There were two others with him. There was the private, Vladislav something-or-other, a replacement up from the rear, whose face was still well-fed and round. And there was Boris, who needed evacuation. The frostbite on Boris's feet was so bad now that he could only stagger.

But no evacuation had come. Only a handful of replacements, a few days ago, with well-oiled rifles and dressed in clean winter camouflage. "Well," one of the veterans had said, "at least once they get killed we'll have new rifles and ponchos. That's something."

"I can almost hear you thinking," Boris said to Czesław, in a voice flattened by exhaustion. "You stupid fucking Polack. You're so dumb I can hear the gears in your brain turn every time you have a notion. Don't do it. This is the forward-most trench. I'm telling you: That man who is calling for help *isn't one of us*. He's one of *theirs*, calling out in Russian to bait you. If you stick your head up over the edge of the trench, you're dead. As dead as this meat will be by tomorrow." He gestured at Vladislav with a mittened hand.

"That soldier could be from one of our patrols," Czesław said. "Or he could be from another unit. The Finns have been circling us for days now, cutting us into smaller and smaller pieces. Who knows where anyone is? He could have been cut off from his own squad. He could have been injured and left behind."

"And if he is? There's probably a sniper team in the trees, hoping someone will be stupid enough to come and get him."

"So which is it?" Czesław said. "Is he a Finn pretending to be one of us or one of our own wounded being used as bait?"

"Let the medics deal with it," Boris said. "It's their job."

"The medics are all dead."

Boris showed him a square of teeth. It wasn't a smile; it was lips drawn back in pain. "Yes. Because every time someone called out for help, they answered."

The call came again. This time Czesław was able to pinpoint its direction. He might even know the distance. No more than a hundred meters. No more than that.

In the silence afterward, the pines creaked in the cold. And

Czesław saw the scene from above, the way he often did. The replacement Vladislav, cheeks rosy with cold, his eyes shifting from one man to the other as he lay against the rear wall of the insufficient trench they had chopped into the frozen ground. The veteran Boris, holding his rifle uselessly against his chest with his forearms, his telogreika bulked up by the wool jacket he wore under it, a jacket he had stolen off the corpse of a Finnish officer. His hands were wrapped in gigantic woolen mittens, also stolen from a dead Finn.

And himself, Czesław, tense, on all fours against the forward slope of the trench, his helmet just below the level of the rotting log they had pulled over to provide more cover. Him—the big, broad-shouldered private in a telogreika that barely fit. Raw, red hands in their fingerless wool gloves, mittens shoved into his belt. An awkward-looking soldier with a boy's head, a boy's underfed face, ridiculous under the rim of the helmet that sat on top of it like a soup pot.

Just a boy, riding atop a man's body. Still just a boy.

Then the boy was up and over the edge of the trench and running. He ran in a half crouch, bent over his rifle, because making himself just those few inches smaller could save his life. He ran, setting a foot and turning to avoid the trunk of a pine. Snow underneath and snow above, and the bars of the pine trunks between.

He ran past one of the dead medics, face turned to the sky, wearing a glass mask of frost, eyes wide on nothing.

Czesław saw himself as if he were just over his own shoulder. Big shoulders that could carry a load. Dodging around another trunk. Sure-footed in snow. If you did not see his face, you would not say this running soldier was a boy.

If these were his last moments, they were good moments. Right moments. A hussar with his horse shot out from under him, running forward with his saber over his head. Running into the teeth of the enemy.

From behind, you could not see the terror in the little boy's face, the terror of death. And if you could not see it, maybe it did not matter.

For a moment, he was afraid he had lost his way, and then the voice came again: "*Po-mo-gi-tye!*"

Help!

Czesław placed a foot, adjusted his weight, angled slightly to his right.

He kept expecting the bullet. As if he would be able to see it, to hear it. But they said you never heard the one that hit you. He had heard so many of them zip past him, cutting through the air where he had just been, where he was just heading.

He saw the man, lying on the ground. One of his legs at an angle that made Czesław's brain scream, *Wrong!*

And the man saw him. Or his eyes were pointed in Czesław's direction, at least.

Was he seeing anything anymore? He took a breath, like a sack inflating, and cried out for help again.

And then Czesław had reached him, was lifting him, struggling to get him up and onto his shoulders. Was running with him, on his back like he might carry a small child.

And the bullet came. The crack, and the whir of it as it cut the air, close.

Nothing to do now but keep running, and hope.

Another bullet. Czesław did not hear this one in the air, but he saw it punch into a tree trunk in a burst of snow, bark, and lichen.

Was he even running in the right direction? In a moment of terror and uncertainty that almost made him stop running, despite the bullets, he was certain he had begun running not back toward his own lines but *deeper into the forest*. Toward the enemy.

But his feet kept moving. And he found it: the fallen log they had pulled over to their dugout for more cover. Then he was over, in.

Boris was exactly where he had been. He and the replacement Vladislav stared in awe at Czesław, gently leaning the wounded man against the dugout wall.

"You'll get a medal," Vladislav said. "A promotion."

"That was the stupidest thing I have ever seen anyone do," Boris said. "So, yes, you'll get a medal for sure."

The man Czesław had saved looked from one of them to the other, his eyes huge in a starved face.

Czesław saw what the man saw: the round, frightened face of Vladislav; the sunken face of Boris, so hollow that his cheekbones jutted out from the side and gave it the shape of a cross. And Czesław, his ridiculous boy's head, smeared with dirt and soot, balanced on the shoulders of a grown man.

"I think that first shot was one of theirs," Boris said, "but the second one was definitely from our side. They almost killed you, running back into our lines like some idiot bogatyr."

The man Czesław had saved opened his mouth in uncomprehending horror and screamed:

"*Po-mo-gi-tye!*"

August 1941

From his hunter's blind, Czesław watched the buck. It had raised its head and was sniffing at the air. But Czesław was upwind from it. Still, it had heard something, sensed something.

Czesław's father had always told him: Animals have smell, sight, hearing, all the senses we have. But also senses we do not. Ways of knowing we humans have no name for. Senses we have lost or neglected. Senses we never had.

The buck *knew*. Knew he was there, sensed it.

Czesław could not get a clear shot. He had set his blind up to give him a shot where he expected deer to show, on a ridge along a clear deer path through the forest.

But the buck had stopped short. His mighty head, with its root-spread of antlers, was obscured behind the trunk of a thick weeping birch. The bulk of his body was screened by brush and a fallen pine. No clear shot.

A knowing we have no name for.

Please. Please. We need this.

He sent the prayer to the only god he had—a nebulous, incoherent god of battle-luck and forest-fortune, a god who might make a bullet miss if he was angry or bring a deer from cover if he was pleased. A god who might nudge a coin flip or put a needed card next on the pile. A god who was capable of little more than that.

The buck turned and crashed through the underbrush. It knew.

Another morning, then.

He had left the girl who called herself Agata sleeping in the zemlyanka. He'd left before sunrise, crept out from their camp with the rifle over his shoulder in the blue hour, when the forest was just taking on its first colors.

She might be up by now, reading that book of hers again or collecting wood near their camp or playing with her crows.

The crows had found her at the new camp, and in the mornings they visited her there, taking her gifts of bread and other food. Sometimes only one of them, sometimes five or six.

When she spoke to Czesław, it was often about the crows. When she spoke to the crows, it was in a language Czesław did not know, although he sometimes heard words adrift in it that seemed familiar.

This morning Czesław had found himself thinking, again, of the Winter War in Finland. Of the man he had tried to save, but who had been beyond saving. Of how the man had continued his calls for help *after* Czesław had saved him. Continued calling for something that had already come but that he could not recognize.

Boris had tried to stop the man by covering his mouth. "He'll give up our position."

Finally they had to gag the man, though his moans moaned through the gag were almost as loud as his screams had been.

Two days later they were relieved. The man, with a splint Czesław had made for his leg, was driven away on a truck. When the medics took the gag off back at the staging area, he resumed his cries for help, just as if he were still lying on the forest floor, surrounded by enemies.

Boris had grinned at Czesław through the slats of the truck evacuating the wounded. "They're going to cut my toes off. I'm going to be back home in Samara with flippers for feet, thinking of all the stupid things you are probably doing, boy."

And then the sarcastic smile dropped from his face. "For God's sake, boy, keep your head down from now on. You'll never get out of this war alive if you keep trying to save people who are beyond saving."

The truck carrying the wounded moved forward with a jerk and went off down the rutted, frozen track, its back wheels sliding, the man whose name Czesław never learned still screaming for help that had already come, Boris's face obscured by a blue cloud of diesel and by the smoke from the cigarette he had managed to get from someone.

But who was beyond saving? And how would you know? Maybe, a few days later, the man's madness subsided. Maybe, while Czesław was here in the forest, that man was back in his village now, saved and never knowing who had saved him, tending pigs as their backs steamed in the early morning cold.

On his way to camp, Czesław stopped by an abandoned farmstead he had visited before. He waited several minutes inside the tree line before approaching, watching the sun turn the dilapidated one-room house and corn barn yellow.

Things that were abandoned did not stay undisturbed for long. Houses were soon broken into and looted, barns emptied of anything people could eat. This farmstead was the same. The house was empty, its floor of pounded earth filled with looters' bootprints, its furniture turned over, its hayloft barren.

There were no farm animals left nearby, and the two shtetlach within a day's walk had both burned—the one "Agata" came from and the one they had later visited. When he had returned to it in late July, he saw that the fire lit in the synagogue had burned everything but a few outbuildings. It had decimated the church and spread across the meadows almost to the forest itself.

But there were farms scattered around the forest edges that were still inhabited. He did not yet dare approach them, but he knew a time would come in the winter when he might have to go to their doors and beg for help.

He and Agata had built an oven in the zemlyanka for making bread, assembled from bricks they took from a charred hearth in the ruins of her own shtetl. So they had bread. And due to their scavenging they had enough flour and plenty of food.

For now. But if he could not bring down a deer, or trap a few rabbits, the winter would be hard.

He had walked far into the woods, away from the camp and the farms, and the forest there grew thicker. Streams cut their way deep into the sandy soil, so that the banks were nearly too steep to scramble down. Several times, he had to skirt around vast bogs edged with black elder, their stagnant waters bright green with duckweed between islands of bullrush and bog rosemary from which frogs called.

He had tried, as best he could, to remember the places where a higher ridge of earth allowed passage past them, to darker and thicker parts of the forest. Places woodcutters had never been. Places where the trees grew thick and gnarled. The old places that kings and tsars had set aside for themselves. The places the deer ran to. If they had to go in there . . .

The forest was not empty. He often caught the smell of cooking fires on the wind, and everywhere he saw signs of people. A week before, several kilometers from their camp, he had climbed a tree and waited as a group of Russians passed below. Not scattered men, from a broken army—these had already reorganized. They were not in uniform, but their civilian belts were hung with grenades, and they had a leader.

He had considered calling out to them. But he watched the leader carefully. He knew a politruk when he saw one, and he knew he was just as likely to be shot for desertion or as a spy as he was to be taken into their ranks.

And even if he did make it into their ranks? What, then, of Agata? They might take him, but they certainly would not take her. And she would not make it alone. No one could.

Later he had come across a rough camp, nothing more than several poorly hidden zemlyankas and moss-covered lean-tos, where some local Belarusian peasants were trying to wait out the Germans.

And a week ago he found something much worse: a family camp, torn apart as if by wild animals. Its former occupants, three generations of them, lay shot dead and unburied in a naked line. They were Jews.

He had told Agata about the Russians and about the Belarusians, but not about that.

Instead, they talked about vigilance. About keeping alert. And lately, Czesław had begun to move fallen logs, creating snags that made the approaches to the camp more difficult.

He had considered sound traps—cans, perhaps, tied to string, to alert them to a stranger's approach. But traps were a warning in both directions: they could give notice, but they also alerted the intruder to human presence, and told them they had been discovered.

Czesław smelled bread baking.

He heard a crow, calling harshly in the trees above him. Not the kind of occasional *krok* sound they might make while playing—it was a warning call, the kind he often heard in the taiga when hunting, as he intruded into a crow's territory. He'd always imagined the bird up in the branches telling the others: *Men with guns! Men with guns!*

Czesław saw the stranger, standing just where the trees thinned slightly, at the foot of the rise.

He stopped where he was, aware of the fact that, for the last minute or so, he had been hurrying slightly. He had not been paying attention and had not tried to conceal the sound of his movements. Distracted. Planning, thinking, plotting. Not in the moment. Loud.

"You can come out, boy," the man said in Polish. "The girl won't come out, but that is all right. You are the one I want to talk to, anyway."

The stranger had a rifle, but it was over his shoulder. He put his hands up, showing Czesław his empty palms. "I'm not here to hurt you," he said. "If I was here for that, I would already have done it."

Czesław slung his own rifle over his shoulder and stepped out from behind a tree. He walked toward the man, his hands also up, in that gesture of false helplessness. Ready to roll to the side, to free his rifle and at least try to survive. Watching the man's hands for the slightest twitch, watching the position of the man's body.

But the stranger seemed almost casual. He was a tall man—lean, but not from hunger. His clothes were clean and well mended. He wore a wool cap and good German-made boots, the kind that laced up the front. All as if he were simply out for a stroll in the forest.

Czesław stopped several meters from the man, waiting for him to speak first. He would not let his eyes go to the wisp of smoke from their hidden chimney, but he also knew it did not matter: this man was *of* this place. Czesław could tell that. The man had smelled the smoke. He already knew who was inside the zemlyanka. He knew when Czesław was returning. He had been waiting for him. And he had visited them before. Staying a bit farther off. But he had been there. Czesław had sensed it and then dismissed it. But now he was certain: this man had been watching them.

"I am going to sit down on this log, here," the man said. "Is that all right with you?"

Czesław nodded. "I sensed someone was stalking us," Czesław said. "You came yesterday. The day before as well. Just after dusk. But how did you know we were here?"

The man sat. He took Czesław's measure for a moment before speaking.

"You did a decent job concealing this place. You made it very hard to approach," the man finally said. "Of course, it was well hidden to begin with—a poacher's hideout. It's been here since the last century. At least, my family has known about it since then. We never let the poachers know we had found them out, of course. It is better to *know* where the poachers are than to try to *guess*. And when I was a boy," the man continued, "there was a hermit who lived alone here for years. A Jew who fled the pogroms after the first war. Half mad. We brought him bread sometimes, but he only fed it to the birds. Then one day he was gone. After him, this place was not used much."

"You are a forester," Czesław said.

"And you are a Red Army deserter. But you are Polish, which is curious."

"My family was deported."

"When?"

"In 1919. From Białowieża."

The forester nodded. "Good forest there. Old. Unspoiled, thanks to the royalty who wanted its hunting grounds for themselves. And you are a hunter."

Czesław said nothing.

The forester waved a hand. "I would not trust me either, in your place. You should not. You are smart. How did you get into the army so young?"

"I lied about my age," Czesław said. "But I am not so young anymore. And I am not a deserter. My unit was surrounded. Most of us were killed. Those of us who survived were trying to break out of the pocket—but everyone had gone mad. Some politruk tried to kill us for regrouping."

"No," the man said. "It sounds like you aren't a deserter. But the Red Army has most certainly deserted *you*. Well. Here is what I came here for: to warn you. You must do an even better job hiding this place. I did not need to look for it, of course, because I know where it is. But if you do not conceal it better, others will find it—Germans, Russians, Poles, Lithuanians, Belarusians, Ukrainians. It won't matter who they are or what side they are on or what side they tell themselves they are on. They will need what you have, and they will take it."

"I won't let them."

"They will be prepared to fight you for it. This forest is filling up with people. Most are from the cities, from the towns. They do not know the woods. They will only be able to survive by taking what other people have."

Czesław tried to say again that he wouldn't let them. But the forester put up a hand.

"And there will be the Nazis," he said, "hunting for the Jews hiding in the forest. The ones they haven't managed to kill yet. And for escaped soldiers, too, and for anyone else who might try to fight back."

"We just want to live."

"Good. That's the best way to fight back. But besides the Germans, there are the Russians. The Russians will be just as bad. My family was also deported—a year ago, in 1940. The Bolsheviks came for us after having registered me. They deported all the foresters east, to Siberia, along with our families. But I was on patrol during the roundup. They didn't find me at home—so they took my family away and kept a guard at my house. When I returned, I saw the Bolsheviks before they saw me. I hid in the woods, and I have been here since."

"For more than a year?"

The man nodded. "But that is just the beginning. Now the Germans have the Russians on the run. But it can't last. They have awoken a sleeping giant."

Czesław thought of the endless train ride, from his home in Siberia to Moscow. Then of the endless ride from Moscow to the Finnish border. The train windows looking out on an ocean of forest in which only the names of trees changed, the way the color on an endless expanse of water might change, then change back again. "No, it can't last," he said.

"And the Poles will be no better. Do not trust them either, even though you feel you are one of them—it is their fate to fight against everyone. They will have no mercy left over for children hiding in the woods. They will most certainly have no mercy for the girl. There is a war in these woods, and it is a war of everyone against everyone. But especially of the strong against the weak. Do you understand?"

"I understand."

The forester nodded. "Good." And then, after a long pause: "You remind me of my own boy. He's not much younger than you. He would do as well as you have, here in these woods. Maybe better, since he knows them well. But I had a dream last night that they threw his frozen body from the boxcar of a transport train. I fear he won't survive out there, in Siberia."

"The forest is the forest," Czesław said. "He will know what to do there, the same as here. The winter is longer, but the trees are much the same. The animals are much the same."

"It is kind of you to say that. But even here, the leaves are changing already—earlier than I have ever seen. There is an urgency in the air, even now at the end of August. The animals know the fat times of summer are fading. Do you sense it?"

"I sense it."

The forester nodded. "It will be an early winter, a cold one, and long. People will not eat well. But the wolves will eat well this winter. And men who prey on others will eat well enough."

Czesław had heard wolves sometimes, singing in the dark.

He had never been afraid of them. But he had never, yet, spent a full winter in the woods. Perhaps he would come to be afraid of them.

"I will keep your secret," the forester said. "For as long as I last. And I have left you a gift, just beyond your zemlyanka, there. For you and for the girl."

Czesław nodded.

"Even when there was no war here," the forester said, "they say these woods were dangerous. The pools of their bogs would shift in the dark to drown a stranger, and people who wandered too far into the woods saw lanterns in the trees, leading them astray. They even say there were werewolves, deeper in."

"Stories to frighten children."

"Maybe. But stories are paths to truth. From now on, trust no grown man or woman. Keep yourselves to yourselves. Bake your bread only at night. Make no fires during the day. Speak only in whispers. Hunt and slaughter the animals you take farther from where you live."

"I will."

"And remember what I said: There is a war in these woods, and it is a war of everyone against everyone."

"But somehow not of you against us."

"Not yet. But even that may change, if things get bad enough. You should run, if you ever see me again. Do you understand?"

"I understand," Czesław said.

"Speaking of werewolves—do you know why our ancestors were once so frightened of them?"

"No."

"My grandfather told me the secret: It is not because they are men who turn into wolves. It is because they are wolves who turn into men."

▫ ▫ ▫

Beyond the zemlyanka, after the forester had gone, Czesław found a deerskin, wrapped around several kilograms of smoked meat.

Inside the zemlyanka, Agata was sitting on the sheepskin. When Czesław came in, she said, "I heard what he told you."

"He meant for you to hear it."

"Teach me to hunt," she said. "Teach me to shoot and do everything you can do. To fight. I need to know these things. And in return—"

"I don't need anything in return."

"In return," Agata continued, "I'll tell you two secrets. One about myself and the other about the crows in this forest. Something I have told no one."

Czesław nodded.

"My name is not Agata," she said. "My name is Neriya, and I am a Jew."

"I know you are," Czesław said. "I have known it the whole time. It doesn't mean anything to me."

"Maybe not to you. But I am also one of those people from the city whom the forester spoke of. One of those people with no experience in the woods. We came to the shtetl every summer, so my father could help the people here. But I am from Vilnius, and I don't know anything about the forest. I don't want to be helpless here. And the Nazis will be hunting for me."

"The Nazis will be hunting for all of us."

"But especially for me. I heard what he said."

"I doubt they will treat a Russian soldier any better than a Jew."

"My parents . . . do you think they are dead?"

"You said before that your father is a doctor. Everyone needs doctors. Even the Nazis."

"My mother knew medicine as well. She wanted to be a doctor too. In a way, she was one. She *is* one," Neriya corrected.

"Then they would need her too."

She wanted to believe him. He could see that. But he thought of the anti-tank ditch in which men, women, and children lay shot to death. Had anyone asked them their professions before killing them?

I did not know what sanity was until I lost it. Now I think of winter. The children from the shtetl would climb the little hill outside town and slide down on whatever they could find—old sheets of tin, crates . . . for the lucky few an inherited sled. Up and down, until a groove was worn, a frozen trough each one followed, and each made deeper.

That is sanity. The rut that keeps our minds from straying any which way. The worn thoughts of those who went before us. But I have gone too fast. I have run up over the edge, out past laughter, into a blank and frozen world.

And then the crows called me to this place, this home in the ground, where even if the rutted track of sanity is lost to me, I can at least be warm.

—from *The Autobiography of a Burned Village*

12
KEZIA

November 1941

THE BEES WERE LISTLESS in their hives. There was no longer any honey to be taken from them.

"Sleep, then," Kezia muttered, through cracked lips.

There was nothing to be taken from this village anymore. She had found everything others had left behind.

She had even gone into the death-stinking church and broken into a cabinet in the priest's quarters, a place other looters had missed or had not dared to touch. There she had discovered mittens, a man's wool coat, a man's wool shirt, and thick pants, which she cut to shorten them.

That discovery had probably saved her life.

But nothing could keep her warm at night.

She now slept buried in a moldy pile of hay in a miserable outbuilding of the same burned farm the beehives belonged to. She slept in all of her clothes, the wool pants under her skirts. But the cold found her there as well. She was afraid of making a fire—many times, she had heard voices in the forest, or out across the fields. Many times, she had to hide while groups of looters searched the burned ruins of the town, or armed men wandered through.

She woke up on a full-moon night to a strange sound. Crawling out from where she lay, she saw what looked like an entire town of peasants on the move through the burned village. The crowd was silent with exhaustion, a full moon lighting drained faces. Women, old men, children. They staggered through the charred, deserted streets and onward into the trees. A procession of the dead.

In the morning, she found the boy.

He was standing in the middle of the street. He must have been left behind by the others.

But how could they simply leave a child behind?

But . . . the way they had looked, barely human anymore. She remembered times when her own band had wandered hungry. Lean months when the food went short and you became mindless, little more than a marionette of tendons moving your own skeleton around.

The boy had fallen out of step, perhaps. Or had collapsed. Had his mother or father been among the villagers? They should have noticed. But perhaps they were not there. Maybe the boy had already been orphaned, just moving with the mass.

He wore a tattered white shirt that hung down to his knees. He had no shoes: his feet were wrapped in rags. He wore pants that must once have been someone else's pants, even more ill-fitting and clumsily altered than the pants Kezia had trimmed for herself. He had no coat.

How had he survived with no coat? He wore a tattered straw hat on his head. The kind of hat a farmer might wear out in the field, rudely made and falling apart. It was crammed with bits of cloth to make it warmer.

She tried speaking to him in all the languages she knew. He did not answer.

"Well," she said finally, "you aren't my problem."

She left him standing where she had found him and went back to her hay.

She had been sleeping more during the day. She was hungry, and that made her more tired. She lay down inside, covering herself with the hay, and went to sleep. It was better to sleep during the day, when it was a bit warmer.

When she woke up she found the boy in the hay as well, curled up against her like a puppy.

She shook him awake.

He stared at her, waiting.

He was going to make himself her problem.

She should take him to see the corpses of the men she had killed, the skeletons that the crows had picked clean in the fallow November field. Take him there and show him the kinds of things she was capable of.

But she had a feeling that dead men, even skeletons grinning up at the sky, would be nothing new to the boy.

Maybe they were nothing new to anyone anymore.

At sunset the crows flew over, in a silent mass, headed into the woods.

During the day, they sometimes stopped to glean the village fields. They always found something—things humans would not eat. Or would not eat *yet*.

Sometimes she would feel eyes on her and turn, expecting a person, with her hand on the gun in her belt, to find herself looking into a crow's eyes. One of them standing on a post or a fence rail, or on the crumbling chimney of a burned house, watching her. Tilting its head to look her in the eyes. As if asking something.

That night she made a fire in the woods and fed the boy the same meager corncakes, the last of what she had been living on for weeks now. Soon enough, even these would be gone.

And then what are we going to do?

She had not intended to think *we*. She had meant *I*.

But across the fire, the boy sat, in his tattered straw hat, eating a corncake.

He had become her problem.

They slept in the moldering hay, the boy against her.

In the morning, she took him into the woods.

She knew the way. If there was a gift Kezia had, it was this: Having learned something once, she remembered it always. Having been somewhere once, she could find that place again.

She had followed a person, one of the looters, when he left the village a month ago. She had stayed at a good distance from him—so far from him that several times she nearly lost him in the trees.

Maybe the looter was a man. He was as big as a man, and carried a rifle over his shoulder, like a soldier or a partisan.

But she saw soon enough that he was a boy, no more than

her own age. She watched him from a hundred meters away as he uncovered a door in the ground and went inside.

A month later she saw him in the village again, sifting through the burn pile of a house. He found two singed boxes there, loaded them into a pack, and took them away.

After he found the boxes, the boy stopped returning to the village. But she had twice gone to where he had uncovered the door in the ground, the hole where he lived. The first time, to see if she remembered it properly: a safe place to return to, once he was gone. She had thought of the gun, of ways in which she could take what he had—with or without killing him.

But without killing him, there was no way. He was the kind who would return. And killing him was not something she was quite prepared to do.

On her third visit to the door in the ground she saw the girl, scattering bread, surrounded by crows. Speaking to them in Yiddish. Kezia recognized the language's cadence. She even knew some words of it—enough to barter a bit. She had learned it by listening closely when the adults sold horses in the shtetlach. When she heard a word once, she remembered. Even if she did not know what it meant, she could reproduce it.

That time she visited the hole in the ground where the boy and girl lived she had nearly been caught. The crows began calling, and one of them flew to a branch just above her, screaming loudly. The girl stopped what she was doing, looking toward the sound.

Kezia had crept silently away, but the damned bird followed her for what must have been kilometers, scolding her from the trees.

Traitor. I fed you. And I fed you more than just bread. I fed you meat.

A few weeks after that, she had felt the madness begin to come on.

The madness had shown itself to her several times since the day she saw it rise, yellow, from the bog where her mother drowned herself.

After she saw the girl, it visited her again.

This time it came with the crows. She was in the field, huddled in front of her outbuilding. She was gathering grass to cut the smell of the mold in the hay.

She heard the sound of wings. The flock was coming in, over the village, the way they did every evening, in a mass with stragglers closing in from all sides. Gathering. But now gathering into what?

Into the shape of a man. Holding that shape, that purposeful shape, though it shivered in the air like a cloud-ship. A man, stretched out, his arm pointing forward, pointing into the forest.

And as the man of crows drifted over her she swore he turned his head so that the gaps of evening sky that were his eyes found her. And then he spoke to her in many voices.

Then he lost his shape, shivering into nothing but a flock of birds again. A flock of birds returning home as the daylight died.

She slept that night with her hands balled into fists, and woke with crescent moons printed into her palms.

Kezia and the boy walked for nearly an hour. She remembered the way perfectly, but sometimes she stopped and listened. There were so many people in the woods now. You could never be certain that, when you looked at the trees, someone was not looking back.

They came to the rise in the ground, the almost-clearing where the trees thinned a bit.

The girl and the boy had moved things to push people away from the place—here a rotting log across the easiest route, there a snag of fallen branches that would guide a person naturally away. An invisible labyrinth. But she found the gaps.

The crows, at least, were silent. Several watched her from the barren branches of the trees but said nothing.

With two hands on the boy's shoulders, she stood him in front of the door in the ground. Then she backed into the trees and waited.

Was it ten minutes before the door opened? Half an hour?

It was the girl who came out. Kezia watched her find the boy. As she crouched in front of him, just as she had, the girl with hair as dark as Kezia's own, who was as tall as she was, thin like they all were now, trying to speak to the boy in every language that she knew.

She watched the girl look around, missing Kezia where she stood, still, obscured by trees.

Then the girl stood, called out: "You can come too," she said. "I know you are there. You don't have to stay out there alone. There is room here for both of you."

How? How did she know?

Kezia turned and hurried away into the woods.

THREE
The Descent of Man

One morning, early in the dawn, I was woken by a tapping. What was it, this sound? Water leaking through the roof?

No. It was from outside. A wooden sound. I dressed in the semi-dark and went out, back through the house to the rear yard. The tapping came from behind the closed gate.

I opened the gate, and a crow walked into the yard. It was not Joseph, nor one of the others I could recognize and had named. There was a dirty spring scum of snow on the ground, and I saw, as the crow walked gingerly across a patch of it, her blood bright on the whiteness.

Carefully, I lifted her to the table. I was able to find the wound after some searching: a gash near the wing joint, caused by barbed wire, or some other sharp thing she had come across on her journeys.

I went into the house and came back out with a needle and thread and the other things needed. As I held her in my hands, she was perfectly still. Even as I plucked the feathers obscuring the wound. Even as I cleaned it with cotton soaked in alcohol. Even as I ran the needle in. She was still, though she gave an occasional croak of pain.

And the entire time, her eye met mine, reflecting myself back to me, bent at my task, my hands steady. Perfect trust. The trust that comes from understanding.

She stayed a week with me, drinking from a bowl in the yard, eating from my hand.

But she never returned, after she was healed. One morning she was simply gone.

What I wanted to know from Joseph, from the others, from anyone who could know such a thing, was: *Who told her I could be trusted? And why had she believed them?*

That was the first time after the war that I was able to look at my hands again, and love them.

—from *The Autobiography of a Burned Village*

13

NERIYA ABRAMOVNA KANTOROVA

November 1971

THE HOTEL was as gloomy as any other in the Soviet Union. The marble floors of the corridors echoed. In the blocks of limestone cut to make the walls seashells glistened, compacted together until they had become stone, quarried to build with but never having quite lost their original forms.

The bell at the reception desk was brass, and old. Not something made in a factory. Something made by hand. Something rung not only by fingertips of the Party nomenklatura but by bourgeois fingers long since purged, old royalties now in ruins, the gloved hands of the extinguished classes.

The woman behind the desk read the name on the passport aloud. "Neriya Abramovna Kantorova. And you say"—she paused just slightly on that word, to imply that no mistake was made, that there must, instead, have been a lie involved—"that a reservation was made in that name. But I have no record of any such reservation."

The woman's eyes met hers. She saw it crawling at the edge of the woman's lips. The suppressed word, writhing there. *I have no record of any such reservation,* Jew. The word the woman had wanted to add but could not.

"The academy made the reservation. I am sure of it. I was in the room when my secretary called, comrade."

"Perhaps you are at the wrong hotel."

"No."

"Well, I have no such reservation. And we have no room for you. It is a busy time here . . ."

As if on cue, laughter echoed down the hall, spilling out from somewhere. A door slammed. She heard the distant wheels of a service cart.

"Perhaps the circus hotel will have room," the woman continued. "I can give you directions."

Neriya took the letter from the inside pocket of her traveling coat and placed it on the counter.

The woman opened the letter and began to read.

Neriya was tired. The train compartment she had traveled in had been cold, and the tea had arrived from three wagons down, lukewarm and tasting of coal, and there had been many other discomforts along the way. And now this woman's ugly tone of voice, her dismissive prejudice, her petty exercise of power . . .

Still, Neriya did not enjoy the changing expression on the woman's face as she read the letter. The settled skein of contempt and bureaucratic power falling away, replaced by a widening around the eyes. Then, as the woman reached the bottom of the letter and saw the name and signature there: fear.

The woman reached for a phone and began a hasty conversation in Lithuanian. Neriya caught chunks of it, phrases:

". . . get out. No, now . . . the bed, have you? . . . Thank God. Just . . . I mean now!"

She placed the phone on its cradle and looked up at Neriya.

"I am so sorry for the misunderstanding."

"These things happen."

"There must have been a mistake." All the woman's power was gone, just like that. Drained away. There was nothing left but fear. Fear of another, with far more power than her own petty rule over this little fiefdom. "On *our* side," she clarified. "The mistake was on *our* side, of course. One moment . . ."

She came out from behind the desk and went down the corridor, moving as fast as she could without running.

In distant parts of the cavernous building doors slammed. There was a brief shouted argument. A cart clattered.

Moments later, the elevator's polished brass mouth disgorged a flustered, sweating woman carrying two suitcases. The woman walked past Neriya without a glance in her direction, an expression of horror frozen on her face, and struggled through the hotel's heavy revolving doors.

The receptionist reappeared, along with a green-faced man who had missed a button on the jacket of his uniform in his haste to get dressed. He grabbed Neriya's suitcase without making eye contact and headed for the elevator.

"Your room," the receptionist said, "is on the top floor. If there is anything you need . . . simply call . . ."

The woman paused. Neriya made eye contact with her. The

woman was simply another frightened, desperate person clinging to whatever petty hatreds, dirty tricks, and mental sleights of hand would keep her and her family afloat in this empire's dark, dangerous water.

"Thank you, comrade," Neriya said, trying for some kind of reassuring tone. "May I have the letter back?"

"Of course. Of course." As the woman passed the letter across, she averted her eyes from it.

Neriya placed the letter back into the pocket of her overcoat. She followed the sick-looking man to the elevator.

In her faux–palace suite, heavy with red velvet and carpets that had somehow survived the revolution, she opened the curtains and looked out over the vacant concrete square.

On the far side, a newspaper kiosk was still open, casting a trapezoid of orange light across the ground. She watched the proprietor and his long shadow fussing with the stacked dailies and the weekly magazines. Then she let the curtain fall back.

After unpacking her suitcase, she settled at the room's writing desk, in a heavy chair, wooden-armed but thickly cushioned in the seat.

She set a thick manuscript in a green cardstock folder on the desk. She opened it, beginning her rereading this time at a page toward the middle.

CZESŁAW

January 1942

Czesław had constructed a kind of travois from birch branches and his coat.

The girl did not resist as he took her from the little shed where she lay in a fevered stupor. The hay clung to her sweat-covered face, the wet mat of her hair.

He had wrapped her in Neriya's quilted coat. She might be sweating, but it was twenty or thirty degrees below freezing out here. He wore a salvaged blanket as a kind of cape, an old shirt tied around his head and ears.

Keeping moving helped against the cold, but he still felt it, freezing his toes in his boots, numbing the tips of his fingers even in heavy mittens, attacking his nose and cheeks.

Move quickly.

Once he had her on the travois, he began to pull it through the snow. He concentrated only on pulling, working the awkward contraption through the trees, dragging it out when it foundered in deep snow, slipping with it on the icy sides of hillocks.

Once, the girl opened her eyes, but he knew she saw nothing. It had begun to snow. The flakes fell onto her eyelashes. Czesław paused to cover her face with the quilted coat. He was worried the snow would cling to her skin, freezing her eyes open.

Her staring eyes never followed any of his movements.

Maybe all of this was to save a person who was already dead. Maybe the fever had already burned her mind away. And of course he was taking her fever to them. Into their home. Was he killing all of them, and for nothing?

Don't think. Move.

He shook away these thoughts. Worry about these things now, and both of them would be found in the spring when the snowbanks thawed, their wolf-gnawed bones settling down into the waters of a spring bog. Cold could kill you while you hesitated, considered what to do next.

He got her home. While Neriya took over, Czesław went back outside and, with a branch snapped from a pine, did what he could to obscure the footprints and the drag marks of the travois, working at it until he was afraid he might not have the strength to get back to the zemlyanka. Working even past that point.

He saw the wolf less than a hundred meters away.

He had already decided to turn back and was sweeping away the prints of his own boots as he backed his way through their maze of false windfalls and snags.

The wolf was big, thick-shouldered in its winter coat of fur, its mouth hanging open, its tongue lying on top of white teeth. It was half hidden behind a tree.

He saw it and did what his father had told him to do: he stood up as tall as he could and looked the wolf in the eyes.

They held that eye contact for what seemed like a minute, or longer.

Then the wolf walked away.

The wolves will eat well this winter.

Yes, that was it. The wolf was too well-fed to bother with them. It had come to see where they lived. To remember the place for later. Just in case . . .

In the zemlyanka, the girl lay sleeping. The boy, still nameless and speechless and so just "the Boy," lay curled up against her on the mattress of hay.

Czesław and Neriya had expanded the zemlyanka, digging deeper into the hillside, lining the walls with wood salvaged from the villages nearby. It was now more than twice the size it had been when they found it.

And in November, when Czesław brought down his first deer of the season, he had not kept the meat. Instead, he had dragged it on a travois to a family camp of Jews a few miles off, where he had been able to trade half the carcass for a good supply of flour.

And for news.

The news was not good. There were no Jews left in the countryside. The shtetlach were all destroyed. Most of the Jews were dead. The only ones left were those who had run off into the forest to join the partisans or family groups, or had been herded into the ghettos in Vilnius and Kaunas. Some who had skills had been shipped off to work camps.

"But most," the man who butchered the deer told him, "are already in their graves. I saw it myself."

"It happened to your shtetl?"

The man paused his bloody cutting. "I *am* my shtetl, boy."

"Have you heard of a man named Abram Kantor? Or a woman named Aderet Kantor?"

"No," the man said. "Who are they? People of yours?"

"People of a friend. They are doctors. The Germans may have spared them. They could be with the partisans."

The man shrugged. "Could be. But the Russian partisans often kill Jews as well. And the Polish partisans often make a point of killing Jews. They say we are all Bolsheviks and this is our fault."

"The partisans might need these two. Everyone needs doctors."

"Perhaps," the man said. "But they might not have thought of that. Sometimes—often—they shoot before they think."

In early December, Czesław returned to the same family camp to trade another deer, the first Neriya had brought down.

But the camp was gone. There were signs of a struggle—the broken door of a looted zemlyanka, a bit of torn cloth on the branch of a tree.

He hoped those in the camp had gotten away. But he feared what he might find nearby and did not search.

Now he watched the new girl sleeping, the Boy curled against her.

"We should light a fire," Neriya said. "I know it is daylight, and we don't light fires during the day, but it is too cold for anyone to be out in this, and too cold in here. She needs warmth, and so do you."

Czesław nodded. "We can risk it."

Neriya dug into the pile of kindling, pulled out a piece of paper. Then stopped.

"What is it?" Czesław asked. The papers they had been burning were mostly old newspapers and advertisements, collected by whoever had been here in the years before—the poachers who had loitered here, maybe even the mad hermit the forester had spoken of.

"This isn't newspaper," Neriya said. "It is something else. It is written by hand."

Czesław looked. It was writing paper. And covered in a cursive script, letters whose forms he did not recognize. "In what language?"

"Yiddish. Have you been burning these pages?"

"No. The pages I burned yesterday were newspaper. We have always burned newspaper. I would have noticed handwriting. This must have been at the bottom of the pile. Can you read it?"

"Yes," she said. She read the words:

איך הער זיי רופֿן צו מיר פֿון טיפֿער אין וואַלד.

"'*Ikh her zey rufn tsu mir fun tifer in vald.* I hear them calling to me from deeper in the forest . . .'"

I hear them calling to me from deeper in the forest. It is the same insistent call Joseph uses, summoning me out on an early morning.

Now it is joined by a thousand other voices. A hundred thousand. There is a rhythm to it. A beat, like the slow thud of a drum.

It comes in the morning, just after dawn, from the heart of the forest. From beyond where I wandered once to find a curtain of black wings that would not allow me farther.

Would that curtain part for me now? And what lies beyond it?

—from *The Autobiography of a Burned Village*

14

NERIYA ABRAMOVNA KANTOROVA

November 1971

THE ROOM had managed to be uncomfortable, despite all its elegance. The bed was like a stone.

She wondered how much work had been put into assembling the springs that stabbed through the thinly quilted surface of its mattress. They would have been better off stuffing it with hay or grass. It would have been more comfortable. She had slept for years on hay or grass beds that were more comfortable.

After a tepid shower she sat, with a slight ache in her lower back, in the hotel restaurant, eating breakfast. She had passed on the buffet of dismal salads and chosen a bowl of lumpy wheat porridge sweetened with a lingonberry jam, which was, despite everything, delicious.

It was early, shortly after dawn. The sun remained hooded by clouds. Although the workday had begun for many in the dark, and although the hotel was full, there were few other guests in the restaurant. Most of the people who stayed in this hotel were nomenklatura. They were able to stay up late drinking and then sleep late, before being collected in their polished Chaikas by chauffeurs for their meetings, which began at civilized hours.

The only people having their breakfast this early were an older gentleman in an outdated double-breasted suit, his hat on the chair next to him, his head gleaming in the restaurant's orange electric light, and a couple in their middle years who spoke Russian when they remembered to do so but kept slipping, in unguarded moments, into the drawling Kresy dialect of Polish particular to Vilnius and this corner of Lithuania.

Neriya's portfolio stood next to her chair, the manuscript inside. She kept finding herself reaching down to touch it, as if it were at risk of being stolen.

She was just finishing her porridge when a young man came into the restaurant. He crossed the room and stood politely at her table.

He was not in a uniform, but he wore his clothes—a worker's coveralls and practical boots—as if they were a uniform. His hair was the color of wet sand on a Baltic beach. The mark of his cap was pressed into its waves.

"You are Neriya Abramovna Kantorova," he said.

"I am." Here she touched the portfolio again, as if at that moment it might disappear.

"I am your driver. My name is Jacenty."

In his car, an immaculately maintained UAZ 4×4, Jacenty

asked her if she wanted to take a tour of the city center, the old town, before they left Vilnius.

"I have seen it," she said automatically. "I was born here, before the war. I saw it after the war as well. I don't need the detour."

They drove out of the city, past the flaking plaster walls of neglected churches, the gaps where synagogues no one spoke of anymore had once been. They drove past wooden fences and concrete construction walls, behind which the burned buildings of the Jewish ghetto mutely collapsed in on themselves.

She had insisted on sitting in the front passenger seat. For a while, as they moved through the city, she watched the scene change, from the warp and tangle of the ancient center to the more ordered repetition of gray-paneled apartment houses.

A light rain overnight had pasted fallen leaves to the road's surface. At the edge of the city, more prefab apartment buildings rose from torn earth. A pile of fallen logs, a surveyed rectangle of forest ripped away, the cranes lifting panels into place to make more identical homes, or to make factories, some of which would produce the panels for more identical homes.

Between the construction sites, where the forest had not yet been torn away, the woods were walls of trunks at the side of the road, topped yellow or orange with the fall, thick and evergreen in places, or dark blue with spruce.

Soon they were outside the city. Here, what had been destroyed in the villages was rebuilt much as it had been. From the road, it seemed nothing, and no one, was missing at all.

She took out the manuscript and opened it to where she had left off reading the night before.

"You can read in the car without getting sick?" Jacenty said. "I can't. If I am not driving, I get ill."

"It's good that you are a driver, then."

"Yes," he said. "It's for the best. It works out well for everyone."

KEZIA

February 1942

In the mornings, once Kezia had recovered from her fever, she and Neriya went hunting. They hunted hares, mostly. There were fewer deer in their part of the forest now. Very occasionally, they saw a wild boar. The boars were mostly nocturnal, but sometimes one could be glimpsed moving from place to place in the early morning. They did not hunt the boars.

Kezia had not known how to hunt, but Neriya was a good teacher. Neriya had learned the places where the hares sought food. The thickets they frequented, the little meadows where the trees thinned. She taught Kezia how to wait in concealment, and how to fire the Mosin-Nagant rifle.

Made to kill humans, the Mosin-Nagant was really too powerful a rifle for small game hunting, Neriya said, with the authority of someone passing something recently learned on to someone else. But they made do.

They always walked far from their camp to hunt. That was a rule. Although there were closer places nearby, the sound of the gunshot could be heard by others in the woods.

Another rule was that if they fired once and missed, they moved on.

Crows accompanied them on every hunt.

At first, Kezia did not notice them. But soon she learned to look for them, up in the branches of the trees or on the ground nearby. As the girls moved through the woods, the crows followed. Always.

And Kezia learned, over the weeks, to identify their calls to one another—to listen to the conversations they were having as they marked the girls' progress through the forest. Their meanings soon became as clear to her as her horses' language had been: a system of meaning not structured in words, exactly, but in *sense* and *tone*, much like music. Songs of danger, safety, caution, the seeing of an unusual thing, warning, joy . . .

She learned the crows' names too. Neriya had named a few dozen of them, and recognized them by the way they flew or walked, or by individual markings. She taught Kezia the names, and Kezia made up her own names for other birds.

On mornings when they did not go hunting—when it was too bitterly cold, or when it snowed, or when Kezia was too tired, they stayed near the zemlyanka. Neriya played with the visiting birds on those days and was joined by the Boy. The two played string games of their invention, tugging bits of food as the birds hopped after them. They made puzzles for the birds to solve and fed them bread.

While Kezia had been in bed with her fever, the Boy and Neriya had bonded over the birds. Kezia was not bitter about this. She did not feel left out.

In those early days, Kezia had still intended to abandon the

Boy and Neriya and Czesław, believing she would be better off on her own. Her plan was to slip away one night, while they were asleep.

Czesław often took the rifle on the coldest days and went off to scavenge. More often than not, he returned with nothing—but sometimes he came back with real treasures.

Neriya said it was Czesław who had found her own treasures, the day Kezia saw him in the village and followed him back: a box of gifts the crows had given her over the years. And another box containing family papers, which Czesław managed to dig out from the burned ruins of her home.

Kezia marveled at the family registrations, the identity cards with photos and colored stamps. She had seen nothing like them before, had not even known they existed. There was one for Neriya's father, and for her mother, and for Neriya herself, in which she was smiling just a little.

People, in the world Kezia had grown up in, were simply born. No pen ever set to paper over it. They carried no cards with them, with their name on them, or a picture. And when they died, they would go the same way.

And there was a picture of Neriya with her family. The only one that had survived the fire. They tacked that picture up on the wall of the zemlyanka, with a nail left over from someone who had lived there before. In the photograph a dark-haired girl, a little blurred, looked directly into the lens of the camera, with a very serious look on her face. Her father and mother flanked her, each with an arm around her.

The picture became a piece of common property for them. All of them caught the others sitting and staring at it, and all of them were caught by the others doing the same, and turned away with a kind of embarrassment, not sure why they were embarrassed, not sure why they returned, over and over again, to gaze at that picture of Neriya in her lace collar.

"Is it your house, behind you?" Kezia once asked.

"Yes. Our house in Vilnius. A man came around—a traveling photographer, knocking at doors. All the neighbors took pictures that day, I think. If you could look past the edge of the photo, you would see a line of families, dressed up to have their pictures taken. I remember my boots pinched. I remember I was irritated about something . . . I had quarreled with my parents over something . . . something about school, which I have forgotten now. I didn't want to have my picture taken. Everyone was so excited, and I hated standing in line with them.

"A few days later, the photographer came back around, with the picture in a little paper sleeve. We set the photograph up on a shelf in the kitchen, always meaning to frame it. In the summer, my father put it in the box with our other documents and took it with us to the village, to place on the shelf in the kitchen there. But this year, he must have forgotten to take it out of the box . . ."

It was as simple as that. You forgot a thing, and it was saved. You remembered it, and it burned with everything else. Or you forgot a thing, and it was destroyed. Or you remembered it, and it was saved. There was no logic, no knowing. Kezia had left a favorite scarf in their wagon when they abandoned it on the road. Where was that scarf now? Wrapped around the neck of a stranger, perhaps. Or burned, or blown to pieces.

On that day, there were no rabbits. They hunted as long as they could but grew cold and decided to return.

"The pages you found, in the hut . . ." Kezia asked on the way back. "Whose are they?"

"I don't know. Czesław says a Jewish man once lived in the zemlyanka, years ago. A hermit. A forester Czesław met told him about the man. He must have just left them behind when he left. The forester thought the man was mad. But he does not seem mad, although the pages are all mixed up, and maybe his thoughts are a bit mixed up too."

You forgot a thing, and it was saved. You remembered it, and it burned with everything else.

"Why would he do something like that? Why would he leave something he had worked so hard on behind?"

"Maybe he believed he would come back for them," Neriya said. "Or maybe he was too mixed up to care anymore."

"Or maybe he knew he wasn't coming back and wanted them to be burned," Kezia said. "Maybe that is why they were in the kindling pile."

"Or maybe they were in the kindling pile because whoever came after could not read them. They are in Yiddish, so . . ."

"Teach me to read." Kezia had blurted it out, not having intended to say it, not planning to ask this question, ever, but it was as if the question had asked itself—had pushed its way up out of her.

"Teach you to read Yiddish? For what reason?"

"While I was in a fever, I heard you reading from another book. In Russian. About how the animals see the world."

"*Umwelt und Innenwelt der Tiere*. The Environment and Inner World of Animals. It's the only one I had with me when I went into the forest. But it's a translation into Russian. You speak Russian. I can just give it to you to read yourself."

"No," Kezia said. "I speak Russian, but I cannot read in

Russian either. Not in Russian or in Polish or in Yiddish or in any language."

"All right," Neriya said. "We can start this evening, if you like."

Kezia did not know what to expect from Neriya. Mockery? Or some kind of condescension? Or some contempt that she would try to conceal but that would come through anyway, making Kezia hate her? She was prepared for something, tensed for something.

There was none of that. There was only—looking back much later on this scene, which played itself over and over again in her memories—a strange change in the tone of her voice.

Kezia understood only later that when Neriya said, "All right. We can start this evening, if you like," it was in her father's tone. That she carried, like all children did, her parents around inside her. That sometimes her parents spoke through her, in the voice and with the understanding of adults.

"Learning to read in Russian will be easy for you," Neriya said. "And the letters mostly match their sounds."

"Well, if it's that easy, you can teach me Yiddish afterward too."

"Only Jews speak Yiddish," Neriya said.

"Okay, then. Teach me how to be a Jew."

And they both laughed.

That evening, they began with Russian. It was easier in the evening, when they lit the oven for warmth and huddled shoulder to shoulder near it.

Neriya picked easy words from the book and sounded them out, tracing the letters with her finger, then had Kezia do the same.

The Boy watched, and Czesław watched as well, though mostly he was occupied with mending his pants, having torn them along the seam that day.

Afterward, as Kezia lay in her bed of sacking stuffed with hay, the letters she had learned floated and glowed before her eyes, writing themselves in the dark in lines of orange fire. She felt warmed by them. And by the sounds of the others, asleep in the same darkness, and by the memory of Neriya's words: *All right. We can start this evening, if you like.*

As easy as that. The letters floated in the dark like the lines the glowing ember end of a stick made in the night, and she sounded them out in a whisper for an hour.

Then she fell silent. All of this was so good. But what would happen to her when the madness returned? Would she hurt them? Would she run away and find herself alone again? Was her madness something that could be stopped? Or would it take her like her mother, and drown her in a bog?

She thought of the man who had left the pages, scrawled in Yiddish, and then walked away from them, gone off somewhere alone. To kill himself, perhaps, the way her mother had.

Very quietly, so as not to wake the others, she wept.

But when she finally fell asleep, the letters returned, assembling themselves into words, then sentences, imprinting themselves in the colors of fire. Speaking. Bringing understanding with them.

The more the letters spoke to her, the further from her mind the madness seemed. The words, in writing like flame, had the power to *organize* thoughts. The writing held things together, linked different parts of her mind.

The words, sentences, paragraphs, chapters, formed a structure. A scaffolding. A wall. An architecture. They had shape. They *gave* shape. They showed her the lines and edges of things, defined them one from the other, gave them their places. Not a wall. A picture. A map of the world was being drawn, in which everything was brought into relation with everything else, and could be made sense of. The tick, the urchin, the hare, the fox, her father, her uncle, her mother's madness, the fear of the horses, the Nazis, the man who once had lived here, the war, the crows of this forest—all of it was related, somehow.

And once she could read everything she wanted, everything there was to be read, she would be able to understand how it fit together. How the whole world fit together.

Spring is a liar. It promises an end to winter. The ice and snow break up. The smallest green appears, the enticement of purple hepatica flowers.

But there is nothing to eat, and under the disintegrating snow the hungry mouths of the bogs hang open, starving as well.

It is humiliating to go to the surrounding farms, hungry themselves, with my hand out. I know what I am to them: the mad Jew from the forest. The one they use to scare their children—children who hide behind their aprons when I come to the door, peering out in fascinated horror.

I return to my home in the soil with my clutch of bread, the torn segment of a loaf. All my human neighbors were willing to give.

I find, on my doorstep, the body of a squirrel.

From the wet, black boughs of oak and maple, the crows watch me accept their gift.

—from *The Autobiography of a Burned Village*

15

NERIYA ABRAMOVNA KANTOROVA

November 1971

THE DACHA, the country house that was her destination, was at the edge of the forest. She recognized the place. She knew that if she walked out into the long, drying grass of the meadows, brittle with oncoming winter, she would find the shtetl. The mounds of what appeared to be earth but were, in fact, heaps of burned boards and beams, the collapsed walls of what once had been homes, left to find their way back to being earth.

Buried streets would still lead through the meadow, between the undulating knobs of the ruined homes, sunk for three decades now down in the soil, broken apart, forgotten by everyone, forgetting their own shapes as well. Containing within themselves, perhaps, something that would be recognized, if they were excavated, as having once been a part of a life. A tin toy not melted by fire, a bit of lace, unburned, pressed into the earth until it was almost, but not quite, a part of it.

And here and there, slivers of bone. Teeth. Traces of those who had hidden, and were burned.

Were they the lucky ones? At least they were buried where they had lived, one with the final destruction of their homes.

The others had wandered through the war years. Had cowered in holes, had lived in fear.

And if they survived? After the war, so many had been naïve. They had believed the gray postwar years after the Nazis were driven out were nothing more than an interregnum between destruction and the freedom to rebuild.

How wrong they had been. There was to be no rebuilding. Not here. Not rebuilding of the kind they had hoped for. What would be reconstructed, instead of their homes, instead of the shtetl, was their entire sense of who it was possible to be. Of, even, who it was possible to *have been*.

The crimes of the Nazis against the Jews would cease to exist, because the Soviet Union decided there were no Jews. There *never had been*. The Jews had become "Soviet Citizens," undifferentiated from the mass of the rest. Crimes that were unspeakable because of their horror became crimes that could not be spoken because the language in which to enunciate them had been destroyed.

The words for nations, like so much else from the past, had become nothing more than raw material: shells, chalk, shale, slate, blast furnace slag to be added to the crushed limestone and sand of ideology, to form the gray concrete of the present and the future—a future like the prefabricated panels of the identical apartment buildings and the samelike factories that metastasized out of the meadows and woods that once had ringed Vilnius.

A future in which everyone was alike. A future in which no one's past had a meaning that differed from the collective.

Even the white church of the local Lithuanian peasants had not survived this remaking. It had outlasted the war, but she did not see it in the meadow. Either it had collapsed under the powers of neglect or a bulldozer had scraped it away.

Bulldozer atheism, people called it. Around kitchen tables, when they were sure no one would hear.

The dacha was a new building. It stood farther along the road, out past the edge of where the shtetl had once been. It was built in an open space formed by a natural bend in the forest's edge, surrounded on three sides by trees and with its back to where the village had been.

Only a few small windows at the rear faced those empty fields. The rest of the house was oriented to the forest. Its porch, front, and side windows looked out onto a stand of silver birch, their weeping branches nearly denuded at this point, readying themselves for winter.

Jacenty insisted on carrying her suitcase from the car for her. Inside, the dacha was dark, wood-walled and gloomy. Like the personal dachas of those who could afford to keep them, it was filled with what appeared to be furniture taken from elsewhere. But usually people took the furniture from their own houses, moving old couches, tables, and chairs to their humble shack in the country, where they bent over a kitchen garden on the weekends, supplementing a barren diet with green vegetables, preserving berries and mushrooms for the winter.

This was not that kind of dacha. The *pechka*, the traditional stove, was there. The furniture inside was mismatched, yes, just as it would be in a typical dacha. But this furniture was all leather and heavy wood: deep, comfortable couches scarred by use; an oak table with four discordant but high-quality chairs around it.

The furniture looked as if it had been salvaged not from someone's meager home but from the lobbies of luxury hotels, the mountain lodges of the shattered upper classes, the apartments and offices of the business magnates the Soviet regime had sponged away like stains from a whitewashed wall.

Above the table was a heavy chandelier of deer antlers—a looming, thorny mass hanging there as if it had drifted in from another time and place.

Care had been taken in the arrangement of things, attention given to making them cohere, but they could not.

"A room has been made up for you on the left," said Jacenty. "I will put your suitcase there. There is running water here and electricity. You may have a shower, if you wish. There is a refrigerator and food. Everything has been arranged for your comfort."

"When will he arrive?"

"Tomorrow, I think."

"You think?"

"He is often delayed, but I know that meeting with you here is of the utmost importance to him."

But—she saw it in his eyes—Jacenty did not know *why* it was important. Who was she, this biologist from Moscow, from the Academy of Sciences? Why was she of so much interest?

Jacenty was, of course, much more than a driver. No one as close to someone in such a high post, no one who walked around this dacha turning on lights and adjusting things as if he were at home, was simply a driver.

She saw in his eyes that he could not place her. It bothered him. He had been told nothing of who she was. He was not used to being one of the ones who knows nothing.

"If you need anything at all," Jacenty said, "you may use the telephone in the bedroom on the right. Ask to be connected to this number." He gave her a card on thick cream-colored card stock.

On the card was only a number, debossed by the printer's pressure. No name, nothing else.

"Thank you."

"I hope," he said from the doorway, "you will be comfortable here."

"I already am," she said.

A few moments later, the UAZ started. She listened to its tires on the gravel drive, the fade of its engine down the dirt road.

Once he was gone, she took off the pinching new shoes she had purchased for this journey, sank into the deep leather couch, opened the manuscript, and returned to where she had left off in her reading.

NERIYA

April 1942

"It's like I understand the words, but I do not understand their meanings," Kezia said. "What good is reading if I cannot understand the things I read? I want to *understand*."

Neriya had never taught anyone anything before. She did not know what teaching consisted of. She had only memories of how her teachers had taught her. None of those memories seemed to be the right way. Her teachers in Vilnius just said a thing over and over, and had you repeat it. Or they just pointed at a thing, jabbed at it, until you said you understood.

And her mother and father? How did they teach? But they hardly seemed to have taught her at all. It was as if they simply left things around so she could find them. So she could pick them up on her own, and then bring what she found to them and share her discoveries.

That wasn't going to work either. But how could she invent a way of her own?

"I wish we had another book in Russian," Neriya said. "This one is so hard. It's not the first book anyone should have to read."

"But at least we have a book," Kezia said. "You could have walked out of your house with nothing at all."

"Yes," Neriya said. "That's true."

As usual, when Neriya and Kezia sat outside the zemlyanka for their reading lessons, the Boy sat with them. It was late in the morning of a warm day. The crows had already flown away. And on this day, the hardest part of winter seemed to have passed. Could it be spring? Was that possible? The forest was filled with the sounds of ice beginning to melt. Shafts of bright sunlight hit the ground between the denuded black trunks of the trees, glistening with meltwater.

"He starts with that part about the tick," Neriya said, "and writes about how it doesn't see anything in its world. Doesn't sense anything much. It only climbs, and clings, and when it senses this—" She pointed to the words.

"Bu-ty-ric ac-id," Kezia sounded out.

"Yes. This chemical that mammals all secrete."

"Secrete?"

"This chemical that comes out of our skin. When the tick senses that, it's like a switch is thrown. The tick lets go of the branch it was clinging to. It drops down. Butyric acid is one of the only things that the tick can sense, and so it's one of the only things that *exists* for it. It can't sense the other things, because those things just don't *exist in its world.* Then the tick senses the hairs of the animal, and the hairs throw a switch that makes it crawl. Then it senses heat, and the heat throws a switch that makes it begin to feed. The tick's world isn't our world. Its *surroundings* are the same as ours, but different things *matter.* And what matters is its world. Its *world* is limited to the things it can sense, and the things it can sense are limited to what it needs . . ."

And then she saw it in Kezia's face: An opening look. A look of wonder. Kezia smiled—a rare enough thing, in itself—and grasped Neriya's knee. Another rare thing: Kezia so rarely touched anyone, only grudgingly allowing the Boy to share her heat in the cold nights when they shivered in their beds of hay.

"I understand," Kezia said.

"You understand what he is writing about? About the tick?"

Kezia grinned. "I understand the tick, yes. But that's not what I mean. I also understand my uncle now. And my father."

Neriya didn't understand this, but she laughed as if she did.

They had grown close over the winter, the four of them. As

close as she might ever be with anyone. She had listened for weeks to Kezia's ragged breathing as she fought fever. She had tolerated, and then accepted, the Boy as he crawled from bed to bed, looking for warmth, though once Kezia's fever broke he chose her to sleep near on most nights.

At night, in the warm glow of the stove, they sat crushing the lice in the seams of their clothing. She had cut Kezia's hair short, down to the scalp, to try to get rid of the lice. And Kezia had done the same for her. It wasn't just the itching Neriya feared—that was nothing more than an irritation that could be tolerated, the way they had learned to tolerate so many things. It was typhoid she was afraid of. She had seen, working in the village with her father and mother, what typhoid fever could do.

As soon as it was warm enough, Neriya wanted to find a way to boil all of their clothes, hoping to get rid of the lice for good. But for that she would need a cauldron, and a fire would have to be made outside. And who knew what the fire would attract?

Together, that winter, they hid in the zemlyanka when the woods suddenly filled with gunfire, as if on all sides, and the screams of wounded people, and later the lost, calling to one another, and the wounded calling for help until they were hoarse. Until they stopped calling.

The help never came. They lay in the zemlyanka looking at each other, not in accusation but in acceptance. There was no question of trying to help the wounded. There were rules that none of them needed to discuss: Stay hidden as much as they could during the day. Hunt far from where they lived. Light the stove only at night. And most important of all, stay away from adults, who all around them were murdering one another.

Death was always close. Once, while Kezia and Neriya were

hunting in the winter, they heard the crows begin to cry out in alarm.

The girls were at the edge of an open space, with nowhere to go, the snowbanks too frozen for burrowing into. But they knew to listen to the crows. The crows had already saved them so many times. So they scrambled up into the black and spreading branches of an ancient elm—climbed as high up as they could.

They watched as below them a dozen men appeared among the trees. A German patrol, soldiers in feldgrau uniforms, the zag of lightning bolts at their collars, their breath clouding in the frozen air, rifles at the ready.

One of the soldiers carried something in his hand, dangled it over the snow. Something that Neriya could not see clearly—or, when she remembered the scene later, something that her mind would not let her see. Something that her mind censored from her memory, blurred out. Something that her mind *would not allow to exist in her world.*

The men stopped below them, as if sensing their presence.

All around them, the crows were silent.

The men were silent as well. They stood, waiting for something, or listening, in a loose circle around the elm, for a period of time that could not be measured.

When Neriya tried to remember it later, it was a limitless interval, a loop to be played again and again forever, all of the sounds repeating themselves. The creaking of branches. The breathing of the men below them. Her own breathing, stifled by her sleeve. A shudder of needles and the rattle of what leaves were left frozen on the trees as the wind picked up, and again subsided.

Then one of the men held a hand up, waved it forward, and they moved off.

And time began again.

It was another long, cold period before the girls dared climb down from the tree.

By that time the numbness of frostbite had begun in their toes and the tips of their fingers. The sleeve of her jacket, which Neriya had been using to muffle the sound of her breathing, was frozen solid.

In the snow, bright drops of blood trailed in where the men had come from and out, following the path they had taken away.

"What did one of them have?" Neriya asked. "In his hand?"

"It was a head," Kezia answered. "A human head."

If it was only the Nazis who hunted in the forest, that would be one thing, but during their hunts the girls came across other scenes.

Once, when Czesław was with them, and only the Boy was left back at the zemlyanka, the three had stumbled on a scene of battle that could be read like a map: Two groups who had encountered one another along a snowy deer track over a frozen bog. Seven men and two women. Four on one side, five on the other. The group of five had been walking along the track. The four had lain in wait behind the massive, rotting log of a fallen wych elm. The five, after one of them was killed on the path, had managed to retreat behind a berm of snow and tangled branches.

The two groups had continued to fire at one another until they were all hit. The last survivor had crawled away a few dozen meters before killing herself with a grenade.

Some other group (belonging to one of these two sides, belonging to another side, belonging to no side at all?) had found them, stripped their weapons, taken any food or valuables they carried, and left the corpses half naked and barefoot. They had frozen blue in the cold.

"Russians and Poles," Czesław had said, after examining the bodies. "Not a German among them. The Nazis are still here, but already the partisans are fighting each other."

"What could they possibly have to fight over?" Kezia had asked.

"They are fighting over what comes next," Czesław answered.

Absurd. It was impossible to think of *what comes next*. To think of any future at all. It seemed obvious, to Neriya, that all of the partisans were—ought to be—on the same side. On the side of life, fighting together against the death sweeping over the land. Because what could possibly *come next* if they failed to defeat death?

What will come next? In those moments, when that question penetrated, Neriya was vulnerable, again, to the thought that her parents might still be alive.

They had already died so many times for her, and been reborn. When she came back to find the shtetl burned, when she saw the charred timbers of her own house, she had mourned them. It had seemed as if the house *was* her family, and its destruction made their destruction a certainty.

But then Czesław had found the boxes—the box of gifts the crows had brought her and the box of family documents. If these things could survive the fire, then maybe her parents had survived as well. Maybe the destruction was not complete.

Maybe her mother and father were out there, somewhere. Maybe Czesław was right. There was always a need for doctors. Even the Nazis must understand that.

But she could not *feel* her parents out there. Shouldn't she feel something *tugging* at her if they were alive? Something pulling her toward them?

She felt nothing at all.

That night after they came back from finding the battle scene between the two groups of partisans, she felt the possibility, the feeling in her, come again. Her parents might be alive.

Because there *would* be a future. All of this had to end eventually. And once it did, one way or another, change would come. A new world would build itself back up again. And it was impossible to think of that world as not containing her mother and her father.

Worlds didn't end—not for good: they were destroyed in part, and then whoever was left after the destruction built the destroyed parts back up again. And the names of things changed, and the languages one needed to know, and the books the teachers taught from at school, and the ideas of what was supposed to have belonged to whom in the past. All that changed.

But beyond all of that, there was just life, simple life. Parents and children, friendships and arguments, and people writing books, and people making films in which people fell in love.

And there was the world of animals, which had not ended with the war. Which had not even paused.

The world of her crows, for example. What was war to them? To Buster and Moses and Madeleine and all of the others?

They had not ceased to live their crow lives when the shtetlach and the farmhouses burned. Buster, who had saved her life by leading her into these woods, and then saved it again and again.

Buster, who watched over her. Who brought gifts now to the Boy as well as to her.

Madeleine, the cookie thief, whose puzzle skills were second only to Buster's, but who didn't feel like displaying them unless she saw which treat she would get at the end.

Moses, the old leader, standing on the table before she came out in the morning, waiting patiently for her to appear. Waiting for their time together to begin.

She was no fool. She knew: Buster was a scavenger. A carrion eater. He would pluck the meat from a human corpse without hesitation. He would jab the eyes out of a human skull and feed them to his children.

So what did war look like to him? Sometimes she saw it from their perspective. From high up above it all, the undulating waves of trees giving way to patches of devastation from which smoke rose. It turned below them, offering here a meal, there an opportunity to watch as more meals were made.

War was a feast. The way the garbage bins of Vilnius were a feast humans had made for crows. Whatever humans did to the world, it seemed the crows understood how to turn it to their own advantage.

But that was not what Buster had seen when he saw the trucks and the tanks coming toward her, was it? He had sensed the danger of it, saved her from it by leading her into the forest.

And a potential feast wasn't what the crows saw when they saw men wandering in the woods toward the children, and called out in warning from the trees.

So what did Buster understand her as? A source of amusement? With games to play in the mornings, if he was not busy elsewhere? A source of certain treats he craved?

More than that. He had led her away because she was more than that. He had given her his gifts because she was more than that.

He was no tick, activated only by a certain signal, no sea urchin from Uexküll's book, pulled along the sea floor by independent automaton legs, reacting to every shadow that passed above it as if it were the same thing.

Buster's world was rich.

As rich as hers?

Richer, maybe, than what her world had been reduced to. As rich, in its own ways, as what her world had been, perhaps. Or as rich as the world she had once believed would be hers.

And Buster's world, and the world of his flock, was richer than the worlds of other crows. Though all crows were bright-minded creatures, Buster, Madeleine, Moses, and the others from *this* flock, from *this* forest, were different.

There were the gifts. She felt a piercing sense of guilt, sometimes, at how much joy she had felt when Czesław returned with the soot-stained birch box of gifts and she held them in her hands again.

The world is changing, Neriya—but I think soon the world will right itself again. There will be a time for exploring things like this, and for sharing them with others.

She remembered her guilty joy at finding that box. A joy almost as great as learning a relative was alive. Her gifts. Her *proof.* Her evidence that it was all real: that she was special, that she had seen things no one else had seen.

Not no one else. The man who wrote the manuscript they had found earlier in the winter had been given gifts too.

The world would right itself again. Her parents would return. And she would visit Buster at his home, somewhere deeper in the forest.

Neriya would survive. The world would heal itself again. It had to. It had to! And she would emerge from the forest with news that would stun everyone. News of something entirely new.

Perhaps—in a year or two—you'll be standing up in front of the Linnean Society in London, presenting your work . . .

She heard her father's voice so clearly. She would make his vision real.

They are rebuilding the shtetl. There are people returning. Not all the buildings were burned. And where the burning was the raw, new wood of construction has appeared, like the pale stems of mushrooms after rain.

I watch from a distance, sure there is some greater calamity massing in the world, waiting for the moment when we feel safe again. Waiting to descend upon us and wipe us forever from the land.

I feel it like an afternoon storm, gathering the humid static of its thunderhead above the fields.

—from *The Autobiography of a Burned Village*

16

NERIYA ABRAMOVNA KANTOROVA

November 1971

HE DID NOT COME that day.

There was food in the ZIL refrigerator, even things that could be cooked, but she did not bother cooking. She ate a plate of cold sausage, cheese, and bread, then wrapped herself in a blanket she had found in one of the wardrobes and went out onto the porch of the dacha, leaning back in a heavy oak chair to watch the day die over the forest.

When was the last time she had paused, for this long, to gather any of her own thoughts? Had it been a decade?

She was not running from anything anymore. She had not been, for a long time.

But still she had the sense of leaning forward, of a watchful, relentless forward motion, of always being on her feet. In the laboratory, in the classroom, on the Moscow Metro, even, as the crowds penguin-walked down the long transfer corridors, no one catching anyone's eye, moving from one place to another.

Leaning forward. Over her work in the evenings, over the papers of doctoral students, over the work of her colleagues, with a red pencil in her hand.

Not running but falling forward through life, keeping too busy to think of herself.

Always moving forward. Purposefully too busy to think of any of this.

Now she sat on the porch and looked out over the forest as the light died. At the crooked trunks of the oldest silver birches, the younger, straighter, more slender trunks rising between them, the generations of trees together. The trunks caught the color of the sunset at her back and turned a fleshy rose in the dying light, then violet against the darkness of the forest beyond.

From here it would be less than an hour's walk to the zemlyanka where the four of them had spent those first two winters together.

She was sure she could still find the way. Even thirty years later, she could find the way back to it. Even in the dark. She could get a flashlight, a lantern, in the dacha, walk into the woods now, and find it.

Her mind began the journey, found the path, imagined the route her feet would take, step by step.

The decades had covered, by now, the last bones of the war's dead in the forest. The bones of everyone who did not make it until the end of the war. The ones no one had found, the ones no one had been left to find. By now the forest soil had reclaimed the lean-tos. It had dropped leaves onto the fire rings until they were stone circles buried in the earth, buried with the rest of the hard traces of the dead. The belt buckles, the salvaged boots, the gold rings and diamond necklaces sewn into seams in the hope for better days.

They were all still there, in the forest. But a part of it now. At peace, woven into the fungal network of the soil, tangled with the roots of the trees.

They waited for nothing, ran from nothing, avoided nothing. Their flesh was forest. They had blurred into and become everything around them, leaving only bones and teeth and the hardest traces behind to suggest they had once been human. Bones, teeth. And trinkets, things that had never been a part of them anyway.

An Order of Saint Anna medal, 4th Class. A relic from the World War . . .

I do not think that whoever once wore it needs it anymore.

And maybe, as a stream flooded or a hard spring rain wore away a hillside, something might be revealed. Something shiny for the crows to use for decoration, or for a gift. But that was all.

She heard them calling before she saw them. A raucous conversation in the sky. Then here and there, a clumsy shape, flapping against the dusk, tilting right and then left, yelling at its relatives and friends to catch up, to come on!

And then blotting out the sky, the mass of them, pouring into the gloaming over the porch, over her head.

So sudden she gasped, grinned up at them as they filled the sky, stood up under the eaves and raised her hands to them.

So near she could hear, in the interstices of their gabbling, the hiss of wind through a million feathers.

The crows.

And not just any crows. *Her* crows. *Their* crows. Not one of them the particular animals they had known thirty years ago, of course—that was not possible. It had been too long, and their lifespans were too short. But all these crows were descended from the flock that, in wartime, had flown this route silently. From the wartime crows who had known not to reveal where they were going. These were the children, grandchildren, and great-grandchildren of the crows who had lived through the war. And further generations, swooping and turning home, now safe in their routine, calling to one another, gossiping in a cacophony of voices.

He had built the dacha not near the burned shtetl, and not where it could look into the forest: those were incidental. He had built it *under the path the crows took when they came home.* Under their flight out over the trees.

A few dropped down, alighting on branches here and there, pausing.

And she saw them tilt their heads, saw their eyes on her, collecting the last light of the sun and reflecting it in her direction.

Taking her measure.

Her crows. *Their* crows.

CZESŁAW

June 1943

A warm summer day.

It seemed impossible, after each winter, for the warmth to

ever return. But it did. And now it was warm even early in the day, even in the morning.

It was warm, and all of them were well. They were alive. They had enough food. They had lived, again, through the darkest part of the year.

He was doing his job. That was what came to him, seeing the Boy and Neriya with the crows, seeing Kezia and Neriya return with a rabbit, or when he was himself returned from a hunt or from an exchange with one of the local peasants. He was doing his job. He was doing what was meant to be done. And he would keep at it until the end of the war. He would keep them safe.

He watched the Boy, who still did not say a word. He had been playing a game with one of the crows, dragging a red thread along the ground as the bird hopped after him. But the crow had grown bored with that simple game and was now perching atop the Boy's head while he walked around in circles, laughing.

Czesław did not play with the crows. But he saw them watching him, all the time. Everywhere he went in the forest, they watched him. At any moment he could stop what he was doing, look around, and find a crow's eye on him.

Observing, but more than simply observing. Standing guard over him, and over all of them. How many times had their calls protected him? How many times had they given him warning, allowed him time to hide?

Had the Boy spoken, before all of this began? Had he been mute since birth? Or was he made mute by experience? This idea did not seem impossible to Czesław, who had seen many men lose the ability to speak, to one degree or another. And had seen others for whom silence would have been better. The man who had called for help in Finland. The man who had still been calling for help when they took him away in the ambulance truck.

Was that man still calling for help, somewhere? In some hospital, far behind the lines, in a ward filled with other men whose minds had been broken by war?

"Why do you think the Boy does not speak?" he had once asked Kezia.

"I think his family were hiding from the Germans. Someone put a hand over his mouth and told him to be quiet. And he is still being quiet."

That made as much sense as anything else.

Czesław still woke in the night, hearing that soldier calling for help from somewhere. When he realized it was only a dream, he was grateful. Grateful for the sound of breathing around him in the almost perfect dark of the zemlyanka. Grateful, even, for the distant call of a wolf that, at least, was not a man.

Everything as it should be.

His family, in Siberia. His mother, who by now must think he was dead. His father and grandfather, who by now were almost certainly dead themselves.

More people he could not help.

The Boy pulled the red thread through grass and flowers. A crow followed the path of the thread, with a dance and a flap of wings. Another crow stood on the Boy's head, cawing, and now had been joined by two more, on the Boy's shoulders. Neriya smiled. And Kezia sat nearby, reading her book.

All of them, at least, were still safe.

They had lived through two winters now. They had lived through men walking around their little clearing in the forest while they crouched underground, silent, Kezia clutching her revolver, Czesław with the rifle, listening to German voices or Polish voices or Russian voices or Lithuanian voices—all of them men ready for violence, all of them at war with everyone else.

They had lived through so much else.

The two great powers of the war had come smashing together and shattered. In 1941, there had been the massive collision itself, the Germans driving the Soviet troops back and back and back. But that first clash had left fragments. Splinters of the Red Army, shards of villages and shtetlach scattered among the trees. Now fragments blew in from the east as well. Men in rags with dead eyes. And the war had fragmented the groups in the forest beyond nationalities and even causes. Lithuanian police patrols encountered anti-Nazi Lithuanian partisans in the woods and filled the forest with gunfire. Polish nationalists hunted for Polish communists, Red Army deserters fought one another for supplies dropped by Soviet planes, and ambushed German deserters staggering back from the eastern front.

And from the cities, terrible news. The Jews of Vilnius and Kaunas had been herded into ghettos. The ghettos were then destroyed, everyone in them murdered.

He had not told Neriya about that. He had kept that news to himself, carrying it alone, along with so many other things. The stacks of bodies from Neriya's village, piled like cords of wood in the tank ditch. A woman he had found, tied to a tree in the forest . . .

He wandered farther than any of them. He heard more. Saw more. He lay outside the camps of partisans, hidden in the trees, listening to them recall the terrors of the forest, and the terrors they had brought on others.

Doing his job.

And he understood that getting his friends through this war meant more than just keeping their bodies intact. He had to preserve their minds as well. So that one day, when all of this was over, they could live again.

Had he become like the Boy? Had he fallen silent as well, lost the ability to speak?

He still spoke, but only about the surface of things. Neriya and Kezia lay for hours in the dark, talking and talking to each other, laughing, sharing stories. Neriya and Kezia had tangled up with each other until their stories were tangled. Until it was unclear to him, sometimes, which of them was speaking.

He listened; he tended the fire. He said less and less all the time.

What was there to say? What was left to tell anyone?

He had thought of his father and grandfather as silent men. He had admired them for that—for the way they could be still and wordless in a hunting blind. The way they could watch for the movement of a deer all day if need be, not making a sound.

But when they were away from the hunt, they were both men full of stories. Easy to talk, easy to laugh.

He was the silent one. Even before the war. Even before Finland.

"Such a quiet boy."

Now he heard it as a chorus of voices. So many had said it of him, over the years.

Such a quiet boy. And he felt himself growing quieter and quieter.

Someone put a hand over his mouth and told him to be quiet. And he is still being quiet.

Yes, perhaps that was how it had happened for the Boy.

But for him, it had been slower.

Years ago, he'd had a place in the world. A small place, but a place of his own. There was his mother and his father and his grandfather and the other Poles they could whisper their own language to. And there were Russians as well, good people just trying to get by in the logging camps, through endless winters, despite the Bolsheviks and the impossible demands.

And then the world had begun cutting things away. The world could not allow him even that small space.

First the world had taken his father and grandfather away. Then it had taken him from his mother. Now it was taking parts of him as well. The world was cutting him down until he was just a fragment of what he had been.

No one was permitted to have anything to themselves in this world.

Sometimes, on a hunt in Siberia, they had encountered a dugout or a lean-to some exile had constructed, in the hope of surviving the regime. Of being left alone. But those places had always already been discovered, the people taken away. Only traces were left behind, like the bricks of an old chimney standing alone in the forest, testifying to the absence of a home.

Now, again, he felt he had a small place in the world. Here, with Neriya and Kezia and the Boy.

But he heard rumors—rumors traveled the forest as if the trees were telegraph poles. The Germans were not defeated. Not yet. Yes, perhaps in the east they were falling back. But here, they were still strong. And they were gathering for an offensive. Gathering to end resistance to their rule forever. To drive the partisans out of the forests. To kill every remaining peasant in the countryside and burn every village left, if that was what it took. Maybe to burn the forest itself.

A German offensive was coming, and the partisans of the forest knew it. They were stockpiling, preparing.

And this place, their little zemlyanka with its weak protection of fallen trees and watchful crows, was too close to the edge of the forest to be safe. The forester had known of its existence. Others would know as well.

Czesław had already begun to think of escaping from here.

"Isn't there any place in the forest to run to?" his father had once asked in Siberia, as the three generations stood around a destroyed exile camp, clothes scattered on the ground, a broken shovel.

"There are places," his grandfather had answered. "Farther in. Places safe from people. But from where there is no coming back."

The shuddering avian wall he had encountered two summers ago, deeper in the forest. Every glossy eye on him, the whole forest winged, alive. Every tree watching him with hundreds of eyes. Every stone with its feathered sentinel. And the threat from a hundred throats.

Farther in. Places safe from people. But from where there is no coming back.

He had a dream in which the four of them—he, Kezia, the Boy, and Neriya—stood before that wall. It shook and threatened when he approached . . . but when the eyes saw Neriya, the wall of wings parted for them like a curtain.

He had that same dream several times. But he always woke before seeing what was beyond.

In the city, that place of forgetting, we were modern together. The world was being reshaped as we were being reshaped. The world, like us, was becoming something new.

But in the trenches, with my hands over my head as the artillery rained down, it was not the sounds of the city that I sought to return to—machine sounds, the distant cousins of explosions—no. It was the shtetl. The rooster's crow in the first blue of morning. The hawker's call. A footstep on floorboards, upstairs. The crackle of the stove.

Sanctuary.

—from *The Autobiography of a Burned Village*

17
NERIYA ABRAMOVNA KANTOROVA

November 1971

SHE WAS NOT SURE what woke her. Perhaps, in the distance, there had been the sound of a car. Or perhaps a piece of furniture had creaked in the other room.

Whatever it was, she found herself suddenly alert in the dark.

There was someone else here. For a moment after waking she was not even sure of where *here* was—she was just in a bed, in darkness, anywhere at all, unstuck in place and time.

But aware of a presence. Aware of someone else here with her, aware of the acceleration of her heart.

Then the world settled around her. She was in the dacha at the edge of the forest. November.

She was under two heavy blankets. It was cold. Was it

anywhere near dawn? It felt like the very center of night. Her eyes adjusted to the darkness, from which emerged the wooden beams of the ceiling, the planks of the walls.

She listened. Nothing. No sound at all that human ears could register. But there was *someone here.*

She sat up slowly, pushing the blankets aside. Wincing as the bed creaked. She paused, listening again. Was there a sound from the other room? Had she just heard something?

She became aware, in the dark, of someone else's awareness, directed at her.

The way prey became aware of being hunted.

And maybe that was it. Maybe she had come all this way, back to this place she had left so long ago, for no other purpose than to fall into a trap.

Had she been wrong the entire time? Wrong to place trust in relationships that were now in the past?

Had those relationships been made meaningless, like so much else had been made meaningless?

But she had to know.

And of course, that was how traps worked. She had to know, and so she had come.

She put a foot on the floor. Placed her weight on it slowly. Added her second foot. Stood in the dark.

No longer dark, really. The moonlight came in through the window. Her eyes had adjusted, and she could see. And there was light from under the door. Yes. Dim, but there. Electric light, a weak bar of it along the floor.

She had not left a light on.

Three steps to the door, as quiet as she could make them. She put an ear to it and listened.

The sound of paper being lifted, turned, set aside.

She opened the door.

He sat at the writing table in the corner of the room. Her bag was open next to the desk.

He was reading the manuscript. The reading lamp there was on, casting shadows out from itself. His back was to her. The bulk of him. As if a bear walked out of the forest, came into the house, and sat down quietly to read.

His shadow, the even more enormous shade of a huge man, fell across the other chairs, the leather couch.

He paused in his reading, raised his head. Then he pushed the chair out and stood, blocking most of the light.

"Czesław," she said.

In the intervening years he had gained mass to go with his height. He had become thick—weighted with power. He had shed anything boyish or quick about him. He left the manuscript on the table, crossing the short space between them.

"And what do I call you, these days?"

Here. Where we are alone, she finished for him.

"Just Neriya," she said.

"All right, then."

"How much have you read?"

He crouched now, in front of the stove, feeding it wood.

"This place is cold," he said. "Did you forget how to light a village stove?"

"I think I did," she said. "I am in the laboratory or at the university or at home almost all the time. Moscow takes care of the heating for me."

"In these last few years," he said, "I have begun to feel the cold in a way I did not before. I am not an old man yet . . ." And now he turned, face lit up by the stove, and she saw him for the first time. A face and head battered by years, grown thick and coarse, but still the features she knew. Still the face from those years, lit by the winding alternations of firelight as he tended the stove that kept them warm.

Your stupid ears. They still stick out like taxi doors.

". . . but I have started to feel old age coming," he said. "It starts in the joints."

She felt it too. It had been decades since the war. But they were not old. Not yet. Because they had been children during the war.

But, no, that was not quite right. They had not been children, any of them. And they had not been adults. They had been the kind of human survival makes. An ancient state of being, in which they were bound to others for heat, food, shelter, and safety in ways the modern human had stopped recognizing. Bound together in the old ways, with every moment one of total reliance on the other. Bound in a way in which words like *friend* or *family* made no sense.

Child. Adult. Friend. Family. Those were modern words made for a modern world. For civilization, which really meant a world carved out of nature like a little dollhouse. An artificial world, with the natural painted and papered away, where each person lived in their own decorated box of a room. Where distance from one another was possible and true relationship fell away.

Suddenly present in the room with them was the zemlyanka of those first winters. And the log bunker they had occupied later, after they ran. And the stone hut they finally reached, in the forest's very center.

All those tiny places where they huddled together in the dark! And finally . . . The room danced in the stove light, the black-winged walls shuddered, the wooded beams reverted to the trees they had once been, and she saw them again.

The palaces.

"I read half of the manuscript," Czesław said. "I have been here much of the night. I came late and did not want to wake you."

Came from where? Came from doing what?

She could not imagine anything of his life now, of who he was now. A letter from him, asking for all possible courtesy to be extended to her, was enough to put fear into others. She remembered the face of the woman at the hotel—eyes widening in terror, her petty power drained away. And the woman carrying her suitcases through the revolving doors, ejected into a bleak night by the force of a letter from him.

He could control people, bring fear to them, threaten them without even being present. With a politely worded letter. *I ask that you extend all possible courtesy . . .*

Or else. The unspoken message.

She realized that in those few moments since she had come into the room dawn had arrived, red at the edges, blue up over the trees beyond the house, lighting the room.

Czesław blew into the stove, deftly adjusted its baffles, and closed its load door. He stood and walked to the window, looking out at the world gaining light and definition.

She had not noticed his uniform jacket over a chair at the table. Or his cap, with its hammer and sickle, its star. And embroidered behind those surface symbols, the sword that kept them all in power.

He did not turn to face her. "Come here. Do not miss this. They are beginning their day."

She joined him at the window and watched as, in the early light, the crows came. First one or two of them, wandering in the air above the forest canopy. Then several, then a dozen. Then a hundred, two hundred, just over the tops of the trees.

And then the uncountable mass of them. Even through the window she could hear them calling. The sky above darkened as they flew over, as if they were some last, ragged piece of night. The mass of them was sustained for a full minute, it seemed, blotting out the sky.

Then there were a dozen of them again, then several, then only a lagging few. One dropped a nut or a pine cone on the roof of the dacha. They listened to it roll down the shingles.

"I saw them returning home last evening," she said. "And I knew. These are *our* crows. Not the very same birds, perhaps, but the same lineage."

"Yes," Czesław answered. "They are the same."

"And there are more of them."

"Yes. Many more. And I have things to show you today. And today . . . or tomorrow, whenever you are ready, we will go into the forest. If that is something you want."

"It is. I do."

"I've prepared packs for us. We'll have to be ready to stay overnight, and it will be cold. When was the last time you slept in a tent, or on the ground?"

She thought, for a moment, that it was a question she could ask him as well. Seeing him at first, with the bulk of age and power added to his frame, she had thought he was a creature, these days, of offices and indoor spaces.

But now, standing near him, she saw that was not true. He was still a woodsman, a hunter, a tracker. Still what he had been when they were together.

He came here often. That was clear from the way he stood in the room, the way he moved in it, the way he had banked and fed the stove. Across the short hall from the room where she was staying, there was a locked door. Behind it would be his room.

"I have a question for you. About the manuscript."

"What is it?" And was she ready to answer it?

"You don't write only from your own experience. You write . . . all of us. Not from outside our minds but from inside."

And now he would ask, *What gives you the right?* Or, *How could you dare?* She steadied herself for it.

But what he said was, "How did you do it? How did you know the things I thought? Things I told no one else?"

"I did not know them," she answered. "But I tried to be true to who we all were. Of course, we talked so much . . . not you, particularly, but it wasn't always about words either. We showed each other who we were at every moment. And I have had so many decades to think about all of it. I was afraid that if I did not write it down, I would lose it all . . . and then having written it, I put it away in a drawer. I put it away and could not read it. Did not even want to. And now . . . I don't know what else to do with it, except to give it to you. I must have been writing it for you, after all. For all of us. But since you wrote to me, asking me to come, I keep taking it out myself, reading parts of it again. It all seems wrong, the way I wrote it down. Like a bad translation. Blurry and indistinct. Words don't describe the world; they just glance off it. But then my whole life seems wrong. It's someone else's life."

He put a hand on her shoulder.

"It is not someone else's life. It is your life. And you have been living it as well as anyone could. I have not done half as well myself."

"If there is something there that is not correct," she said, "if you want something taken out, or changed, I can do it. But the book is for no one but us. Once you have read it, it can be destroyed."

"I think enough has been destroyed. We have lost enough. And I want nothing changed in the book."

"You haven't finished it."

He continued as if he had not heard her. "I don't know what magic you used, but you know the boy I was better than I knew him. And even my father and grandfather live again, in those pages. And my mother. It has been so long since I saw her . . ." He broke off. "Breakfast," he said, and clapped his hands together in a way that indicated, *This openness is done; this vulnerability is over. We will speak no more of this for now.* "I have brought the best of what the farms around here have to offer. We will need our strength."

NERIYA

July 1943

They ran until they did not know how long they had run for.

The sound of crows was what woke them that morning: an absolute cacophony of cawing.

Once they had fumbled in the cavern-dark of the zemlyanka

and dressed, they emerged to find hundreds of crows around them, screaming at the tops of their lungs, calling with their entire bodies bent over.

Czesław tried to start in one direction, but the crows blocked their way.

Moments later they heard gunfire from there.

So they ran in the directions the birds allowed them to run. And several more times, as they ran, crows would rain down in front of them, blocking their way. Guiding them elsewhere.

The violence in the trees was close enough that they often smelled cordite or saw the flash of an explosion. The woods were filled with shouted orders in German and in other languages. They seemed to come from every direction at once.

Time and time again, the crows would block their way, push them off in another direction. They knew better than to disobey.

"Your documents," Kezia said to Neriya.

"They are here." Neriya put a hand to her chest. The documents were under her shirt. And she had taken the photograph as well. The picture of herself and her parents in Vilnius. But not the box of gifts—and she realized that she might never again see the gifts that the crows had given her.

They ran all day, trying to interpret the signs the crows gave them. Kezia and Neriya were usually in the front, Kezia with her revolver in her hand. The Boy stayed slightly behind them. And Czesław took up the rear, turning to look back repeatedly.

After what seemed like endless running, they found themselves much deeper in the forest. The trees here were larger. The pines were taller, the ash and oak thick and twisted. Trees that had been struck by lightning lay burned and tangled in the underbrush.

In a low area they came to a bog that surrounded them on three sides. The water was alive with the call-and-response of frogs, dotted with stunted and drowned spruce and pine. The sun poured down on bright green duckweed, cotton grass, and cloudberry.

Nowhere to go forward.

When they tried to turn back, they found hundreds of crows behind them, darting and jabbing, herding them toward the water.

Neriya recognized birds among them. Buster was here, and Moses and Madeleine. And so many others she had named.

"We can't go back," she said. "They won't let us."

And she remembered the first day. The day she lost everything, and found herself in the forest, trapped by Buster, who had saved her life by trapping her there. How he had saved her on that day and so many times since. Here he was now, in the closest fringe of birds, yelling and darting, herding her forward into the plant-choked water.

They see things we can't see, she wanted to say.

But there was no need for that: The others understood it already. The others were moving. Kezia was knee-deep in the water. When Neriya looked at her, she saw terror in the girl's eyes, but Kezia kept moving forward, holding the pistol high in one hand, her pack tight and high on her shoulders, her other hand in the Boy's.

The bog water was warmed by the sun. The duckweed clung in bright green rings to her clothes as Neriya waded deeper in, moving the precious documents from under her shirt to under the fisherman's cap Kezia had taken from her own head and given to her.

Soon they were in water up to their armpits. The Boy wrapped his arms around Kezia's back and swam clinging to her.

The crows flew in guiding lines, circling and returning.

Around them, on all sides, were the sounds of gunfire, of shouting in several languages, and the engines of planes.

A bomb was dropped close enough that they could feel the pressure wave of it cross their faces, and saw the expanding circle of its power in the bright green vegetal surface of the water.

The mud of the bog tugged at their boots. Several times one or another of them had to dive down to retrieve a boot that had been trapped. Soon they were all wet from head to foot, streaked with mud, duckweed, and algae.

It went on and on. Until the sun was overhead, and then began lowering toward the western horizon.

Finally, they saw a hummock of land in the bog, its edges marked by dwarfed trees and drifted snags. An island.

As they approached, dozens of frogs hopped into the water. One swam past Neriya so close that she could have reached out and touched it.

She dragged herself out onto the shore and collapsed. It was nearly evening now, the long-shadowed time of the day, and the stunted columns of the pine copse that clung to life on the island sent bars of shadow across her body.

She rolled over and felt the sun on her face. She inhaled the scent of bog rosemary that grew thickly on the island.

The Boy laid his head on her abdomen. She put a wet arm across him.

She was not thinking of what they had survived, not thinking of the next steps they would need to take to keep living. None of it. She had gone from that moment.

She sat at the table in the sitting room of their home in Vilnius, where her mother and father sat also. They were writing up notes on the patients they had seen that day. Neriya listened to the scratch of her mother's fountain pen, and to her parents' hushed voices as they discussed the cases.

While she listened, she was leafing through a notebook from her father's childhood, in which were neatly pressed samples of plants from a forest bog, each labeled with its scientific and common names: *Andromeda polifolia . . . Bog rosemary . . . Scheuchzeria palustris . . . Rannoch-rush . . . Drosera rotundifolia . . . Round-leaved sundew . . . Rubus chamaemorus . . . Cloudberry . . . Vaccinium oxycoccos . . . Small cranberry . . . Eriophorum angustifolium . . . Common cotton grass . . .*

She looked up to find her parents both smiling at her, and realized that she had been reading the Latin names out loud.

"Those," her father said, "are the names that knit our world together. One day, if you meet another biologist, you will be able to communicate to them in that language, no matter where they are from."

"And you will be able to have an argument with them," her mother continued, "about some of the most boring subjects in the world."

She laughed. The Boy laughed with her, not knowing what he was laughing at. Simply happy to be with her, and alive.

So many times, during those years, she had returned to that table, to that room, or the other rooms in their Vilnius home.

In her memories she was divided—she was the girl at the table, the girl in her bed, staring at the crack in the whitewashed ceiling, the girl putting her coat on to go to the movie theater, the girl bored over her dreary homework, the girl clearing dishes in irritation—and she was also herself as she was now, a presence somewhere in the scene, seeing herself inside that quiet, ordered life.

If you had known—she thought, addressing her own self as if the girl were a stranger—*if you had known, you would have clung to even the dullest of these moments.*

But now she thought of the words she had read in the manuscript, found under newspaper and scrap for kindling. The Yiddish words written by another person driven out into the forest—this forest—by violence.

> *We become real only at the moment of our ruin. Our shtetl takes form at dusk, as the Cossacks ride into its outskirts.*
>
> *We become solid as the shutters slam, as our shaking hands extinguish candles and the pogrom begins.*

If you had known the world was tilting (the Lithuanian nationalists marching down the street, blaring a brass anthem out of tune, while her father pulled her away, down an alley) . . . *If you had known . . .*

> *All between is shadow. The silversmith taps at his mold, a sound as spectral as the finger of a séance ghost behind a wall. Grain is bought and sold by spirits. Tinsmiths guide their shears through metal as frail as cobwebs.*

If you had known the world would lose its cohesion (the red flag raised above the palace in Vilnius, and her mother shaking her head, hurrying Neriya along) . . .

From Tu B'Shevat through Yom Kippur and Hanukkah the holidays cycle, year after orbiting, insubstantial year. A dream of home and safety.

If you had known this quiet world was only temporary (a Jewish peddler in her family's examination room, holding a cold compress to his bruised face), *you would have clung to it more tightly, and made it last forever . . .*

We wake to reality and the reek of fire.

Bog rosemary, pine. That smell overwhelmed by the smoke that drifted from the burning forest around them. Cordite and gasoline, and worse things.

Reality and the reek of fire.

Yes—that was the problem. None of that was real if *this* could also be real. Only one of these realities could be the truth. The other one had to be something insubstantial. A dream.

She saw again the world from above—the world of the crows, looking down on them. Looking down on the great green ragged eye of the bog in the middle of the forest, with this iris of island in the middle. The place the crows had led them to, to keep them safe.

What scientific name would she give, one day, to the birds

who could do something like this? What name would stitch her crows into the world? Make them something that could be understood? Would there ever be a human world that could understand them?

After the war. There had to be, after the war.

Kezia and Czesław had already gone into the copse of pine at the center of the island. They were the practical ones, already thinking of what would come next. Of shelter, and sustenance. Of survival.

She joined them.

This was the real world. And if she wanted to live to dream of that other, insubstantial world again, she had to survive this one.

Our history can be summed up in a single sentence: We arrived, we lived awhile, and again we were driven out.

—from *The Autobiography of a Burned Village*

18

NERIYA ABRAMOVNA KANTOROVA

November 1971

WHILE CZESŁAW MADE BREAKFAST, Neriya went outside. She wore her overcoat.

Dawn's red edge hung over the forest.

The dacha had no yard to speak of. Unlike a typical country house, there was no garden here.

But not only was there no garden—there really was nothing here at all. A stump with an axe sunk into it, scarred from the cutting of wood. Firewood stacked against the outer walls of the dacha, almost up to the eaves.

This was not a place in itself. It was an outpost. A waypoint, between the world at its back and the forest it faced. A waypoint along the crow road, which was above it in the air.

Around the side of the house was a table. And scattered across the ground, a few feathers. Bits of stale bread. The half shells of walnuts.

And on the table, a gift.

This one was shaped like a wheel. It was carefully made of dozens of small, peeled twigs, selected for their size, woven together into a garland just larger than the palm of her hand. Other twigs passed through them, like the spokes of a bicycle tire. Moss was woven into them, and a single feather. Not a crow feather, but that of something smaller. A sparrow?

She picked up the gift and turned it in her fingers.

It had been so many years since she had seen one.

"They left another one," Czesław said from behind her.

Well, he had not lost his skill in perfectly quiet stalking. When she turned, she found him just a few meters from her, although he had made no sound at all.

During the war, none of them had ever heard him coming. He was suddenly just there. And if he went on a hunt, early in the morning, the three of them woke to find him simply gone. They never heard him leave.

"There is a crow," Czesław said, "that I call Charlie. In honor of Buster. They are so alike, I swear that she's Buster's grandchild. Or great-great-great-grandchild, maybe. It's something about the way she struts around after she's won a game."

"A game?"

"Checkers, mostly," Czesław said.

She looked at his face to see if he was joking with her.

"I tried to teach Charlie chess," Czesław said, "but she kept stealing the pieces. Something about their shapes. I guess she likes them too much. She stole the queen first. But that was just the start. Somewhere in the forest, she has half of a very nice set of ebony and bone chess pieces. Not the pawns—she left those to me. They were too boring for her taste."

"So you play checkers instead."

"Yes."

"And does she win?"

"Most of the time. We play for walnuts, which she likes enough to keep her attention. Usually."

"And she *wins*." Neriya was turning the wheel in her hand. "Really? She understands the object of the game?"

"The object of the game," Czesław said, "is to get a walnut. She understands that very well. And, yes, sometimes she wins fairly. But she also cheats, if you don't keep your eyes on the board. And I have to admit that sometimes I just let her win."

"You *let* her win?"

"Yes. Charlie is a very poor sport, and she shits on the board if she loses. And sometimes on me. It's easier to let her win and give her a walnut. I think she knows I let her win, and why. And that is a kind of strategy as well, isn't it? She has us figured out. Breakfast is ready." Czesław turned back toward the house.

Breakfast was fried eggs, bread, and jam. Not unlike what they might have eaten on a very good day in the war. Eggs were a rarity, in those years, but could sometimes be had if Czesław managed to trade nearby.

When they were living in the zemlyanka, anyway. Once they were on the island in the bog, things were much harder.

"They still bring you gifts." She turned the spoked hoop in her hands.

"They do," Czesław said. "I have quite a collection. And I have something else to show you."

He returned after a few minutes from the room that had been locked when Neriya arrived.

He held a box she recognized.

The sight of it was a shock. Like seeing someone who was dead resurrected. She put a hand on its stained birchwood lid. "It survived."

"Not only the box survived. Open it."

Inside, the compartments were filled with the gifts. In the first compartment was the Order of Saint Anna medal.

And although there were things missing, much was preserved. When she removed the top tray of compartments, there they were: the woven, made things the crows had brought to Neriya before the war. Hoops and the figures they had called "crosses," but had later found out were more like dolls. The gifts the crows had made of twigs, of moss and dried grasses, of feathers and found objects. Nearly all the gifts given to the four of them in the forest. Gifts for which they had exchanged bread and games and finally . . .

As she cried, she kept waiting for his hand to touch her, to descend on her shoulder. For him to say, "Everything will be all right," in that strange, automatic way he had always said it to them during the war, when they were near giving up.

"Everything will be all right"—a phrase that, she had come to understand, did not mean anything would be all right but instead meant "We must go on." As if the only lesson he had learned, and could pass on, was that one.

He did not touch her. And he did not say it.

Maybe he had lost the ability to say it. Everything, after all, had not been all right. There were many things that would never be all right again.

Instead, he cleared the plates and washed them in the small sink. He tended to the stove. He did not leave the room.

When she had finished crying, he said, "We will go into the forest tomorrow."

"Not today?"

"You have lost your weather sense," Czesław said. "It will rain today. But that is all right. The rain will give me time to finish reading the manuscript. By the way, I read your book, *The Unnamed Senses.*"

"The parts of it that survived the censors, you mean."

"I can't imagine they would have censored much," Czesław said. "In a book about human and animal perception."

"You would be surprised," she said, "at the writing that fails to ever escape the academy. You would be surprised at how political the field of science can be."

"I would not be surprised," he said. "When has science been anything but political in this country? When has anything *not* been political in this country?"

"They took so much out that *The Unnamed Senses* is half a book. But thank you for reading it."

"I don't know if you know this, but *The Unnamed Senses* has a following in . . . my profession."

"Does it?"

"I suppose we like to think of ourselves as seeing parts of the world that other people miss, and so it appeals to us—this idea that there is a secret world of feeling most people are unaware of. And this idea that in the end, all the senses converge for a single purpose. It was interesting to find that theory in your book."

"Thank you."

"That was my grandfather's theory as well," Czesław said. "He told it to me while we were hunting . . ."

"I know. You told it to us." *You passed it down to us*, she had wanted to say.

"I felt like I never spoke. I don't remember telling you that, or much of anything. That is why I called you here, you know. There were other reasons . . . but that was my most selfish one. I need to speak about these things with you. It is as simple as that. I need you to know what happened . . . after. I feel like I have spent over a quarter century waiting to speak of it with you. But that is why *I* called *you*. Why did you *come*?"

"I needed someone to read the manuscript. And to take it from me, so I will stop reading it . . . I needed that. But I also needed to come back here. To see the places where we survived. And to see our crows again. To go to the center of the forest again. And to see *you* again, Czesław."

She paused, searching his face for some response to this last. But he was looking slightly away from her.

"You know," she continued, "you almost never spoke in the daytime. But in the zemlyanka, and then in the bunker on the island, when it was dark, we all shared stories."

"I only remember the two of you talking, while I listened."

"I often remember it that way as well—I mean that I often remember the two of *you* talking, while *I* listened. But we all told our stories. We told each other everything. There was nothing else to do—"

"Except kill lice."

"Except kill lice, yes." And she could feel, under her fingernail, in that moment, the fat little body along a seam of clothing. The pop as she crushed it with the hard edge of her nail. *One more thing I can never forget.* "One night," she said, "you told us your grandfather's theory. About how animals sense their place in the physical world. And about how humans sense their place in society. And I wrote about that second part in my book too—not revealing my source, of course. But the censors removed much of the second half of *The Unnamed Senses.* They didn't want me to speak about human culture."

"You'll have to tell that part to me," Czesław said. "I've been trying to understand human culture all my life."

CZESŁAW

September 1943

"I remember one hunting trip my grandfather and I took alone," Czesław said, as they all lay together in the dark of the bunker on the island in the bog. "I think I remember it because it was almost always the three of us hunting together—me, my father, and my grandfather. But that time, my father was ill. Like my mother, my father was hardly ever sick. Whenever one of my parents was ill, it was as if the family had lost an arm. I remember that it was frightening to go with my grandfather, by myself. I don't know why. Everyone said we were so alike, the three of us. They saw us that way, but it wasn't exactly right. My grandfather spoke more, for one thing. Not as if he liked talking, but as if he were *compelled* to speak. As if it were his job to pass things on.

"He told me stories of Poland in the old days. They were like fairy tales, almost. He told me about drunken noblemen at the hunting lodges playing cards all night long, then through the next day and the next night. About a man who lost at cards so badly that he lost his family home—a whole house! The winner's workmen came and took all the furniture away, the paintings, the tapestries, the candlesticks and chandeliers . . . and then the parquet floors, and the roof, and the walls. They carted it all away, board by board, wagonload by wagonload.

"He told me stories of terrible doomed love affairs he had witnessed. A man who bathed and dressed in his tailcoat one morning, then cut his own throat with a razor, after his brother's wife had refused his advances. And he told me stories of war: He told a story of a man who led a cavalry charge in the Great War and was shot through the head. He did not realize it until the battle was over and his lieutenant told him. Then he replied, 'Oh, I see . . . That's why I feel so strange . . . ,' and died.

"On the last day of the hunt, when I missed a shot, and the buck fled into the forest, my grandfather told me to use my *sense*. I wasn't sure what he meant. 'I thought I was,' I said. But he told me no, that was not what I was doing. I saw the deer, but that was only part of it. I needed to use my *sense*. I needed to be aware of the position of my body on the ground. Of the way the wind blew on my face and ears, telling me its direction. Of the feel of the rifle in my hands, the sound of the hooves of the deer, the small sounds made by my breath. Even of my memories of what I had done before, in similar situations. All of it—everything together—was my *sense*, telling me where I was in relation to the deer. And not only to the deer. 'What your sense is telling you,' my grandfather said, 'is exactly where you are in relation to the rest of the world. To what you are stalking, to what is stalking you, to your friends and relatives, to the Communist

Party, to your boss. It is the sense we use for hunting and for trapping and for planting in the garden, but it is also the sense we use among other people. In your classroom. In society. All the tools we have for learning about the world—our vision, hearing, touch—are only parts of this one sense. And because people rely on one or another of these tools, without using them together, they fail to know where they are. But if you can learn to use your sense—all of it, together—you will always know where you are *in relation to everyone and everything else*.'"

As Czesław told the story, he felt its truth again. The way it had felt like the truth of everything to him, like a secret passed down. He felt the positions of the others' bodies as they huddled together for warmth. The Boy between him and Neriya. Kezia against him. All of them woven together into a single being, eight-legged and eight-armed, trying to survive. He sensed, in the dark, the position of the others' heads as they listened. Of their limbs, their elbows and knees. Their attention on his words. The way their breathing was angled in the dark.

He felt his desperate, idiotic attraction to Kezia—the poison of it, asking him to do things he knew he should not do.

And he felt the razor across his throat—across all their throats, together—if he ever acted on that desire.

That, too, was listening to his sense.

After the words *in relation to everyone and everything else*, he had paused, waiting to see if anyone would say anything. From the rhythm of the Boy's breathing, Czesław could tell he was asleep. Neriya was as well: she always slept quietly, almost silently.

After a moment, Kezia said: "My mother called it *the whisper*. She said it told her what the world wanted from her."

It was the only time Czesław ever heard Kezia mention her parents. Or anyone in her family.

▫ ▫ ▫

September had brought a sudden cold. The frogs had grown quieter. When they first came to the island, the frogs had been so loud some nights that they could hardly hear one another at all.

The first days had been hard. They were lucky to find a log bunker on the island that someone had dug out many years ago, but it was in terrible shape: flooded at the bottom, its roof collapsed. For several days, the main work was in repairing that. They slept out in the open in the meantime, mosquito bitten and miserable. The battles in the woods around them had subsided after those first days, but they would sometimes hear an eruption from one direction or another. And planes still flew overhead, from which they scrambled to hide underneath the stunted spruce trees.

They had good luck too. There was a small boat on the island. Flat bottomed, little more than a raft, and missing one of its oars, likely disappeared along with the second oarlock, which had been torn from the gunwale. The boat leaked enough that it had to be bailed out continuously, and it could only take one of them comfortably, but it was a way off the island, allowing them to scout and forage. On Kezia's instruction, Czesław gathered tansy, which they rubbed on their skin to keep the insects away.

He gathered, he hunted, he watched to see what had changed in the woods. After the German assault in the forest, there were fewer deer to hunt, and fewer rabbits. Parts of the woods were burned. He found places where all the trees were knocked to splinters, whole groves shattered and stinking of death. Holes had been opened everywhere in the woods, eaten away by fire and war.

They learned to eat frogs, spearing them with sharpened sticks. The Boy, especially, became very good at this. And the bog had—at least in that height of summer—a never-ending supply of frogs, which, though all of them were sickened by the thought of eating them at first, roasted up nicely.

"And every time I eat a frog," Kezia said one evening, "I tell myself it's one less of the bastards left around to keep me up at night with its croaking."

The visiting crows saw them eating frogs too. They watched the Boy kill frogs with his little spear and began to do it themselves, darting down from the spruces and snatching frogs from the shallows.

It was Kezia who found the roll of pages, stuck in a bottle they dug out of the wall. She had learned to read Yiddish by then, the way she had learned to read Russian—hungrily, as if making up for years of lost time. It was the way she learned everything.

אונדזער געשיכטע קען מען פֿאַרסך־הכּלען אין איין זאַץ: מיר זײַנען אָנגעקומען, האָבן געלעבט אַ ביסל, און ווידער האָט מען אונדז אַרויסגעטריבן.

"'*Undzer geshikhte ken men farsakhaklen in eyn zats*: Our history can be summed in a single sentence,'" Kezia read out loud from the first page, part of which had been eaten away by damp. "'We arrived, we lived awhile, and again we were driven out.'"

"How is it possible," Czesław asked Neriya, "that the same man lived in your shtetl and then in the zemlyanka and then here on this island as well?"

But it was Kezia who answered. "It is the crows. They protected him too. They led him to the zemlyanka, and they led him here as well."

Having extracted the pages from the bottle, the two girls were on their knees in the grass trying to peel the damp pages apart, to save what they could of them. Worms had eaten parts of them, leaving pages where there were only a paragraph or a few words left. But there were pages, too, where almost everything survived. They flattened the sheets that could be saved and let them dry in the sun.

"Does he say who drove him out of the zemlyanka?" Czesław asked a few days later, watching Kezia read the dried remains of the pages.

"Yes," she answered. "It was foresters. He thought they were friends of his, but one day they came with torches and threatened to burn him out if he did not leave."

It is not because they are men who turn into wolves. It is because they are wolves who turn into men.

A few days later, Czesław woke to find himself alone in the bunker. By that time much of the repair was finished. It was becoming a new home for them. They had filled in the earth to stop the flooding, rebuilt the walls and roof, made beds of reed to sleep in. And they had tacked the picture back up on the wall—their collective picture of Neriya and her family.

Czesław heard the sound of laughter from outside. Blinking in a late morning sun in front of the bunker's entrance, he saw Neriya, Kezia, and the Boy, their arms full of the crows' gifts.

"They dropped them all over the island," Neriya said, holding up an old medal from the First World War. "All of the gifts that we lost. They gathered them from the zemlyanka and brought them here, to us. I thought they were lost to us forever, but we have them again."

The Boy was carefully arranging the gifts on Neriya's jacket, which lay on the ground. He placed each in sequence on the jacket's bright purple lining. Hoops of woven, peeled twigs, some with spokes, others without. X-shaped figures of knitted grass. Stranger figures, sometimes laced with found things—a bright yellow thread, a bit of colored paper or foil. Nest-like objects, but not nests or parts of nests. More like tiny bowls, filled sometimes with colorful things: petals, broken bits of colored glass.

When Czesław looked at them arranged together against a field of purple cloth, in a way he had not seen them before, they looked like letters in an alphabet, or like the Egyptian hieroglyphs he had once seen in books.

As if they could be read, somehow. Solved. Spoken out loud.

Now, in September, he lay in the dark. The cold was coming. It could be felt in the evenings, eating away at summer's edges. And night was already winter's territory.

The bunker was not as warm as their zemlyanka had been. They huddled together for warmth under a single blanket.

The others were asleep. He lay awake, feeling their lack of food, the new difficulties in hunting in the damaged forest, the new dangers, the changed map of everything.

Sensing their position in the world. Trying to plan their way ahead through winter.

Among the Jews, I saw the world as a Jew. Among the soldiers, I saw it as a soldier. But when I returned to the shtetl after the war, I could see as neither Jew nor soldier. I had double vision and was lost. I needed to find a new way to see the world.

And now? Winter is coming. The bog is freezing over. What am I now? Still a man?

Still a man, but last night I dreamed I was a scrap of the night sky, flying above the trees, and below me was a map of the world no human eyes had ever seen.

—from *The Autobiography of a Burned Village*

19

NERIYA ABRAMOVNA KANTOROVA

November 1971

CZESŁAW READ ALL DAY, turning each typed page neatly as he finished and placing it atop the others.

As he progressed through the manuscript, Neriya's sense of dread increased.

Finally she could not take it. She could not be in the same room as him.

On the porch she laced up the good East German boots she wore on expeditions. She went for a walk.

She forced herself to walk through where the shtetl had been, to find the overgrown path that had once been the main street, the flatter area that had once been the little main square.

This hump of earth was a synagogue, that one the house where the butcher lived.

Neriya had lived over here, and these humps were the farm where Kezia had lived awhile, taking honey from the bees, until the Boy appeared.

Here was where Kezia had killed the two villagers who tried to attack her.

Here was the whitewashed church, which had survived the war, but had not survived Communism. They must have torn it down. Whoever had torn it down had even taken away the material: there was no hump here to mark the site of the church's existence, or even of its destruction.

Without the map of this place in her own mind, it would have been impossible to know anything of what had once been here. Impossible to know that generations had lived in this place. That it had been filled with human voices for hundreds of years. That wagons had been built here, clothes mended, grain traded, weddings celebrated until the latest hours of the night, politics discussed, children educated, griefs shared and kept secret, joys shouted and silenced.

There was no sensing any of it, without her own lived connection to the place.

And she understood why the church, too, had been taken down.

It was so that this place would have no landmark that could be seen from the road. So that it could not even be found. So that it would cease to exist forever. So that once the few people who had survived this shtetl's burning were gone, it would be gone as well, never to be rebuilt.

Could something so terrible happen to you that you not only died but disappeared forever? Something so terrible that it erased you, as if you never had existed at all?

She went into the forest, but not far. After walking for several minutes, she found her hands shaking.

She knew the way to where the zemlyanka had been, perhaps even still was, but she could not bring herself to go there. She could perhaps even find her way, after the many years that had passed, to the bog. And farther in.

She sat down on a stone among silver birch. She could not go farther.

She was not afraid, exactly. She simply needed to have someone with her. That was all. It was not a thing that she could do alone, although many times she had imagined her return here, imagined coming back to the forest and the crows, and in those daydreams she was alone.

In the early evening, she returned to the dacha. It was full of cooking smells. The manuscript was face up again. Czesław was at the stove, his massive back to her.

But aware of her, she knew. Aware of her as he was always aware of everything and everyone around him. Of his place in the world, in the room, in his chair. Or who was watching him, and who he needed to watch. None of that had changed about him.

She felt the audacity of what she had done. The intrusiveness of it. She had not only written herself, her own thoughts, her own life—she had written all of them. Reassembled who they were, out of the stories they had told one another, out of her observances of them.

What she felt was guilt. As if the writing of this book had been a crime. In the true sense—if it were found—it *was* a kind of crime. It contained the wrong kinds of stories about the partisans in the forest, the wrong history of the war, the wrong endings to it all.

But it was also a crime of another kind. It contained the secret of the crows, and it would endanger them if anyone ever discovered it.

And it contained her own crime, a secret that could destroy her completely.

But it contained another crime. A crime of the worst type. The sin of trying to tell the story of another. Of speaking in the voice, and in the name, of another. Of speaking for the dead, because they could not speak. Of speaking for the living—for those who could not speak, for those who had chosen not to speak, and for those who refused to do so.

What she wanted to say, watching Czesław's hands as he placed the cloth-wrapped clay dish on the table, was that she had *guessed* at nothing. In the writing of the book, she had *returned.*

She had gone back to where they were together. To that space in their lives where they were not children and not adults, and not separate from one another, but together. Not only together—one. A single entity.

She had gone there to *bring them back.* And she had never guessed at their thoughts: She had written what she knew was true. Even the things they might not admit to themselves were true.

"Why did you bring the book to me?" Czesław asked her.

She seated herself at the table, only then noticing that there were three places set, not two.

She had gone over what she would say next many times in her mind, in the days after she wrote to him requesting they meet. On the train. "I know this book is not safe. Not now. Not with the world as it is. But if I did not write it, these things would be lost forever. I said before that once you read it, it can be destroyed. But that's wrong. It needs to be hidden, until the world changes. And I don't know anyone who has the kind of power it takes to do that . . . to keep it safe, and then to make sure it can be found, when the time is right."

"Except me."

"Except you."

But had she made a mistake? It was possible. Who had Czesław become, in these decades? He'd had the time to become anyone at all.

She felt the draft on her neck and turned to find the door of the dacha open.

As Czesław had predicted, it had begun to rain. She heard the drops, larger and larger, striking the roof. The sun had gone down behind the trees already. The crows were in the sky, hurrying home, gossiping loudly about their day.

And the uniformed man in the doorway was a person she recognized immediately.

She made a sound of surprise and joy. She ran across the room to throw her arms around him.

She had not known, until that moment, that he was still alive.

THE BOY

January 1944

Quiet.

He still heard his mother's voice. He still felt the silencing hand clamped over his mouth. The desperate hand.

Quiet.

Desperate, because not obeying the command meant death. And he had seen the consequences himself—the baby that had not stopped crying, the hand over its mouth and nose, suppressing its wailing forever.

All of them in the barn, in the dark. Outside, the engines. The sound of a horse in terror. Outside, noise. A cow that had not been milked, lowing and lowing.

Quiet.

They hid in the barn, behind the false wall. Light bled through gaps. In those slashes of light he could see the eyes of the villagers, wide with fear.

Quiet.

That was before. Before, not now. Before.

Quiet.

All those people were gone, and the hand that had held itself over his mouth, and the woman that hand had belonged to, gone.

Gone in fire.

But the hand was still there. He felt it over his mouth.

Quiet.

And he obeyed. Never, ever spoke a word. Did not cry. Did not reveal their hiding place to others. Did not.

But still they had burned the barn.

And still she had left him behind.

Now, in the freezing dark, he put his clothes on, and was quiet—so quiet that Kezia, Neriya, and Czesław could not possibly hear him.

He crawled from the bunker in the dark.

Outside was Marusya, waiting for him. The Boy placed a finger over his mouth.

She understood. She did not call to him the way she usually did—she just flapped her wings and curved in the air, came down a bit farther away, in a place where they had cut a path through the snow.

He was aware of the bog as he crossed it. Underneath the snow, underneath the ice he was crossing, was water that was still not completely frozen. Underneath that thick, frozen layer was a slurry of sleeping things and darkness. Down there were things so slow in the winter that they were barely alive, like toads asleep in the ground for years and years.

They were like that in the log bunker now, the four of them. Neither dead nor alive. So slow and weak that soon they would be unable to move at all.

But they would not live in the ground the way toads lived, able to wait for another spring.

No. They would die. If he did not find help for them, they would die.

Marusya would lead him to help. She had told him this. She had been trying, for days now, to make him follow her. She had been trying to take him to her home, to lead him to help.

And when he found Marusya's home, he would be able to show the others. He would save them all.

Quiet.

Even snow was too loud: It squealed and crunched under his feet. The brittle skin of it shattered like glass in the early morning air.

So early—not even dawn yet. The coming of the sun still

only a single color in the forest. A lightening, really, more than a color. White added to the night's darkest blue until the human eye could see.

Marusya led the way—across the frozen bog, into the denser trees. Away from where standing water choked and stunted the forest. Away to where the pines grew tall and thick. On, and on.

She was joined by others, calling from low branches, dropping to the ground beside him, behind him, ahead of him, flying with her and walking with him. Leading him, encouraging him, letting him know he was on the right path.

There were dozens of them around him now. Then hundreds. Then thousands of them, the branches of the trees heavy with them, the forest heavy with the rich smell of them, the snow dark with needles they had knocked from the canopy, twigs, feathers not yet gathered.

There was a depression where the snow was deeper, where his feet passed through rotten layers. A foot punctured the surface. From underneath came the sound of running water. A stream, half frozen but still moving over its stones.

Then the bank on the other side. A bank like a cliff. He had to work hard to climb it, to push and find and form handholds and footholds in the snow, compact it down to make a staircase, a ladder he could climb.

Under the snow he found the roots of trees, found and clung to the rocks the roots clung to. He hacked the snow away. His fingers stung, lost feeling.

It was not a high cliff, but he felt his own weakness. It seemed impassable. He would not be able to go on.

He had been concentrated on moving forward. But now he felt the cold all the way through him, and wanted to scream to let it out. As if screaming were the only thing that could bring warmth back into him.

Quiet.

There was no such thing in him that could make a sound. But the crows did it for him, yelling from the trees in the dawn, in the light that had gone yellow and green and other colors, flooding in.

Encouraging him. Driving him on. He scrambled upward, finding tree roots buried in the snow, finding stones to rest on for a moment. He pulled himself up, slipping, struggling for handholds.

The crows were there in the thousands. Every branch filled with their presence, from the dead white of the forest floor to the green of the canopy above. Wings wheeled around black and gleaming eyes. Eyes, wings, and the sharpness of beak and claw, all moving.

They had been calling to him as he climbed.

But now he stood at the top of the cliff, with the ancient pines all around him, and there was no sound from them at all.

Quiet.

And then the forest itself moved. All of it, at once. Shattered, lifted, spiraled up into the sky.

Opened to him.

I am not afraid to die. I am afraid *they* will die. That the shtetl itself will flicker out. That *all* the shtetlach will flicker out: every rabbi and every tailor, every husband and every wife, every bathhouse and every cantor, every miller and every laborer whipping his laden donkey home.

I am afraid that everyone will become nothing. A scattering of moldering pages no one finds, in a language the pogroms have murdered. Unfinished work the worms will eat along with my flesh, unread.

—from *The Autobiography of a Burned Village*

20

NERIYA ABRAMOVNA KANTOROVA

November 1971

WHAT SHE WANTED WAS TO HOLD HIM, the way she had when he was a boy. The way they had all held each other when they needed to.

But they were changed now, in a changed world. So she let the Boy go. She held him at arm's distance, searching a face that was grown now but that she still knew as well as she knew her own.

"His name is Innokentiy now," said Czesław. "They gave him that name at one of the state orphanages. He still does not speak. Not in the way you or I do, anyway."

"Innokentiy," she repeated. Yes, it sounded right.

Maybe it had always been his name.

"After I was separated from all of you, it took years to find him," Czesław said. "I thought, after the war ended, that it would be simply a matter of making some inquiries. That if I spoke to fifty people, or a hundred, I would find him. But I wasn't aware of the *scale* of what had happened to the world. There weren't a hundred thousand people missing, or two hundred thousand; there were millions. The Nazis had smashed and burned their way through Poland, the Baltic states, Russia—through so much of the Soviet state.

"The lost choked the roads after the war, trying to find their way back home. Everywhere I searched, there were horse carts filled with nameless orphans. It was like looking for a particular snowflake in a snowstorm. I was searching for one nameless orphan in a country of orphans. And I was doing it while trying to stay alive myself."

She thought of her own registration, after the Red Army took control. Of standing in the lobby of a building in Vilnius, all of its windows broken, the cracked tile of its floor covered in muddy bootprints. Standing hungry with all the others.

The tangle of lost children, their noses running, clothed in lice-ridden rags. Filthy, half-starved children gathered together by filthy, half-starved adults in uniforms that, in many cases, hardly looked like uniforms anymore.

She associated her registration with a sound—the sound of someone with a broom made of twigs sweeping up broken glass.

She remembered finding herself at the front of that ragged line, staring into the eyes of a woman with a terrible red scar down one side of her face. Not even a scar: a red gash more wound than scar, still healing, too fresh to be called a scar yet.

"Name."

Handing the documents across to the woman. Documents she

had kept safe under her shirt, carried for months against her skin. Documents she held out now with a shaking hand. Watching as the woman copied into a ledger. *Neriya . . . Abramovna . . . Kantorova.* Watching as the woman wrote a number next to the name.

That sound of broken glass being swept up, behind her.

Wanting to tear the documents from the woman's hand. Being desperate to have them against her skin again, to hide them away again. The documents were all she had left of all of them together. They were all she had left of a self. And if they were lost? What then?

Then she had nothing. Then she was nobody at all.

The woman finished writing the number. She handed the documents back, along with a card with that same number written on it.

She remembered looking at the ledger. Seeing where blots of ink had smeared other numbers into illegibility. Seeing where the woman's hand had shaken, turning a five into a six, leaving something on the page between a seven and a nine.

Mistakes that might alter entire lives. Broken threads to pasts now lost forever.

No way back.

In another room someone gave her soup so thin it was almost water. A cabbage leaf floated in it. A sliver of potato. The table crawled with slow spring flies.

No one looked at anyone else. Everyone here was alone. Everyone had lost everything but, by some terrible miracle, themselves.

And what were those selves worth, if they had lost the place in the world where they belonged?

"After we took Vilnius," Czesław continued, "we kept moving. It was hard fighting. Terrible battles, every single one of them. The Germans never gave up easily. We had to break them, every time.

"We took Kaunas, and Klaipėda. We ground on, headed to Berlin. All I thought of was staying alive. Finding you all again. The guilt was terrible. I had abandoned you. I had left you alone. I had left you undefended . . ." He broke off and turned his face away from her.

It was well into the night now.

Under the electric bulbs, she saw that Czesław's hair had thinned. His scalp gleamed underneath it. His forehead was lined. There were vertical bars from his nose to the edges of his mouth. His eyes, narrowed by their swollen lids, red rimmed, were discolored near the orbital bones like a bruise.

She had missed his youth. He was still a boy when he was taken from them. Now he was middle-aged. *As am I*, she reminded herself, thinking of the gray that had seeded itself through her hair, of the knee that ached every winter morning. It did not seem possible.

She looked at Innokentiy, who was listening as well.

Innokentiy's face, chapped by the sun and wind of life outside, was less lined. His eyes were less tired. But he, too, had passed through most of his youth. How old was he now? Past his mid-thirties. She knew men that age who had died of heart attacks.

She wanted to hold them both. To stop it. To reverse these changes in all their faces, this unraveling of who they had been, when they were together.

"I never stopped looking," Czesław said to her. "I never stopped looking for all of you. It took me years to find you in Moscow. Even so simple a thing—to find a woman studying in university—took *years*. I thought it would be easier, after the war. Years later.

But there was no 'after' the war. Not really. The conflict died down to embers, but it continued. Nationalists hiding in the forests. Revolts in the countries the Soviet Union had absorbed into itself."

You never came to see me, she wanted to say. *You never sent word. Why?*

But she knew why. Because it would have endangered her.

"And no one wanted to remember what had happened," Czesław continued. "As soon as the guns stopped—even before the guns stopped—the war stories began to change. Everyone had something to hide. So many people had done terrible things to others. Even good people." His eyes met hers, but not in accusation. Still she heard the tired old line rise in her mind:

We did what we had to do.

But had people done what they *had* to do? Or had they gone further than that? Used the excuse of war to do other things—things they had always *wanted* to do but had never been allowed? There were people who seemed so happy, once the war had started, to see civilization peeled away. There were people who shed civilization like reptiles shed an old skin. People who leaped into violence gleefully.

As if they had been waiting their entire lives to hurt others. To wound, burn, and kill.

"It took power," Czesław continued. "Finding you. Finding Innokentiy. It took power. To do it I had to get that power. I had to become a part of the system."

"That can't have been the only reason you joined them," she said.

She watched his face tighten. She saw for a brief moment, maybe, the mask that other people might have seen, before they were condemned.

But the mask came, and was gone. He met her gaze and held it.

"No," he said. "It was not the only reason. I also wanted revenge. Against the SS men who fed their uniforms bit by bit into their stoves so they could get away with what they did to us. Against the Lithuanian police who spent years hiding the truth of what they did to the Jews. Men who were worse than the Germans. Revenge against the monsters, the collaborators who burned the shtetlach and filled tank trenches and sand pits with the bodies of Jews who had lived alongside them for six hundred years, then—once the war was over—pointed their fingers at the Nazis, as if they had done it all alone.

"I wanted revenge against the villagers who denounced the families hiding in the woods near their farms. Against the bureaucrats who tallied up the dead like stacked coins. Against the nationalists who shook their heads at the Holocaust and its excesses, but still hoped to be handed a state that was *Judenrein* after the war, and were glad someone else was there to do the dirty work. Against every Polish partisan who executed a survivor of the ghetto or a family of peasants burned out of their farm because they were an inconvenience to them or might give away their position in the forest.

"After the war, the collaborators and the monsters were all still there. They hid their pasts under floorboards, thinking they could wait us out. I wanted to put every single one of them up against the wall."

She wanted to protest. To say the weak, obligatory, forgiving words. *Some helped. Some hid us. Some gave us bread. Some risked their lives.*

Those words were meaningless. Yes, it was true—some

helped. There were always some who remained human, despite everything. There were always some who were brave, some who risked themselves for others. But it was only *some*. It was never *enough*. Most did nothing. Many helped in the killing.

"Revenge isn't possible," she said instead.

"No. Revenge *is* possible," Czesław replied. "Believe me. It is possible. I exacted it from hundreds of people. But then a decade went by. More. The people I wanted to take revenge on, the people who once had been powerful, became weak themselves. They became pathetic, hunted. Hollowed out when they lost their power. Hiding in cellars, as their victims had done. Hiding in the forests, as their victims had done. As afraid as we had once been. As the people they murdered had once been."

And for some reason, she found herself thinking of crows, mobbing a hawk. She was a girl again, in the forest, looking up into the sky, watching the crows as they swooped and dove, scolding and harassing the larger, more dangerous bird, avoiding its beak and talons, banking in the air and twisting, working together to drive it away. Seeming to take joy in the chase, in harassing the bigger bird, that could kill any one of them. And then breaking off.

Still alive, all of them. The crows. And the hawk, which snatched their babies from their nests and sometimes even killed an adult if it could catch them unaware, was still alive. All of them were still alive, left to continue the conflict forever.

Czesław had been next to her, watching as well.

"I don't understand," Czesław had said, "why they don't just kill that hawk. They could do it so easily, if they all worked together."

The crows circled. One crow dropped down and landed near their feet, turned a half circle in front of them, nodded its head.

She was not a crow they had named yet. She was one of the new ones, just grown into the quick adulthood of the flock.

"Why don't you just kill him?" Czesław asked the crow.

But the hawk was already forgotten. The crow ignored Czesław, picking up a twig and beginning to dig with it in the snow.

KEZIA

January 1944

The three of them followed the Boy's footprints through the snow.

The island had become nothing but a hump in the larger maze of snowdrifts that formed the frozen bog. They had trod paths in them, trails to rabbit traps that had now been empty for months. Trails to hunting blinds that had been fruitless since November, when Czesław had killed their last deer of the season.

As winter deepened and the bog froze over, they had thought they would be able to range farther to find food. But the snows had come, falling day and night, constraining their movements.

Czesław had made them all rudimentary snowshoes, of bent branches and deer hide, but still it was hard going. And the snow changed the landscape, made it easy to get lost, turned a straight line into a maze.

"Where are the deer?" Kezia once asked. "Where are the rabbits?"

"There are too many people in the forest," Czesław said. "The animals have moved deeper in, to the most impassable places. The ones that remained behind have already been eaten."

And there *were* too many people in the forest. They smelled their campfires, heard voices, heard gunfire. Sometimes they lay flat while on a hunt and watched a column through the trees. Partisans, on a patrol. Or a ragged group of peasants, dragging their belongings with them.

On the day they woke to find the Boy gone, they ate the last slivers of meat.

Slivers were all they had now. So many of their days were spent in the dark: the sun came up late and went down early. In between they stayed huddled inside, where at least there was a fire to keep them from freezing. Where there was some warmth, even if there was no food.

They sensed that the crows were struggling as well. Fewer came. Buster, Moses, Madeleine, Marusya, Enoch, and a few of the curious young ones still visited, but even they looked ragged and hungry.

"They have to compete with people now," Czesław said.

They followed the Boy's snowshoe tracks, with Czesław in the lead.

Neriya was the weakest. Sometimes Kezia had to stop to help her pull free a foot that had gone down through rotten snow and gotten stuck, or had stumbled into a tree well.

When Kezia looked into Neriya's hollowed face, or saw Czesław's wrists, like the comic bones of a drawing of a skeleton jutting from his telogreika, she was afraid.

They were her mirrors. And in their skeletal reflections, she saw that she, too, was dying.

And there was the madness.

Kezia had seen it again a few days ago. She had left the shelter to go to the bathroom, just after dawn, and had seen the madness spread over the snow of the bog: a yellow haze between her and the world, filled with voices.

They were voices she almost recognized. They whispered in circular sentences, parts of things people had said to her before, but broken off and tied into nonsensical loops, shaped into unrecognizable things.

"You are not here," she said, out loud.

And the voices rose in volume, in answer, insisting on their reality. Formed sentences, thickened in the dirty fog, trying to make themselves clear.

The end! Of all of it!

Again! It is in the genes . . .

Sure as the coloring of a horse or its temperament.

I told you not to follow us . . .

Oh, child. What have you seen?

"You are not here!" she had said, over and over again, until she could be back inside the shelter with Neriya, with the Boy, with Czesław, and safe from them.

They walked for hours in the maze of drifted snow. Sometimes Neriya and Kezia lagged so far behind Czesław that they almost lost sight of him. But he always waited, or circled back to help.

Then they were across a stream on rotting bridges of water-hollowed snow. They were climbing a cliff. A frozen ladder of ice, roots, and stone. Climbing for so long.

Near the top, Czesław helped Neriya up, then reached down and took Kezia's hand.

A thousand crows were there to meet them. Among them Buster, Moses, Madeleine, so many others. A feathered, surging wall in the forest.

Neriya sank to her knees in front of Buster.

"Is this where you were leading me, that day?" Kezia heard her whisper. "Do we finally get to have that cup of tea together?"

When Neriya tried to stand, she could not. It took Kezia and Czesław both to help her to her feet.

As they stumbled forward together, the birds in the trees dropped to the ground around them, some walking ahead of them, others to the side, opening a way farther in.

What was beyond was the forest . . . but changed.

The trees here were thick with new structure. At first, it looked as if they had grown in some strange new way, bulged out, connected with one another. But then Kezia saw that it was not the trees themselves that had grown.

They were nests. Nests that had grown huge, interconnected. Nests woven together, one into another, into great spiraling, twisting towers.

A town of crooked buildings, leaning on one another for support. Winding tree-streets of towers, twisting among the branches of ancient elms. Massive, elaborate, sometimes linking one tree to another.

Not the nests of crows at all but battlements and castles. Palaces.

And from those palaces, eyes looked down at her. At all of them.

Under one of the elms was a rough stone structure, more lean-to than hut, built at and against the base of the tree, roofed by branches, the chinks in its stone walls filled with old moss. A human shelter, battered and old.

And out from it came the Boy.

When Neriya went to him she fell, and again had to be helped up. The Boy held something up to her mouth.

Bread. A hunk of bread, from half a loaf held in his hand.

Not stale: fresh.

"Freshly stolen," Neriya whispered through cracked and grateful lips. "By our friends."

The grove rustled a thousand wings. Kezia looked around her. Everywhere, there was structure. Everywhere, there was movement.

They got Neriya inside the lean-to and onto an old pallet of reeds that had once been a bed.

It was dark in here. What light there was came slanting down through gaps in the damaged roof, settling on the dusting of snow that had gotten inside, on the Boy trying, with Czesław's help, to start the hovel's rough-built stove . . .

And on the neat stack of human bones in the corner. The long bones of the limbs and the smaller bones of hands and feet tucked inside the rib cage, the skull balanced on top.

The sockets of its hollow eyes glinted back at Kezia in the half dark. And she saw that the skull had been filled with glittering things that caught the light. Bits of glass, a rhinestone button, the brass of a rifle shell, the fancy porcelain stopper of a bottle.

Gifts.

Kezia helped feed twigs into the fire. She covered Neriya with her own coat, and shivered. She put bread between Neriya's lips, and accepted bread from the Boy for herself as well.

But her eyes kept coming back to the skull, staring at her from its corner niche. The fire was well lit now. Its light danced yellow in the sockets of the skull.

What am I now? the madness whispered. *Still a man?*

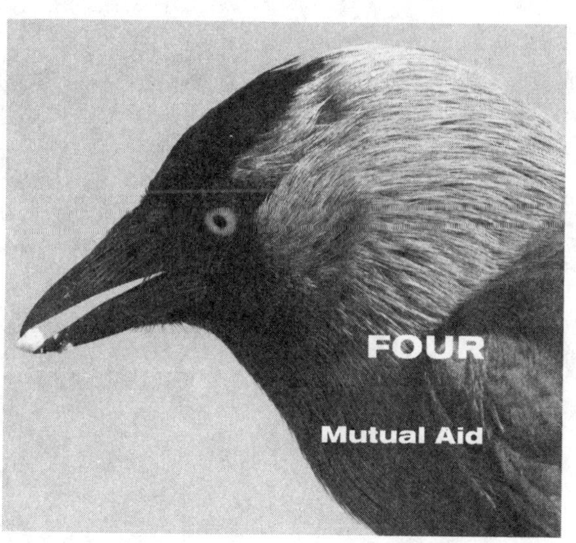

FOUR

Mutual Aid

I remember, as a boy, waking early in the morning. I do not know why: I simply woke in the dark. There was a weight on me in the house. I needed to be outside, and walking.

I dressed in the dark, silently, not to wake the rest of the family. As the first light of dawn lit the shtetl, I walked out to its edges. To where the Jewish homes ended and the Lithuanian farms began, their fields cut down to stubble.

A mist was over those fields. A fog had risen from the ground or fallen from the sky. And there in the fields were shapes, larger than I was. Shapes that walked like men but not like men. Folded things that clacked and strutted on stiff legs. That flapped and stabbed sword-faces into the ground.

They shuddered, stopped, turned to me in a whorl of wings and eyes.

And Ezekiel saw the wheel.

And I remembered Isaiah:

Each had six wings: with two he covered his face, and with two he covered his feet, and with two he did fly.

Then the seraphim were hidden in the guise of storks again. Storks about to leave for their long journey to Africa, gleaning the harvested fields for sustenance.

But for a moment, between sleep and wakefulness, I had seen them for exactly what they were.

—from *The Autobiography of a Burned Village*

21
NERIYA ABRAMOVNA KANTOROVA

November 1971

THEY ENTERED THE FOREST in predawn half-light. A forest of blue shadow, in which the deciduous trees had shed most of their leaves. Every breath brought cold to the nostrils and stole heat from the body. The ground was thick with fallen leaves. Among the stripped webs of branch and trunk were dark clusters of spruce.

They had eaten breakfast in silence. Not a tense silence, though there might be tension between them—rather, it was a silence of anticipation.

The feeling was familiar to her, from those moments when she was setting off on a biological expedition, on the cold train platform among the bags and boxes of equipment and supplies, breathing in the smell of coal from the furnaces of sleeper wagons on a siding, waiting for a journey to start.

There was a slight decline to the ground at first, as if the weight of the trees had depressed the surface of the earth. Then a rise in land, farther into the woods. The undulations continued, with Innokentiy leading them along a path obscured by fallen leaves.

With perfect clarity, she found the map of the forest in her mind. Where the bunker was. The many blinds of their hunting grounds. The clearings and hollows where partisans and family groups had camped. The winding way to the bog.

And from there, the path to the deep woods where the larger stream cut its trench in the soil. The ladder of roots and stone up the steep bank beyond.

They were half a kilometer into the forest when she heard the flock approaching, overhead past the winter-stripped canopy, the birds calling to one another at a distance.

Then they were there, beyond the pattern of denuded branches, darkly massed against a dark sky. Individual crows broke off from the group, dropped down into the trees around them.

Several came down around Innokentiy. One landed on his hat. Innokentiy reached up to stroke its back.

Several more were in the lower branches and on the ground around them now, harassing the leaves and one another, watching the three humans passing through their land.

The bird on Innokentiy's hat spread its wings, hopped from his head to his shoulder, then dropped down to the ground.

The bird tilted its head at her. She bent down and returned its gaze.

The crows they had named must all be gone. Most hooded crows lived less than a decade. Some might live a bit longer. But she recognized the movements of the birds they had known in these birds, the same way you might see the gestures of a parent or grandparent reflected in a child.

The difference between these crows and the others she had studied, over her many years, would be something difficult for her to describe, if she were to put it in a paper. It was . . . what? A *calculation* in their movements. An *intention* that would not be visible, perhaps, to most observers. A *directedness*. Their movements were thought through. Everything was done on purpose, not by routine.

"Do you have names for them?" she asked Innokentiy.

He nodded.

"Who is this one?"

He drew a cheap, gray-papered *bloknot* from his pocket. With a stub of pencil, he wrote:

Adaiah.

"Beautiful," she said.

Adaiah flew up onto a lower branch, then danced up into the canopy with the others and leaped into the air to follow the rest of the flock.

"I think the last winter we spent together in the forest is the one I remember in the most detail," she said. "The four of us among the palaces. The way we studied the crows. The dreams we had for a future after the war. The two of us would become biologists. And you two . . ."

". . . would be allowed to be your lab assistants," Czesław finished for her. "Yes. I remember. There was nothing to write with, so you girls would lie in the shelter at night, reciting the observations you had made during the day, trying to memorize them. That was Innokentiy's lullaby, all winter. Your field observations."

"Years after the war," she said, "when I was a postgraduate, I wrote it all down. And it was as if I were here again. I wrote about every teaching tool they made. I sketched them: the hoops of feather and twig, the models the crows made of people. I sketched their palaces too. I sketched the classroom ring, where the adults taught their red-mouthed fledglings about the world. I sketched the work teams, repairing a tower . . . And then I burned it all. I was afraid . . ."

"Of leading someone here?" Czesław asked.

"I thought that was what I was afraid of at first. But I think I was afraid of remembering it all again. I wanted to remember our time *here*, but not the time *after*. I wanted to remember that winter, when we were together and we had a future. But I did not want to remember what followed."

Innokentiy put a hand on her shoulder. The three walked on in silence. The sun came up, dull citron through morning haze, its light scattered through the branches.

And then they were there. At the zemlyanka.

She had not expected it so soon. She realized that the map in her head no longer fit. The size of everything had shifted slightly. She was a few inches taller now than she had been. Her pace had altered. She was an adult now. Was that it? Or had the forest expanded the space, over the years, that it occupied in her mind?

She was not ready.

Someone had built a sanded and painted wooden door where their improvised door of planks had once been. The new door was fitted. It had a handle and a lock, which Innokentiy now turned with a long key.

"Go on," Czesław said. "There is nothing terrible in there. I tried to keep things as they were, for the most part."

She took the flashlight Innokentiy held out to her.

Inside, it was decades ago. She passed through the door and was there again. She could swear that the smell still lingered. The unwashed smell of war: dirty clothes and dried sweat, covered over by the smell of fire, the odor of precious bread they had cooked here, the bits of meat they had rationed. The smells of sleep and darkness, dissipated by seasons but still clinging to the surfaces of the clumsy beds of larch and pine needle, the crude hearth.

And here was the nail in the wall where the photograph had hung.

No. Stay with us. Czesław will come back. He has to. He knows how to get out of things. He knows what to do. He can take care of himself.

No one can take care of themselves.

How long was she inside? A minute? Five minutes?

She tried to make herself stay as long as she could. She had dreamed of returning here for so long. She had come back so many times in her mind.

But that place she had returned to was different. This felt like . . . what? Like a museum of itself. Like the museum house of some writer or poet or politician. A faded copy of what it once had been, even if nothing about it had changed.

Was it that? Or was it that time had collapsed, in here? Decades had become days, and she had heard voices. Had heard, in here, a voice she had not heard so clearly in a long time.

She realized that, emerging, blinking in the bright light after even that short time, she had expected to see him as he was then. Her mind had slipped, in those short minutes, back in time. Innokentiy would be dragging a red thread through the grass, with Buster hopping after it. Czesław would have his rifle over his shoulder, about to leave on another hunt. And . . .

"I can't stay in there for longer than that either," Czesław said.

"On the train here," she said, "I finally allowed myself to think it. To really let it sink in. *She has now been dead much longer than she was alive.*"

Innokentiy held the bloknot out for her to read:

She's not dead while we are not dead.

Then he wrote:

The crows still visit this place too, though none were alive then.

"If you are ready," Czesław said, "we should continue. The days are short at this time of year."

They left the zemlyanka behind. The maze they had created to lead intruders away from their home was also still here, though many of the logs had decayed back into the earth, and everything was covered with seasons of leaves and windfall.

She recognized the feeling she had. A cemetery feeling.

The last place you saw someone was a kind of grave as well. Especially if you did not know where they were buried.

Or *if* they were buried.

CZESŁAW

March 1944

The stolen food the crows brought them was never quite enough, so Czesław left the others asleep in the hut and was up early every morning, hunting. The sound of the crows bursting into the air was what woke him, most days—the collective rush of predawn wings that marked their daily departure.

He always slept in his clothes—all four of them did—so all he had to do was put his shoes on in the dark. Outside the hut the tangled, spiraling tower-nests of the crows, twisted through the trees all around him, were quiet.

But they were not empty. Here and there he could see eyes peering down at him. Old crows who could no longer fly, the sick and wounded of the flock, cared for and fed by the others, left behind during the day as the rest foraged.

A cloudy-eyed head peered down from a high tower, watching him cross underneath. Neriya called that one Zaydeh. It seemed to be the oldest of the crows, or the oldest they knew of, anyway: there might be other, older crows being cared for in the labyrinth of interconnected nests above, hidden from view.

Neriya and Kezia had hundreds of names for the crows now. And names for the different areas of their strange city in the forest. There was the kitchen, the workshops, the schoolroom, the hospital. There was the orphanage, the nursery, the amphitheater. Human names, applied inexactly to things they were trying to understand. Approximations.

But there were things the crows did that were perfectly recognizable. They taught their young, for one. Czesław watched, one day, as Buster carefully laid in a cleared area several of the X-shaped gifts that the crows made and went through some elaborate lesson, swooping over them, stabbing at one of them, cawing, as three pink-beaked and blue-eyed fledglings watched.

He wondered if they were Buster's children, or if he was simply the "schoolmaster" on duty that day.

They cared for their elderly. He saw Madeleine at a nest low in one of the trees on a winter morning, with a beetle in her beak. He had thought it was for a baby, but no: she was feeding an old and battered crow.

And it finally became clear, as well, that Buster and Madeleine were more than just two crows who showed up together. They were mates: Czesław helped the girls locate their nest, high up in a primordial elm, from where the two looked down at them and Buster gave a croak that seemed clearly to mean: *Mind your own business, kids.*

The crows came to Neriya and Kezia for medical care, as if this was what they simply assumed a human was for. The girls stitched wounds, removed burrs and splinters.

The birds were often accompanied during these medical visits by other members of the flock, who jostled and commented as thorns were extracted from feet and tiny splints applied to broken toes. The girls began to call the little hut their "operating theater."

Czesław's main hunting grounds were down beyond the stream. He had found a place to cross where a fallen larch angled over the water unsteadily. He could straddle the trunk and inch across, his feet dangling over the rotten ice below.

He was halfway across the stream when he saw it.

It was two hundred meters or more from him, screened by trees. It was crouched over something.

Czesław finished crossing the stream in silence. He took his rifle from his shoulder but did not cock it, afraid the thing would hear. He moved in an arc, circling it at a distance, pushing his boots slowly into the snow at each step, as quietly as he could.

He had seen it the day before, but it had been much farther away and screened by trees. He could not have known what it was at that distance.

Now it was close to them, almost at the stream.

He reached an area of windfall, where a winter storm had blown down a line of spruce, tearing their roots from the frozen ground. Another storm had already coated them with ice.

He was behind the thing now. He depressed the trigger on the rifle to silence its cocking, then set the bolt while wrapping it in his shirt, to dull the sound.

Raising the rifle, he took aim at the thing's humped back.

It raised its head, as if it had sensed the point on its back where the bullet would go in.

Even at this distance, Czesław could make out the scarlet-smeared gore of the lower half of its face. Its eyes searched the forest.

They had been the eyes of a man, once. But they were not a man's eyes any longer.

Wind moved through the trees and filled the woods with the glassy sound of icicles clinking on frozen branches.

The thing's head remained raised. The lower half of its face was obscured by a matted beard. The hatless head was a greasy mass of tangled hair.

It stood up to its full height, head still raised, tilted in a posture that Czesław recognized as canine, feral.

Would it be able to see the rifle barrel through the iced-over spruce he was concealed behind?

He expected that it might call out, but it did not.

Could the thing speak anymore?

It had no rifle, but Czesław saw the knife in its hand. And

he heard the words, spoken to him years ago, as clearly as if the thing were speaking them now:

You should run, if you ever see me again. Do you understand?

Just as his finger moved to squeeze the trigger, the thing moved, ducking sideways and loping off into the trees.

The way it moved was not human. Czesław was reminded of a bear. A thing that could be upright but was not a man.

Not anymore.

He did not exactly hunt, that day. He wandered the woods with his rifle, but without being able to hunt for anything except the thing that had once been a man.

Where it had been crouching, he found a body. A partisan, out on patrol? A deserter, wandering the woods? It was hard to say. The man was not freshly dead, and many animals in the woods had been eating from him, besides the thing.

That evening in the hut, Czesław lay listening to Neriya and Kezia talking about the shapes of the towers, and the way the teams of builders, whenever they reconstructed one, took what was broken apart and built it larger than it had been before. They talked about the way several crows worked together, shifting materials, weaving new tower stories atop the old ones, buttressing earlier layers. They talked excitedly, totally engaged in the story they were telling about the crows, about what was going on here, in this place. Exchanging ideas, theories, explanations.

As if there were no war going on at all. Or as if that war were happening in someone else's world entirely. And why not? This *was* another world.

He had long ago stopped looking at the bones in the corner, the eye sockets filled with glittering bits of the crows' treasure. But now he found himself looking at them again, in the embers of the dying fire. Along with the bones, there had been, wrapped in the scraped skin of a doe, dozens more of the pages from the man's manuscript. All winter Neriya and Kezia had read them together. He had been half listening.

Kezia read now, as well as Neriya ever had, in Russian and in Yiddish.

But what had *he* learned? Kezia had learned to read from Neriya. Kezia and Neriya had learned to hunt from him, and were as good as he was. But what had *he* learned from *them*?

Very little. A door had closed in him, years ago. It felt like it would never open again.

"We have to leave here," he said in the dark. "It isn't safe anymore."

He expected questioning, protest. He had been preparing for a difficult discussion, trying to search for what he might say to them that hid the truth of that awful thing out there but also moved them.

But there was none. What did they hear in his voice? Why did they trust him?

After a long silence, Neriya said, "All right. We'll leave tomorrow."

The Boy wept.

Here, time has slowed. Here, I can think and dream again. I can remember, again. Time once moved in an exhausted line, like a chain of soldiers returning at dusk to their entrenchments. No longer.

Time loops and whirls. Today arcs backward into yesterday, and the seasons are nested one inside another.

I mend wounded limbs and wings. And in return they allow me a place among their palaces.

—from *The Autobiography of a Burned Village*

22
NERIYA ABRAMOVNA KANTOROVA

November 1971

"DURING THE LAST MONTHS of the war," Czesław said, "I sent letters home but received no answer. In the wreckage of Berlin, just as the Soviet Union was raising the red flag over the Reichstag, I received a letter from a neighbor who still lived in the Siberian logging camp. My father and grandfather had died of typhoid in the camps, she said. My mother had been resettled in Kazakhstan. She was killed late in the war, in a factory accident.

"So then I had no family of my own. All I had to hold on to was finding you. As I rooted the last of the nationalists out of the forests," Czesław said, "I was working my way up in the ranks. I was gaining power, connections. I was building a network that reached across republics. I was able to make inquiries. And I needed all of that. I had only one full name: *Neriya Abramovna Kantorova*. The other two people I was looking for were a nameless boy—one lost boy among a million lost boys—and Kezia, a Roma girl with no surname. One lost girl among a million lost girls.

"What I hoped for in those first years was that somehow the three of you had stayed together. That if I traced one name, I would find the others. That you had all made it out of the woods together, ended up in the same orphanage or were somewhere out there as I imagined you, wondering about me and unable to locate me.

"But that was when I had time to think of such things. So much of my time was spent hunting. Hunting men in the forests of this new Lithuanian Soviet Socialist Republic. Hunting the nationalist, collaborationist murderers who called themselves 'forest brothers' now.

"And the forest brothers hid well—these were their woods. They'd had years to dig in. They knew the landscape and the ambush points. And they had the loyalty, much of the time, of the local population. They hit our units and ran, gunned us down in the streets, shot our convoys up on the roads.

"After the war, they fought us harder than they had ever fought the Germans. They fought desperately, and well. When we finally found groups of them, the battles were as savage as any I fought in Finland. And at first, they were almost like a real army—with uniforms and good weapons. But over the years, their equipment grew worse. Their leaders died, and their supporters grew tired. Tired, and afraid: tens of thousands were deported; whole communities who supported the partisans were razed. And I was a part of all of it. I was doing it, I told myself, for you.

"I woke up one day and it was 1950. The war had been over for years. I was a man. A leader of men. I was feared. And I realized that I had not spoken Polish for years. I looked in the mirror and tried to speak my native language, even to myself, alone, but it came out distorted. Broken. And the face it came out of was not a Polish face anymore—so how could it be expected to speak such a language? It was no longer my father's face in the mirror, looking back at me. It was no longer a younger version of my grandfather. I had become someone else.

"On that same day I received a letter from a woman who had fought as a partisan here. A contact of a contact, now working in Rostov as a mechanic. She said she had known a girl called Neriya in the late days of the war. A girl they had found with a little boy. She and Neriya and the boy had been together in a partisan group, where Neriya worked as a nurse. And before the group they were with joined the assault on Vilnius, the boy was sent to the rear, on a truck full of orphaned children, headed for a village near Minsk. She knew the date, because it was just before the storming of Vilnius, and because it was her birthday.

"So I had something, at least. Finally. But it took me two more years to locate Innokentiy. By the time I found him, he was a young man. He was living in a barracks with other war orphans, laying concrete for one of the new cities in Siberia. And do you know the surname they gave him?"

They were at the edge of the bog now. Innokentiy was unlocking an aluminum boat, which had been chained to a tree and concealed with branches.

"Neriya. Do you know what surname they gave Innokentiy?"

She had thought, for a moment, that she had heard gunshots in the forest. No. It was nothing more than an echo, come down through the years, of that day when they had fled the zemlyanka and run through the woods. That day they had run, with the grinding roar of German machines all around them, with the woods filled with explosions, gunshots, the shouts and screams of men.

For a moment she almost saw them as they had been, the four of them, coming to the edge of the bog. Not this present bog, this silent gray expanse of late autumn water, but the living green bog of that summer, its surface skeined with bright green duckweed, frogs calling from the bulrushes.

"What surname did they give him?" she said.

"Voronov. The crow."

They got in the boat and Innokentiy pushed them off, climbing in and taking the oars. He paused to write in his bloknot for her:

They named me after the Red Army artillery commander, not after the birds.

As they drifted out into the bog, a crow landed on the gunwale. Innokentiy stroked its back. The crow played a game, for a bit, of flying up and then landing on the shaft of an oar—first one, then the other. Then it tired of the game and flew away.

"I brought Innokentiy back with me," Czesław continued. "By then I had a plan: I was high up in the KGB in the Lithuanian Soviet Socialist Republic now. I would turn this forest into a reserve for the KGB. Like the royal hunting reserves that had once protected forests in Europe. I was done with revenge. All I wanted now was to keep this one place safe. It was the only use left for my power that made sense: To keep the crows safe. To protect them. To keep them safe as they had kept us safe. And I could keep Innokentiy safe too. He would be a forester and have a home here. We would be together again."

"You must have found me as well."

"Yes. I found you at the Academy of Sciences."

"When?"

"In 1952."

"Almost twenty years ago? But you never contacted me."

"Your name came up on a list. I got on a train for Moscow immediately. I saw you coming out of a building with several other young researchers. I followed you to a park, where you sat in the grass, still wearing your white lab coats. You were sharing sausage, cheese, bread, and kvass, laughing together. I wanted to approach you. I wanted to. But . . . you were *there*. You were *with them*. And who was I? A ghost from another time, and not even the boy I had been but something so much worse than I had been then.

"I remember that your coats were so white, I could barely look at them. Then it started to rain, and you scattered, laughing. I stayed across the street from the academy building, in a café, with the rain streaming down the windows. I waited for you to come out in the evening. And you did come out. I had been hoping you would be alone. I thought, *If she is alone, I'll be able to talk to her.* But again, you were with people. And you were happy."

"How could you think I was happy? Knowing what you knew? What you saw? I was afraid every day."

Czesław shook his head. "No. I know fear. You had learned,

by then, to blend in. To be a part of the group. And you had found a calling. I had read your thesis. You had become the person you both spoke of. Given time, you would stand at a podium, just as the two of you had dreamed, and tell the world great things."

Was it true? She tried to imagine what day that had been. Looking back at her academy days, what she remembered was dead birds on tables, dead birds under bell jars. The smell of formaldehyde. Invitations to parties that she refused. A violent moment with a professor who had tried to shove his hand up her dress. The purges in the Academy of Sciences: Professors suddenly gone. Students suddenly gone.

And the fear, all the time—because the Black Marias still roamed the streets. Because someone could always find out . . .

But, yes, there were other days. Sunny days. You could not be miserable all the time. You could not be alone all the time. You could not work all the time.

So, yes, there were days when they all went to the park. Days when people laughed, and people gossiped about little things, and people got on trams together and gave each other gifts, and people baked cakes for birthdays, and drank tea in cramped kitchens, and shared jars of preserves from the dachas of their relatives, and sang and played guitar, and went out on dates, and did all of the other things that people always did and probably had done even in Moscow when the bombs were falling in the worst days of the war.

And she was a part of that too. Laughing and doing everything people did when they were happy. Acting like they did. Blending in. That's what she told herself.

And not wanting to spoil things, to bring others down.

Pretending to be happy for the sake of those around her, so that they would not be lonely and afraid. So that her own feelings would not infect them.

But was that true? Or had she made herself happy by pretending to be happy? Thinking back to that time, it was impossible to tell which it was.

All around her, others had seemed happy. But were they doing the same? Pretending to be happy for the sake of others?

She had heard, once, on a train, a conversation between strangers. One of them was telling the other that, in fact, nobody believed in God. Not a single priest, not a single member of the flock. All of the so-called faithful were only pretending to believe.

Most were not charlatans. No. They pretended not out of some desire to lie but out of love. They wanted other people to have faith in something. They wanted others to have something to cling to, though they themselves had nothing.

Even Jesus himself, the stranger said. He never believed he was the son of God. He died on the cross to give us hope. He died knowing we were, every one of us, alone in the universe. He did not want to infect others with his loneliness—and so he pretended to have a father who loved him. A father who could save him.

How could Czesław have known, from the outside, what she was feeling? The gnawing terror of it all? What he had seen was her laughing, her happy with others, her blending in. The opposite of everything he felt.

But he of all people *should* have known. He was a part of delivering terror to people. Of bringing it into their homes at night—tearing parents from children in the name of revenge.

He must have seen so many of them smile into the faces of their children as they were taken away, and tell them everything would be all right.

She felt sick. "I was so horribly alone," she said. "All that time. Especially then, when I was surrounded by others. You could have saved me from that."

"I know that now," Czesław answered. "But how was I supposed to explain to you the murderer I had become? What I had been doing, in the years after the war?"

"And who was I? What things did you assume I had done?"

"In those days," Czesław said, "I thought I was the only one who was alone. And then the decision was made. I walked away. Then time went by. Years passed. I thought of returning to see you. I thought of inviting you here. But I told myself it was too late. It took me until now to understand that, while we are still alive, it is not too late."

CZESŁAW

April 1944

He heard the crows' alarm.

It was distant—half a kilometer off? But he had come to know that call well: what Neriya called the "bad man" call.

He had been in the deer blind, waiting. It was still cold, but in the brighter places where the sun managed to find the ground were clusters of snowdrops, and on some of the most optimistic trees, the fleeting new green of spring.

The call came from an area between him and the zemlyanka, to which they had returned after leaving the crows.

That was what worried him most. He abandoned the hunting blind, moving as silently as he could toward the sound.

He heard the call shift position, moving through the trees.

The crows were scolding. They had formed a ring around the intruder. They were following his movements, yelling down from the trees.

Had Neriya heard the call? Had Kezia? Had the Boy? It was still far from them but heading in their direction.

Czesław was moving now in a half run. Moving with a loping pace, as quickly as he could while remaining quiet.

Now he saw crows in the branches above him. They did not call at him. They looked down silently. They knew he was on the hunt.

The alarm calls were still moving away from him. He slowed slightly, lifted his gaze from the placement of his feet.

And he saw it.

It did not move like a man anymore at all. It was still upright, but only for a few steps at a time. Every few paces it crouched, knuckles in the dirt. Cocked its head, listened. Sniffed the air.

Between the matted smears of hair and beard were bright, feral eyes in a filthy face. It was covered in muddy, wet rags, barely identifiable as human clothing anymore.

As its head began to turn his way, he concealed himself behind a tree. He was downwind of it, but he knew it sensed him.

It understands the crows are helping someone.

He stayed silent for a minute. Then two. The crows had gone silent as well.

When he looked from behind the tree, it was gone.

Then there was a burst of alarm sounds on his right. He saw it—close now. Moving fast, straight for him. In the middle of the dark, terrible mass of hair that was the lower half of its face, its teeth showed.

It was so fast, leaping off the ground. On all fours and then on two feet. Close enough now that he could hear the sound it was making, the chuckling, gibbering sound that once had been a human voice, able to structure words, and was no longer.

You should run, if you ever see me again. Do you understand?

He saw the knife, like a claw in its twisted hand.

He raised the rifle and fired.

It kept coming.

He had hit the thing. He was certain he had hit it. But it kept coming.

He fired again. It leaped into the air, huge, so close to him now that he staggered backward.

Almost on him.

He fired again.

Still coming, and making louder sounds now.

You should run.

Inside that sound there were bits of words. Not language anymore, but parts of it. Like the fragments of something half digested.

He tripped and fell. Expected it to be on him. Found himself looking up into the sky and the tops of the trees. Knew he was dead.

But when he finally sat up, he saw it in a heap, twenty meters from him.

The last shot had caught it in the throat. It had fallen, half upright, against the trunk of a larch. Its head, tilted at an angle, stared off at nothing.

Czesław stood up.

He had hit his shoulder falling, and his hip. The bruises would be bad.

His ears rang. Had he hit his head as well? He felt something hot on his scalp, touched it, came away with a red hand. A nasty cut. But he was whole. He was alive.

And the thing was dead.

But the crows were still calling, all around him now. Warning.

Then he heard the voice, from behind him, in Russian.

"Lay the rifle on the ground, and put your hands up."

He did as he was told.

"Turn around."

The men were dressed in old Red Army uniforms from early in the war, but with new tunics and new boots. There were two of them. They both carried submachine guns.

"I, too, am a soldier of the Red Army," Czesław said. "I have been in these woods since 1941."

"Who is with you?"

Czesław thought of the corpses he had seen in the forest over the years, their hands tied, shot in the back of the head. Men, most of them. But women as well. And children too.

Secrecy was more important to the partisans than mercy. They had always known very well that staying away from the Soviet units in the woods—deserters or partisans—was as important as staying away from the Germans.

And so now he was dead. But they were still far from the others. The partisans might not find them. The others, at least, might live. *Fine. Fine. It's my time. Fine. I have done enough for them, taught them enough to make it. They won't have my rifle, but they have Kezia's revolver, and spring is coming . . .*

"I am alone," he said. "I have been alone for three years now, since the Germans destroyed our unit in 1941."

"And who is this man you killed?"

"That is not a man anymore. Once, he was a forester and took care of these woods. But the war has turned him into something else."

"It has done that to many people."

One of the men made a wide circle around Czesław. He picked Czesław's Mosin-Nagant up off the ground and examined it with professional, military interest.

"I think this is the cleanest rifle I've seen in the forest in years. Even the commander might approve."

"So we have a good rifle," the other said. "And him?"

"We can let the commander decide."

He had thought it was all right. But suddenly he was filled with a terror that was greater than his fear for them. It was the terror of losing them. Of being alone again, among strangers to whom he meant nothing at all.

He could not be alone again. And for a second, he thought he would run. That he could find it in him to run. That maybe he could get away, get back to them.

But he did not run. There was no getting away. Not for him. Not now.

They tied Czesław's hands.

Czesław looked up into the trees to find a circle of crows, quiet now, watching as he was led away.

He thought of the crows' city in the forest, complete with its schools, its hospitals, its laws, and its trials. Of a crow he had seen surrounded by others and pecked to death, for some incomprehensible transgression. Of how the crows had surrounded it, in a circle. For an hour, there was a conversation. A clacking of beaks, a shivering of wings. Minor fights broke out.

The bird in the center, through all of this, was perfectly still.

A trial, Czesław had later wanted to call it.

The jury closed in. There was a swarming of feathers and wings around the defendant bird. Strangely silent and businesslike.

Afterward there was blood on the snow, and the limp, dead bird who somehow had transgressed and paid the price.

The crows looked down at him now from the trees, watching without a sound.

You have your politics, and we have ours.

This is my shtetl now, and finally I have my place among the flock.

—from *The Autobiography of a Burned Village*

23

NERIYA ABRAMOVNA KANTOROVA

November 1971

"THEY TOOK ME to the camp," Czesław said, "where I waited to die. I sat against a tree for hours with my hands tied together, an old man pointing my own rifle at me. And all I can remember thinking is that I had left all of you without a rifle.

"Finally, I was brought before their commander for questioning. I remember so little of that interview. The commander was so unexceptional. A man just like any other man, though later he would be remembered as a Hero of the Soviet Union."

The prow of the boat bumped onto the island in the middle of the bog. They got out, and Innokentiy hauled the boat up a bit farther onto the sandy soil.

"I would come to know the commander as well as anyone

who served under him," Czesław continued. "He was not cruel or kind or anything at all. He was empty. He was no one. Whether it was war or something else that had emptied him out, I do not know. But he was the perfect man for war. He knew what was useful in the moment—what was needed to win. He cared for nothing else. He listened to my lies, impassively, and finally waved a hand, having decided not to kill me. I do not think he believed a word of the story I told him. He simply decided I was of use."

The forest had warped in its proportions. Parts of it now seemed telescoped in size as they were walking through it. But other parts were claustrophobically small.

The zemlyanka, which then had been like a home, with room enough for all of them, had seemed to her like a cage. Unable to stand up in it, she had crouched in its darkness and thought of the four of them, crammed in together. Had there really been space for all of them?

Now, stepping onto the island, it was shrunken, distorted. Where was the beach where they had sometimes lain together, soaking in the sun? The little hummock of sand jutting from the water had once been a world. Most of its features had since been erased. Blurred.

"I was brought past an area where people were being shot. There was a trench dug there, a slit in the earth half filled with corpses. They were the ones who the commander had decided were not of use. Their faces, white with lime, stared up at the sky. There were men there, and women, and children too. I remember all of them clearly, because I searched each face to make sure it was not one of you."

It was only a few dozen strides to the center of the island.

The log bunker had collapsed long ago. Its bottom was flooded, as it had been when they found it, decades ago. The island was choked with dry bulrush, the bleached and colorless stalks of bog rosemary, fallen leaves that had drifted here on the wind, and the needles of stunted pine.

Innokentiy wrote in his bloknot: *I can still taste the frogs.*

"Me too," she said—and smiled for the first time that day. "It wasn't until years later that I found out the French eat frog legs as a delicacy." She made a disgusted face.

Innokentiy wrote: *I thought they tasted good. But maybe I was just hungry. I haven't tried them lately.*

"After the commander finished with me," Czesław continued, "my hands were untied. I was given a bowl of soup. I ate by a warm fire, listening to the sounds of others, not as lucky as myself, being shot.

"All I could think of, for the first months, was escape. Returning to you. Making sure you were all right. But then the Red Army arrived in the forest, with tanks and trucks and all the heavy equipment of war. We began preparing for the assault on Vilnius. I was reregistered, assigned to a unit, absorbed back into the mass of the military machine. I became like the men around me: a part of a wave. Particles in a massive, forward motion.

"We were inevitable. A Soviet victory, though it might be years away, was inevitable. We knew that. And I knew I might have years of fighting ahead of me, but the wave of victory had already swept over the forest. You were probably already saved, already put on trucks and brought to the rear. That is what I told myself. I might die before I ever saw you again, but you three would live, and that made my death worth it.

"That's what I told myself. You would live. And once the war was over, if I did live, I would join you."

The crow who had landed on the gunwale of the boat earlier now settled on the rotting logs of the bunker. Czesław followed it with his eyes.

"It wasn't until years after the war that I realized *the crows were the ones who led me to the zemlyanka in the first place.* In the days when I was alone, before I met any of you, I followed a group of them calling in the woods. That was how I found the zemlyanka. Several of them were standing around it and walking back and forth near the door. There didn't seem to be anything unusual about that. Just crows, in the forest. But that place saved our lives, and now I am sure they led me to it on purpose, though I never knew it then. And then they led us here, to this island, and then farther, to their home, where they sheltered us among them for that last winter, when we would have died if we were left on our own. But I never understood *why.*"

"There are many possible reasons," she said. "But I think it was simple: They had enough to live, and we did not. They had a surplus. And we were kind to them. And maybe most important, *he* had been kind to them, before. So why not help us? It cost them little, and in return we amused them. And sometimes we could be useful."

Like pets? Innokentiy wrote.

"Maybe. I think it could have been as simple as that, yes."

"Or a stray dog you leave a bowl of food out for?"

"Why not? Isn't that good enough? The stray dog doesn't complain."

"I have always felt," Czesław said, "that there was a deeper reason."

"There has never been a deeper reason necessary for cruelty. Why would a deeper reason be necessary for kindness?"

The crow hopped down from its log and danced around Innokentiy's feet, trying to untie his shoes.

I come here sometimes and catch frogs for them, Innokentiy wrote. *Maybe she thinks I have one hidden in my pocket.*

But then the crow darted in, grabbed a beakful of bootlace, and pulled. It flapped off, calling with a cackle that sounded like a human laugh, circling overhead to watch Innokentiy retie his boot.

KEZIA

June 1944

In late June, when the leaves of the trees were full and had lost the gold of spring, Kezia and Neriya brought down a deer—a young buck, his antlers still sheathed in velvet.

It was the first deer they had seen in this part of the forest since winter had ended. They had managed to bring it down with the revolver, by some miracle. And they desperately needed it.

They had survived for months now on what they could scavenge and forage, and on the gifts the crows sometimes brought. But those gifts were meager. Spring in the forest was not a generous time, and early summer had been little better.

Czesław had been gone for months, but Kezia felt he was

still with them. He was there in the things he had taught them: As Kezia field-dressed the buck, her hands moved the way he had taught her to move them. The motions of her hands were Czesław's motions.

But the knife she used was the antler-handled knife she had taken from the peasants who had attacked her years ago. The gun they brought the deer down with was the one she had taken from her uncle, who had died in a time and place incredibly distant from here.

Those events—the death of her family, her time alone in the village—did not seem like they had occurred years ago; they seemed like things that had happened to someone else entirely.

This Kezia, missing and remembering and mourning her friend as the knife in her hand mimicked his efficient hand, cutting through the deer's belly and spilling its entrails on the ground, certainly could not be *that* Kezia.

This Kezia had learned everything Czesław had taught her. From him, she had learned how to stalk a deer. How to hunt and shoot. How to track any animal or any person in the woods. How to know when someone was tracking her.

This Kezia, who could now read and speak in Russian and in Yiddish, who understood the way ticks and sea anemones and bees and foxes saw the world and knew every plant and tree in the forest by their Latin names because that was how Neriya knew them, and that was what Neriya had taught her, could not be *that* Kezia—that illiterate girl who had watched her mother pulled from a bog and seen the madness curling after her, searching for the next mind to infect.

This Kezia was a new person. She could not be, either, that feral girl from the village, the one who had spent an autumn living on the honey of abandoned beehives, sleeping in a pile of hay, killing men without flinching.

Neriya was several meters away, collecting feverfew in a sunny spot.

The Boy had been running a fever for several days now. Nothing seemed to help.

Last night, he had ceased to respond to either of them. This morning, the Boy was alternately so hot that he soaked himself in sweat or so cold that his teeth chattered and clacked together.

Part of the deer would be for them, but part was for trade. For years now, the girls had avoided the peasants in the forest and those still living in the few huts that survived.

But now Neriya was determined. "There is one family," she said, "that my parents helped. My father performed surgery right on their table and saved their daughter's life. They must still know me. If there is anyone left in the world who might help us, it is them. We need real medicine, not just a tea that makes headaches go away. If we don't get it, the Boy will die."

"Then let *me* go," Kezia had said.

But Neriya refused. "I am the one they know. I have to be the one who goes."

They dragged the deer on the improvised travois they had made, getting it as close as they could to the zemlyanka. Kezia pulled while Neriya obscured the drag marks, sweeping them away with a pine branch. Kezia butchered the deer while Neriya boiled water and made the tea.

In the zemlyanka, the Boy had somehow managed to get out of all his clothes. He lay naked in the middle of the floor, his skin dry and hot to the touch, his eyes staring wildly at nothing at all.

Neriya took up the pack, filled with meat.

"No. Stay with us," Kezia said. "Czesław will come back. He has to. He knows how to get out of things. He knows what to do. He can take care of himself."

"No one can take care of themselves," Neriya said. "We have to take care of each other. The Boy won't drink. Can't drink. I'm going *now*. Before it is too late."

Neriya pushed through the door.

And what was there to do? Kezia tugged at her jacket, but she was gone.

Kezia sat with the Boy on the floor. Sat looking into his staring eyes. His mouth opened, and she thought for a moment that he was going to speak. Finally speak. But he said nothing. He looked from her face to the door and back to her face. That was also a kind of speaking.

"Let's go outside, at least," she said to him. "In the shade. It might be cooler there."

She dressed him and carried him out into the clearing and lay him in the shade.

Only then, she saw the men.

There were eight of them. They were armed. They were in uniform, but the uniforms were not whole. They were pieces of uniforms, the insignia torn off. German uniforms, and the uniforms of the Lithuanian police. They wore salvaged boots. Most of the men were blond, light eyed, though one had darker hair.

Kezia stood with her hands in the air while one of the men patted her down. While he took the pistol that had been her last defense, her last way of providing food for them, and handed it to another man.

He said something to her that she could not understand. She

had expected German. She had thought of the men walking through the clearing while she and Neriya hid up in the tree. The men with the severed head.

But the man spoke in Lithuanian.

No matter. Another language of killers. Another language that confirmed they were dead. She was dead, the Boy was dead.

At least Neriya had gotten away.

Kezia looked into the trees and saw several of the crows there, looking down at her and the Boy.

The Boy was crying. He was doing it as he always did—in perfect silence.

"I am sorry," Kezia said to him in Polish.

"Be quiet," one of the men said, also in Polish. This one stood in front of them. He was probably their leader.

Another of the men had gone into the zemlyanka. The one with darker hair. She heard him tossing things around.

He came out a few moments later with Neriya's box. And with her documents. He and the man who had told her to be quiet went through the documents. Finally he found one of the identification documents with a photo and held it up. He looked at Kezia, at the photo. Back at Kezia.

He sees the Jewish name.

The man went through the documents again, shuffling them, then coming back to that one, holding it up.

"This is you?"

And Kezia understood. They were looking for Jews.

Everything was falling apart. The Red Army would be here any day now. The world of the Germans and their Lithuanian collaborators was ending. They were making sure no one was left to speak of what they had done. They had to be sure.

Their mismatched uniforms, the insignia torn off. These were criminals, covering up a crime. Making sure there were no witnesses left.

And when she denied the documents were hers? When she tried to save her own life? What then?

They would hunt for Neriya, or wait until she had returned. Finish what they started.

She and the Boy were already dead. But these men would wait for Neriya. Make sure there was no one left.

And if they looked a little harder, they would see it was more than the two of them who lived here.

"Yes," she said. "That is me. I am Neriya."

For a moment, the entire world shuddered. She felt it, inside her. The thing she had repressed for years now—the madness. A yellow fury, seeping from the soil.

She wanted to laugh at them. At these men, at the other murderers in the forest, at the false crows who had betrayed her and the Boy, not making a sound as their enemies closed in, turning on her after all of these years.

She looked at the Boy. He was staring back at her through tears. But he did not shake his head. He did nothing at all.

"Who is this?" the man asked, pointing at the Boy. "Your brother?"

"No," Kezia said. "He's just some goy I found in the forest."

I was planning on drinking his blood, of course, the madness wanted her to say. *Isn't that what you think we Jews do?*

"What's your name?" the man asked the Boy.

"He doesn't speak," Kezia said. "He hasn't spoken since I found him."

The man said something in Lithuanian to the Boy.

The Boy shook his head.

"What are you asking him?"

"If he is your brother."

"I don't have a brother," Kezia said.

"Were you with anyone else?"

"We were," Kezia said. "But they were killed."

"Who killed them?"

"Men like you," Kezia said.

The man's face did not change. "Where did you get the gun?"

"I took it from a dead man." *Another man like you*, she wanted to say.

The man looked at her. And she looked into his face for the first time. Smeared with dirt, narrow lipped, his hair a dirty off-blond under a shapeless garrison cap. Blue eyes. A broken nose.

War had eroded away any expressive qualities his face might have had. There was no cruelty in it, and no kindness. It was the face of a man who gave orders, followed orders, pulled triggers.

And now he would kill her.

And the Boy?

Maybe not. Maybe not, if they believed the Boy really was a Lithuanian, like them. And he probably was. Kezia realized she had never thought of what language he would speak, if he could speak. He had always seemed to understand everything said to him. And since he never spoke, understanding had been enough.

"All right," the man said. "Let's go."

When Neriya returned, the zemlyanka would be empty. She would see their things scattered around. But she would never know what had happened.

Neriya would be alone again. But she might live to see the

end of the war. At least there was that. And maybe one day Neriya would find the Boy again, if they both survived.

But for me, it is over now.

One of the men reached down and picked the Boy up, as if he weighed nothing at all. To Kezia he had seemed so heavy. She had struggled to get him outside.

But, she realized, *that is because I am dying. I am using up my last strength. The whole world is heavy. Even the smallest pebble.*

And so what, then, does it matter? At least I can make dying mean something. At least I can die in someone else's place.

What have I discovered, living here among them?

If I had only one sentence to explain what I have found here, it would be this:

Every time I watch them, trying to understand what they are doing, I find them watching me, trying to understand what I am doing.

—from *The Autobiography of a Burned Village*

24
NERIYA ABRAMOVNA KANTOROVA

November 1971

IT WAS PAST MIDDAY when they reached the stream.

They had not followed a path: There was no path to follow. Innokentiy and Czesław had carefully destroyed all paths into the heart of the forest. They had arranged windfalls, snags, moved fallen logs to confuse any poacher who wandered too far into the woods. Everything wound back on itself. All the apparent tracks came to impasses where deadfalls or the torn roots of trees rose up and blocked the way farther in.

Most poachers would stay away anyway: This forest was the reserve of the KGB. It was where the men everyone feared supposedly took their leisure, hunting in the style of European lords in centuries past.

That was its public reputation. But Czesław had ensured that the reputation of the forest in the KGB was a poor one. That the officers who might have come here believed it to be nothing more than a dreary tangle of bogs and stinging nettle, set aside not for their pleasure but as a strategy for denying it to what might be left of Lithuanian bandits and nationalists.

Innokentiy led them through the labyrinth of misdirection. And finally, to the stream.

To a place she recognized. Here, the trunk of the fallen larch still lay across the water, as it had for decades. And once they had crossed it, there was an invisible ladder of roots and stone, allowing them to climb the steep, cliff-like cutbank on the other side.

It was hard going. Footholds had been removed. Stones had been loosened on purpose, handholds cut away. Innokentiy guided her up, traversing to the parts of the ladder left intact, too secret to be found by a stranger.

At the top, he reached a hand down to her.

There was no wall of crows, as there had been during the war. No wall, and no welcoming committee.

But the palaces were everywhere. Where once there was a town, there was now a city.

There was not a branch or an angle in the trunks that was not filled with the crows' constructions. Multistoried towers, towers balanced on towers, walls of conjoined homes wound among the ancient trees of this oldest part of the forest.

And the crows had even built structures on the ground, among the roots. They appeared to have dug down into the earth and constructed what looked like small, arch-topped huts of sticks, roofed with mud, feathers, leaves.

It was all there, as it had been—but now there was so much more of it.

The burned village in the fields at the edge of the woods. The humps where the houses had once been—the lost world of the shtetl, the burned synagogue, and the market and libraries destroyed, the fallen lintels and the charred doorposts with their mezuzahs buried with them forever in the earth.

All of that was gone.

But here, a whole world had been saved. And not only saved: a world had grown and thrived in this secret, sheltered space.

A crow waddled slowly toward them. It had emerged from among the roots of one of the nests on the ground. It was old and walked stiffly. One of its wings had, long ago, been torn away.

Innokentiy bent down and ran a hand over its back. He took a walnut from his pocket, shelled it, and held it out to the bird, who ate it slowly.

Innokentiy wrote: *I saved this one from a hunter's snare a decade ago. I call her Baba.*

"The crows take care of their sick, their elderly, their wounded," Czesław said. "They always did, but they are better at it now than they were before. The nests on the ground are for the crows who can no longer fly. The oldest among them, the wounded, those born without flight. They are safe here now as well."

At the center of it all, built solidly of planks and stone, with a roof of wooden shingles, was a small cabin, which had not been here during the war. It stood next to the hut where they had spent so much of that last winter together with the crows.

Innokentiy picked Baba up. Cradling her in the crook of his arm, he led the way to the cabin.

Above them, around them, quiet daytime routines continued. There were no alarm calls. Here and there, the faces of crows peered down from the palaces. On the ground near the door of the cabin, a group of juveniles, their young eyes still blue, their ruffled plumage dull brown-gray, were playing with a hoop of straw. They stopped for a moment and stared warily at the three humans as they passed.

Inside, Innokentiy set Baba down on a big rough-hewn table strewn with notebooks. There were a few chairs here. In one corner of the room was a small wood-burning stove. In another, an old army cot. A smaller table against the wall had things for food preparation. Next to it was a water tank on the wall with a spigot, a sink underneath, and a bucket beneath that to collect the drained water. Pegs on the walls held many things, some of them clearly toys or games.

She dropped her pack and sat in one of the chairs. Collapsed, almost.

Suddenly she was very tired. It was a familiar feeling—the feeling she often had during a long experiment, when she could not leave the laboratory for hours, or sometimes for days. Or on return from an expedition, when she closed the door to her apartment and nearly fell onto the couch.

It was the tiredness that came from holding herself together for too long, banishing all possibility, for days on end, of rest because something needed to be done.

Often, afterward, the exhaustion was total. Not only physical—emotional as well. After long expeditions, even when they were successful—maybe especially when they were successful—she felt herself plunged into a gloom that threatened to widen into depression. Sometimes, it did.

Innokentiy lit the stove and placed a kettle on top, filled from the water tank.

For the next several minutes, none of them spoke. Czesław stood, leafing through one of the notebooks on the table, his back slightly turned to her. Innokentiy tended the fire in the stove. She cradled her head, her eyes open. A bar of sunset-colored light came through the cabin's single small window and fell in an oblique bar across the table.

This was the place she had needed to come to. And now she was here. She had crossed the bog, and the stream, to the center of the forest. To as far as they had come as children.

To the place where the two of them, Neriya and Kezia, had played their most elaborate game of the war, in which they had imagined that one day the world would be entirely different. That somehow a war, having torn everything into shreds, would result in a world that was *better* than the one before. And a Roma girl and a Jewish girl would emerge from the woods and tell that world about the miracle they had discovered: the civilization of crows that had saved their lives, fed and sheltered and preserved them while humans ripped everything apart.

Why had they believed that, having been smashed and broken, torn to rags, the world would somehow end up *better* than before? It was never true of people, was it? Never true that, once abused, once hurt, they became better people. They became more defensive, more concentrated on preserving what little they could of themselves. More insular, more determined never to let anyone hurt them again. More determined not to remember what had happened: to close off every part of themselves that could be exposed to hurt.

And as with people, so with whole nations. The Soviet Union fought the Nazis off and then slammed the door shut across all of Eastern Europe to keep their enemies out. Then they got to work weeding out from their collective memory all the things that were hurtful and inconvenient to official history. Tearing up by their roots the memories of the shtetlach of the Pale, of the millions of prisoners of war, of the nations who allied themselves with the Nazis, willingly choosing Hitler's sadistic, genocidal terror over Stalin's murderous repression and brutality. They rooted out the memories of the incompetent Soviet leadership that led millions to the slaughter, the generals brought back from the gulags, their hands shaking, their teeth rotted by famine, to take over the command of shattered armies.

After the war, their story, the story of what happened in the forest, would become just one of many stories that could never be told.

And on the other side, in the West, she was sure they were doing it too. Hollowing out the war so they could fill it with a more convenient story. Something with more convincing heroes, and more inhuman villains. And the people who had lived through a completely different kind of war—the real war—grew more and more silent.

When she finally raised her head, she found Baba standing in front of her, one eye looking inquiringly at her.

She reached out and stroked the bird's chest. Baba leaned into it, the way a cat or a dog will lean into being pet.

For the whole journey here, beginning with the train in Moscow—no, before that: beginning with the moment she had received the letter, hand delivered by some KGB functionary across the threshold of her apartment door—she had been tense, collected, not letting herself lose focus of what was in front of her. Aware of the danger, at any time, that came with changing one's routine. Of the questions that might be asked, and the answers she would need to prepare for them. Aware of the coming reunion with Czesław, the unknown territory of the questions he would ask her.

She had stepped onto the Moscow–Vilnius train at Belorussky Station with that tension in her, settling into her compartment and ordering a cup of tea from the steward. She had watched the megalopolis's outskirts die away in crumbling brick and rusting metal that seemed, like the city they surrounded, to go on forever. Had stared out at the forests and the lonely station platforms standing in front of them like stone molars. Dark forests of evergreen, punctuated by white stands of birch, a repetition of forms stretching on in insular totality. Whenever she thought of where she was going, of what lay ahead of her, her hands shook.

She had disembarked in Vilnius with that same tension, checked into the hotel with that same tension, sat with Jacenty in the UAZ with that same tension.

And now it was broken. And she felt immobilized. Exhausted. As if she would never again rise from this chair.

But there was something else inside that exhaustion. Down inside it. Another shape, rising.

Anger.

How could Czesław have come to Moscow, have seen her, have believed she could possibly be happy among others? Knowing what he knew? Knowing the story she carried with her? How could he, whose job had become the reading of other people, the *unmasking* of other people, have made such a mistake?

All she had wanted, all that time, was to be back with them.

To be reunited with them. Instead, he had left her there. Alone, among strangers.

He and Innokentiy had two decades here, together, protecting this place, helping the crows thrive, helping preserve a world where they could build and grow, while she was alone. While she was banished.

Yes, that was the word. *Banished.*

I suppose we like to think of ourselves as seeing parts of the world that other people miss, and so it appeals to us—this idea that there is a secret world of feeling most people are unaware of. And this idea that in the end, all the senses converge for a single purpose.

How, then, could he have missed it in her? The fact that, at every moment of all that time, what her senses were telling her was not *where she was* and *how she related to that world* but instead screaming to her that she was *in the wrong place.*

But then another thought occurred to her, interrupting the anger.

The Unnamed Senses had never been her book at all. The theory at its core was not hers. It was a theory belonging to a man she had never met. A theory that belonged to a Polish noble who died of typhoid in the gulag. It was a theory passed down by him to his grandson, who . . . in the midst of war, in a dark space underground . . . passed it on to her.

And she had kept that theory, like a coal carried from a fire, protected from rain and weather, used to light the next fire. She had carried it, and so many other things . . . so many other stories that belonged to someone else . . .

Baba tugged at a lock of her hair.

She had stopped stroking the bird's chest. She laughed at the bird's indignant posture.

Do your job, Baba said with a look.

"All right, all right." She went back to petting the old bird's feathers.

Part of me never walked out of these woods. Never left them at all. And that is why I needed to come back here.

To retrieve the rest of me. The other half of me. The one who didn't make it out of the forest.

The anger was gone now. She could see what the anger had been concealing, like the gray ash concealing a glowing coal beneath.

Grief.

KEZIA

June 1944

The men did not bother tying Kezia's hands behind her back.

As they led her away from the zemlyanka, she felt it: She would never see any of this again. She would never see the places where they hunted deer or trapped rabbits together. She would never enter the door of the zemlyanka again. She would never see Czesław or Neriya again.

She looked at the Boy, being carried by one of the soldiers. He appeared to be asleep, or half asleep. Would they save him? Would he, at least, survive? And how many times would she see his face again, before they shot her?

Would they throw her into a grave, among strangers? She did not want to be buried with strangers. She did not want to be left alone, to rot among people she did not know.

An absurd thought. Like a person about to go to a festival who thinks, *Let me at least make it to the festival before I die*, as if dying the day after would be better.

She was dead already.

And it didn't matter where they buried her: She would be alone. She wouldn't be *with* anyone else. She would be outside of all of that. She would be nothing at all.

Czesław was gone. Was he dead already? Nothing, already?

Neriya would come back to the zemlyanka and find herself alone. The last of them.

Neriya might survive. At least her. At least she would live.

Maybe the Boy would live too. The men had spoken to him in Lithuanian, and he had understood. Maybe they would think, at least, that he was one of theirs, and save him.

And then maybe, one day, all of this would be over. And Neriya would find the Boy again. And they would write out the story of how Kezia had saved them both.

They would remember her.

Didn't that make it better? The idea that she would be remembered by the people she had cared about?

Maybe. But she was terribly afraid.

They had come far, while she was thinking of all these things. Now they were at the edge of an encampment. There were many people here.

One of the men in uniform who had taken her stood, with a rifle, watching the two of them. The others went on, taking Neriya's documents with them. Taking Kezia's revolver, taking the good knives she had saved. Everything she had left, all the tools to get them through another winter.

And she found herself thinking: *What will Neriya use to hunt? If the war continues for another winter, how will she survive without the revolver, without the knives?*

One of the soldiers had placed the Boy against a tree.

He looked at her, and she placed a hand on his head and smiled. "It's going to be all right."

But he did not nod in return. He just stared into her face out of fever-swollen eyes.

He knows. Even in his fever. He knows it isn't going to be all right.

A woman came into the clearing. She, too, had a rifle, carried over her shoulder. She had the documents in her hands.

She wore a stained German tunic, the buttons torn away at the throat. "You are Neriya Abramovna Kantorova?" she asked in Russian.

"Yes," she said. Straightening up as she said it.

Then the woman was holding her, pulling her into her, crushing the breath out of her. "Oh, child. Your father wanted so badly to see you."

"My father . . ."

"He held on for days. He was so certain we would find you. But we didn't. Not in time. He died this morning. Come. I will take you to him. At least you can see his face again."

The woman turned to the man with the rifle and said something to him in Lithuanian, the only word of which Kezia understood was "food."

"You are safe now," the woman said. "As safe as any of us are, anyway. We will feed your friend. Now come with me."

They wove through a massive camp—here were many people

in uniforms, but none of the uniforms were whole. They were all assembled from bits of other uniforms, from the uniforms of every side that had been fighting here for years.

And then she saw two women standing in front of a fire, warming their hands. They wore new Red Army tunics, fresh boots.

And she understood: These were not Germans. And these were not Lithuanian police. They were Soviet partisans.

Outside a gray army tent, a young boy sat winding bandages. In a pot in front of him, bandages writhed in boiling water. All around him, they hung on lines to dry. Streamers of bandages, none of them quite white. She wondered how many wounds they had wrapped.

The woman knelt in front of Kezia. "Before you see your father, I want you to know something. Your father was a hero. He *is* a hero. He saved so many lives. So many. He was with us for the entire war. And because of him, hundreds of us survived. So, I know it is painful to lose him like this. But I also want you to know: I was with him all these years, and he never stopped talking about you."

"And my mother . . ."

"Your mother was killed before your father even reached our camp. He saw it happen. And I am so sorry, child. But he never stopped believing *you* were alive, somewhere. That kept him going. He told every patrol your name and asked them to search for you. To ask everyone. Every day. For years. It became a tradition—before every patrol went out, he would say, 'Don't forget,' and they would laugh and repeat your name, your whole name, and your description, before they left camp. He never, ever gave up on you."

The woman held the tent flap open. "Now be brave. Go and say goodbye to him."

It was dark inside the tent. A few rips in the fabric sent slashes of light across the floor. Across a clothesline with a stained coat on it, a pair of pants, an apron that told terrible stories of injury and desperate attempts to save lives.

The tent smelled of illness, bleach, iodine. On a low army cot, a man lay unmoving. The man's hands had been placed over his chest. His eyes were closed. Had someone closed them?

Kezia told herself that she had to approach the bed, had to look at this man.

For Neriya. It was important that, whenever they were finally reunited, Neriya know what her father had looked like in death. Know all the details.

Kezia would tell her everything. Gather this man in, keep these images for her.

She remembered the picture on the identification card Neriya had. But this man did not look anything like that picture. This man just looked like any other man, killed by sickness during the war. He looked tired, hollow cheeked. How many days had he been suffering from the fever that finally killed him? The fever, or the work, had taken away so much of him.

His face. She would have to try to remember it. What was special about it. Did it look kind? Concerned?

But death had subtracted any of that. It was just a face.

She thought of all the things Neriya had said about this man, Abram. Her father. She thought of all of the stories Neriya had told about him.

The things they had done together. The things this man had taught her.

Those details should make this face come alive—lend it more humanity than it had. Make the waxy, unreal skin seem more human and meaningful.

But those stories didn't seem to belong to this corpse. They weren't stories that could belong to a dead man. This was just a corpse, like any other corpse.

But the stories Neriya had told her about him were present and real to her. They were as clear as if Kezia were remembering them herself. She could hear his voice.

I think soon the world will right itself again. There will be a time for exploring things like this, and for sharing them with others. Who knows? Perhaps—in a year or two—you'll be standing up in front of the Linnean Society in London, presenting your work . . .

And Neriya had kept that idea with her and shared it with Kezia. And now it would be the two of them, standing up there. For him.

Kezia came out of the tent, blinking in the sunlight. The woman was still there, standing with her hands clasped in front of her, waiting.

"I'm so sorry, child. But you should know—you were his inspiration. You have to understand that. He stayed alive for you, and because he stayed alive, hundreds are alive. And because you are his daughter, everyone in this camp is your family."

"I need to go," she said. "I have a friend. In the forest. I need to find her."

The woman shook her head. "That's not possible."

"I have to find my friend. I can't stay here without her."

Kezia tried to walk past her. But the woman's hand came down on her arm like a clamp, and she was turned around, found herself looking into a face that was harder, and less feeling, than it had been just seconds ago.

"Neriya, listen to me. We all have friends out there. But there is no leaving this camp. I convinced our leader that you are worth keeping with us. That your father taught you medicine, and you can be useful in the field hospital. But people who try to leave here are shot. Those are the orders. We can't afford to have people in the woods who know where we are. There is no leaving."

"My friend . . ." she said again, weakly.

"What is her name?"

"Kezia. She's alone out there."

And for a moment she believed it herself—believed that *she* was Neriya, and that it was really *Kezia* out there, alone. She even saw Kezia's face—her face—as she returned to the zemlyanka and found her friends gone.

Stop.

The woman bent down. "Listen."

She did. And she heard it: a sound on the horizon, like thunder.

"What is it?"

"It is the artillery of the Red Army. They are only days away now. They will be here soon. If she can survive until they arrive, your friend will be safe. But right now, what is important is that *you* are safe, and the boy you saved is safe. We have to save people one by one. That is all we can do. One by one. If you went wandering off into the forest—even if you did get past the guards—who knows what might happen to you out there? Kezia would want to know that you are safe here. She would want you to stay with us."

I am Kezia, she wanted to say. *It is Neriya, the girl who kept that man alive all these years, who is still lost out there.*

But there was a burst of gunfire, nearby.

"What is that?" she said.

The woman shook her head. And then she spoke, suddenly, in Yiddish. In the language that, until that moment, had seemed like a secret shared only between Neriya and Kezia. A language spoken only by the two of them, and by the writer of the book they had found. Now it was in this woman's mouth: "*Yene zenen shpyonen, vos vern dershosn.* Those are spies, being shot. There are plenty of people in this forest who are not who they say they are, Neriya. Bandits, marauders, collaborators. The ones who helped the Germans do this to our people. They know the end is coming for them. Plenty of people are taking off uniforms, forging papers, pretending to be someone they are not. We cannot afford to have any mercy for them."

There was yelling somewhere, and the woman squeezed her arm. She spoke in Russian again. And when she did it, her face changed. It was as clear a change as someone putting on a mask. *She has already become someone else.* "I have to go. I am needed. Get some food. Get an hour of rest. That's about all I can afford to give you. After that, we'll need you working."

Kezia went back to where she had left the Boy.

He was not there. The man who had been guarding them with his rifle was now sitting against a tree, eating soup from a battered tin bowl.

"Where is my friend?" she asked him in Russian. "The boy who was here?"

"Amazing news," the man said. His grin showed where several teeth were missing on one side of his mouth. "The Red

Army has broken through south of here. They took the boy with the other children from the camp. They're moving them behind the front lines."

"What?"

"It means your friend will be safe," the man said.

"They *took* him?"

"And all the other little ones."

"And the rest of us?"

"The rest of us," the man said, "will be supporting the assault on Vilnius. It will be any day now. I hear you are our new medic. I hope your father taught you well, because we're going to need you."

She went to the place where she had last seen the Boy. Leaning here, against the tree.

Or was it this one?

Or this one?

There was no telling.

She chose one of them, the one most likely to be where she had last seen him, and collapsed against it. Held its trunk and wept into its bark.

No one in the camp thought it was strange. They had, all of them, done plenty of mourning.

What I dreamed last night, in my fever, was that I awoke here and dressed and went out to look at the crows asleep in their nests, the quiet of their strange town at night.

But the town had changed. Gone were the spirals of nests, the towers with their interlocking coils. The crows had replaced them all with the buildings of the shtetl, in miniature, up in the trees.

Here was the synagogue, balanced on a branch. There, a wealthy family had built a two-story home high up, where they could lord it over the rest.

And in the hollow V of two trunks was my own home, with an orange rectangle of light in the window. I looked inside and saw a crow bent over the table, his concentrated face reflected in the polished curve of the samovar.

He was writing something, but as in all dreams, it was dream-writing, a blur of shifting loops and whorls that changed every time my eye focused on it.

—from *The Autobiography of a Burned Village*

25
NERIYA ABRAMOVNA KANTOROVA

November 1971

INNOKENTIY AND CZESŁAW SLEPT on the floor, their bedrolls near the wood stove. She could tell they were asleep almost right away by their breathing. She wondered at it: How could they sleep at a time like this?

But then, the only new thing for them was her presence. The rest of it was already habit to them. Their friendship, this cabin. Nights here with the crows.

Baba, too, was asleep on the table, her legs tucked under herself, both eyes closed, in perfect trust and safety.

The crows. As evening came, she had heard their calls approaching. And then they were there. She'd left the cabin to watch them, a black spiral over the leafless trees, a winding dark in the evening that disintegrated into scraps of life, dropping onto branches and the ground, calling out to one another.

A dozen or so had approached her, investigated her. One bold one landed on her shoulder and tugged at a button on her coat that must have gleamed temptingly in the dying light. But mostly she was ignored. Accepted, but unimportant to the cacophony of their busy evening settling.

The trees were filled with birds, as if their winter branches had suddenly leafed out in black and gray. Leafed into crow. And for an hour, at least, it was a bustling city. So much meaningful activity that it was hard to track it all. Their calls when heard, overlapping and intermingling with one another, became background noise, like the conversations of passersby in any human city.

But in the notebooks, in a careful hand that seemed to fit him well, Innokentiy had been recording the meaning of it all. Seated at the table while Innokentiy and Czesław slept, she turned the pages of one of them.

Gifts are only exchanged in the early morning. Just before dawn they come to a place I call "the marketplace." It is a circle of flat ground they have cleaned of any fallen leaves or twigs. Here, a crow who wants to trade brings a gift. Many of the gifts are found things. They love buttons, bottle caps, bright bits of metal of all kinds, but also fancy bits of cloth, candy wrappers, and so much else. I have seen bone chess pieces among the items they stole, a silver teaspoon. And more.

Some of the things they bring are also made. Hoops of

twigs, sometimes figures made of feathers. And sometimes the gifts are a combination of both found and made: a button with twigs pushed through the holes, or one of what I call the "mats" woven from pine needles and found thread, horse and human hair, down or sheep's wool.

But I do not think there is a concept of "value." They leave one thing and they take another. Nothing is exchanged in the marketplace that is of "use" as we might think of it. No food, and none of the tools they make: no jabbers, no hooks, no probes. And no teaching hoops or things they use in the area I call "the schoolhouse." In the marketplace, only decorative things are exchanged.

The exchange is very serious. Sometimes several crows will be in the marketplace, pacing around, examining what is on offer that morning, like customers in a village market testing the quality of berries or apples. Finally, having closely examined everything, they will decide, taking something up and flying away with it.

"Exchange" may not even be the correct word. Most of the time, a crow will leave a gift in the marketplace before flying off with something else. But there are crows as well who come with nothing and take something away. And there are crows who come with something and take nothing away. Once I examined an object in the marketplace more closely—a rhinestone brooch that must have been quite prized by the woman it was stolen from. I later found it left on the doorstep of the cabin for me, although I know it was something many of them must have coveted.

I am beginning to feel that the problem with trying to

understand them is that I keep thinking of our own economies. Of our ideas of exchange, which are not their ideas. Things in their marketplace are left. Things in the marketplace are taken up and coveted. Things are returned, to be taken up by another. And the meaning of the leaving and the taking up is not, I think, about exchange. It seems to be about the admiration of new, strange things. It is about a shared, and sharing, curiosity.

A few mornings later, I placed the rhinestone brooch back in the marketplace.

The notebooks were filled with passages like this. But in one, she found another page.

~~*My first memory is*~~
~~*My first memory is*~~
~~*My first memory is of my mother.*~~
~~*My first memory is*~~

I keep thinking that if I write these words, a memory of my mother will appear. As if through the magic trick of writing "My first memory is of my mother" I can conjure her.

But there is no such memory. I remember a voice. One word, in Lithuanian. "Tylėk!" Quiet!

And her hand. Clamped over my mouth. I remember the feel of it. But not the look of it. I do not remember the look of that hand, or of her face, or of anything else about her.

I remember the sound of the engines.

I remember the baby, as much as I do not want to remember the baby.

I remember outside, a horse in terror. Outside, a cow that had not been milked, lowing.

The eyes of people I may have known or not known. Eyes in the dark, where light fell through the slats and into the place we were hiding.

Then fire.

But these do not feel like memories. They feel like shards. Broken things you pick up off the ground, bits of something destroyed that you never saw, and so cannot identify, because there are not enough fragments left to even know the shape of what they might have been.

Was it my mother's hand at all? Or the hand of someone else? Someone from my village? A stranger who found me and took care of me on the road? Was that word whispered by my mother? Or by a woman I did not know before that day?

My first memory, the first that is whole, and clear, and belongs to me, is of Kezia.

I remember walking through a field: an autumn field, still alive with the last, listless bees and butterflies.

Kezia is slightly ahead of me, leading us somewhere. As always, leading us.

She will not hold my hand. I want very much for her to hold my hand. But it does not matter: I feel the bond between us, as sure as an invisible rope tied around our waists, linking us forever.

She will not abandon me. I will not abandon her.

This is my first whole memory, and my first whole family.

NERIYA

June 1944

She had planned how it would go. The father of the family would open the door. He would not recognize Neriya at first, because of how much she had changed. He would not recognize her, but the wife would. She would remember Neriya, the girl whose father saved their daughter. Saved their family.

Immediately, seeing how thin she was, the woman would try to feed her. But Neriya would refuse. She had only a few words of Lithuanian, but maybe they would be enough. She knew the word for fever: *karščiavimas*. She knew the word for friend. She knew a few other words. And certainly they must understand a bit of Russian or Polish.

So she would be able to explain. And they might not have medicine, but they would know where to get it.

She saw how it would be. Saw it perfectly. The father would be afraid to help, at first. He would argue with his wife, trying to convince her to send Neriya away. A Jewish girl. Helping her meant death . . .

But their daughter would intervene. She would lift her shirt. She would show them the scar, the cicatrice, the mark of how Neriya's father had saved her life. The physical sign of their debt to Neriya's family.

That would convince the father. He was a good man, after all. He was just frightened, like everyone was frightened. All he wanted was what was best for his family. All he wanted was for them to live.

In the end, they would do everything they could to help her.

The father would come with Neriya. He would carry the Boy himself back to their house, where the mother had soup waiting. Where there would finally be medicine. Food. Help.

It was so clear to her, it was as if all of it had already happened.

So when the trees at the edge of the forest began to thin, and she saw the farmstead, and the blackened pile of shattered beams that had once been their farm, it did not seem possible.

She remembered the desperate, red-eyed face of the father, all those years ago, standing on their doorstep. The man's hay cart, the ribs of his horse straining against the harness. The poor farmstead, the one-room house, the feverish little girl, her abdomen as hard as a rock.

Neriya's father had put Neriya's hand on the girl's abdomen so she could feel it. So she could know, if she ever felt it again, the signs.

The smell of the ether, her mother sewing the girl up, the stitch as neat as the one she used for mending dresses.

And the girl's little grandmother kissing her father's hands, her mother's hands, wrapping a newly knitted shawl around Neriya's shoulders.

And the girl's father, roaring into the room, lifting Neriya's father up, holding him so high that he knocked his head against the rafters.

She must have stood there for several minutes, unable to move. It was impossible that the Boy was going to die at a time like this: past midsummer, with the air warm and the nights sometimes hardly cool enough to sleep in, the forest full of berries, the trees filled with songbirds again, the field around that burned house as green as any field had been before the war, as green as fields would be after.

The whole world was full of life. But these lives, the lives that had once tended this farmstead, were over.

And Czesław was gone. And the Boy was going to die.

No. She retreated back into the forest. There had to be something that could be done. Someone in the woods, then, who could help. There were partisans. She could explain it to them. They had avoided the partisans until now, but they had never been this desperate.

There had to be something left of human kindness. Someone to help them.

All the bodies they had come across. The camps destroyed, the corpses stripped of their clothes.

There was no help.

But she could not return empty-handed either. And now she quickened her pace, moving deeper into the forest.

It was not possible that they would die. This war was going to end. It would happen soon: She had woken in the morning a week ago and heard a sound she had never heard before. Like thunder, far off. A trick of the air, maybe. But then it had come again.

Guns to the east. The guns of the Red Army. Still a great distance away, but something about the morning atmosphere had carried their sound and carried its tatters to them.

A sound that said: *Soon.*

She knew where there was a grove of linden trees deeper in the forest, on a sunny knot of high ground. *Tilia cordata.* Their leaves could bring down fever.

She would head there, then. It was something, at least.

She walked for another hour, more, in the forest. Was she tired? Tiredness seemed like something for someone else. She could not be tired, could not afford to be tired.

Buster was up in the trees, flying from branch to branch as he often did, keeping a distant company.

She did not hear his warning call soon enough. She had just crested a hummock of land. The linden grove was close. She knew where she was going: she was following a path they sometimes took on their farther hunts, that skirted the bog and ended deep in the woods, near the crows.

Buster was screaming at her, but she did not hear him. Her mind was fogged with fear. The Boy was going to die.

The linden leaves were something, at least. Boiled into tea, if it was made strong enough, they could be enough. They could be.

The five men were around a campfire. She would have smelled it, but the wind was in the wrong direction: they had been downwind of her. And she had not been careful. Moving fast, not thinking.

They saw her at the same time she saw them.

They were in German uniforms. Camouflage uniforms, with helmet covers. The lightning bolts on their collars told her who they were.

She ran. But they were already on their feet, running after her. Yelling at her to stop.

She turned in the direction that would take her back to the zemlyanka. But one of them had flanked her there, so she turned again.

If she ran much farther in this direction, she would run into the edge of the bog. She arced, instead, toward the stream.

How far was it to a point where the stream could be forded? If she could get far enough ahead of them, make it across and up the cliff, make it to the crows, they might save her. Mob the Germans, chase them away.

Would they do that? For her?

She ran in that direction, then. The men were right behind her, close enough that she could hear them calling to one another as they spotted her.

Why? Why was her death so important to these men, so far from their homes?

She saw the stream on her left. But here the bank was steep, and there was nowhere to cross.

When she glanced behind her, she saw one of the men, not a hundred meters away, raising his submachine gun. She moved right, away from the stream, as the bullets tore into trees around her.

And then she heard the man yelling in pain.

Buster.

She did not turn around to confirm it: she heard Buster calling, and heard answering calls in the forest.

She kept running.

Finally. Here. Here was where she could cross. Glancing behind her, she saw no one. But she could hear the crows calling to one another, and the men calling to one another.

She ran across the log at nearly full speed, and was at the bottom of the cliff.

But the men were closer than she had thought. As she found the first handholds, she looked over her shoulder and saw them. Two were in the water itself. One was up on the far bank.

The two in the water were waving arms above their heads. The crows came down in waves, two or three at a time, changing direction, swooping down at the tops of their heads, at their faces.

It was going to work! She would get away! Where she was

now, there was a slight angle in the cliff that concealed her from them. And they were distracted by the birds, waving their hands and yelling. Like children.

She found a loop of root. She pulled herself farther up, keeping as close to the cliff as she could.

They could not possibly follow her for much longer. They were in the woods, a small group of men. Partisans were everywhere. It was foolish of them, chasing a girl. Even if they did know she was a Jew—and how would they even know that?—what use was this hate to them now? They were endangering themselves, drawing attention to their own location.

For nothing.

The Germans had to break off the chase. They had to!

There were more crows now, coming from several directions, joining in to attack them. At the top of the cliffs, she would be safe. They would not follow her.

She heard the submachine gun fire again. She pressed herself into the soil of the streambank. But the bullets had not been fired in her direction.

And now she dared to look around the angle.

Feathers, floating in the air.

The machine gun fired again. The crows were thick around the men now. Four men, in the river and on the bank. A moment ago the soldiers had been ducking and waving their arms, helpless.

They were not helpless now. They fired into the attacking crows, again and again.

She saw a hit bird spiral off into the air, turned backward by the force of a bullet, tumbling over and over. Hitting the ground where she could not see.

Dead.

Dead for her. Dead in her place.

Was it Buster? Was it Moses? Was it Madeleine?

And when she reached the top, and the men kept on coming, kept on killing? How many more crows would die?

She thought of the bullets tearing through the delicate palaces the crows had been constructing for generations.

Tearing through the blue-eyed fledglings, the hope of the flock's continuation.

Tearing through the old crows who no longer flew far enough to get away from them.

She climbed down. She stepped out into the stream.

It was deep here. The water was over her knees, swollen by recent rain, the current tugging at her.

"Hey!" she screamed in German. "I am here! Over here!"

They did not see her immediately. Their faces were turned upward as they fired at the birds.

"Over here!"

She reached and pulled a stone from the bank.

"Over here, I said!"

"I see you."

The voice was close to her. The fifth man stood on the bank above her and to her left.

He had gotten around the others. And the crows had not yet found him either.

Then she saw Buster, coming toward them. Fast, aimed at the man, adjusting velocity with a flap of his wing.

The man followed her gaze, lifted the submachine gun.

Her rock struck him in the side of his head.

He staggered, turned.

And fired the bullets meant for the bird into the girl in the stream.

He watched as the force of the bullets knocked her back. As she tried to stand again, for a moment.

Then she collapsed into the current. The water washed over her, turned her over. Her body was carried, face up, eyes open and staring at nothing now, downstream.

The bird hit him on the side of the face. One claw glanced off his helmet. The other found his cheek, and tore. He swatted at it, raised the gun again.

But it did not return to the attack.

Instead, it followed the girl down the stream. Calling, as if calling directly to her.

Other birds joined it now, a ragged line of them, trailing the drifting body of the girl.

He held a hand against his bloodied cheek. He watched the body of the girl drift away, trailed by the birds.

"We have to move," a voice said.

He turned. He had been distracted, for a moment, by the strangeness of the scene, the ragged line of birds following the girl as if she were a part of their own flock, leading them away.

The other four had caught up with him. All had blood on their faces and hands.

"Someone will have heard our guns. We have to move."

"The sooner we are back home," one of them said, wiping at his bloodied forehead, "the better. I hate this forest. I hate these people. I hate the East. Even the animals here are insane."

"We'll be home again soon enough," another one said.

"If we have a home to come back to."

"If any of us are left to make it back."

For a while the image lingered in the man's mind: The girl's body floating in the stream, face turned up to the sky. The ragged line of crows tracing her path in the air above her, calling to her as one of their own.

He thought of that scene at strange moments over the next several days. It caught him unawares. It tugged at something in his mind. Some human feeling not entirely scraped away by the other things he had done.

He turned it over in his head, returned to it. A puzzle he could not solve.

Even if he might have been able to, he did not have the time.

He had only a week left to live.

Not one of them made it closer to home than Vilnius. There, torn into pieces by Soviet artillery, tanks, and machine guns, their bodies were left scattered in the city's ditches and buried under its rubble.

As I lie here in a fever, I hear them landing on the roof of the little shelter I built—my nest among their nests. I hear them walking on the floor around me.

I feel the weight of one of them walking across my chest.

—from *The Autobiography of a Burned Village*

26
KEZIA

July 1944

THE ENTIRE CAMP was in motion, in the dark.

A hand shook her awake. "Neriya—it is time."

Later, only a few moments remained distinct, moments of clarity in a blur of activity. Commands shouted or whispered, things pushed into her hands, instructions on where to put things, where to go, delivered by others.

She was always so tired now. There were the terrible surgeries she assisted in, and between them the work: the washing of bandages, the preparations, the constant peeling of potatoes, the carrying of messages she did not understand from one stranger to another.

And always, every time she fell asleep, a hand shaking her awake and telling her to do yet another thing.

What was dreamlike about everything that happened in the camp was its logic, external to her. There may have been order, but it was not visible to her. It was not of her own making.

She worked without stopping. People and objects appeared and disappeared. The wounded staggered out of the trees, gray and broken. The dead were taken away. The soup of bloody bandages, the scattered sunlight through the trees falling across a fresh-dug grave, a patrol returning triumphant, wearing boots they had not left in.

In the clear moments, she wanted to ask: Where was the Boy taken? She wanted to ask: Where was Czesław? Was he with another group? Had anyone seen him? A man with a boy's face, a boy hidden in a man's shape? Had any of them seen a girl in the forest? A girl, the same age as her, a girl who could easily *be* her, wandering alone?

There was no one to ask. The camp grew. There were more Red Army women and men among them now. There were new guns, new structures of order crystalizing among the partisans, new growths of command.

The shooting, too, went on: spies, people suspected of disloyalty. New men came to keep a new kind of order. Kezia felt, at least once a day, the urge to scream, *I'm not her! It's a lie! She's still out there. You must let me leave, so I can find her.*

The desperation broke through the exhaustion. But she knew what would happen if they found out she was not who she had said she was. She heard the gunshots several times a day.

She understood what was done to liars. And she had lied to

them for so long. Dying like that would mean dying for nothing at all.

"It is time," the voice said.

Now, on this morning in July, she was pulled into a group of others and herded onto a truck. When she asked where they were going, she was told simply, "Vilnius."

This was the moment when Neriya would walk out of the forest and join them. She had to find them. She had to. And when Neriya appeared, they would be able to explain it all. They would run to each other, be reunited. They would tell their story.

I am holding your place. Saving this living space for you. For the moment when you return. That is all. I am only keeping it safe.

They were supposed to be together, the two of them together. They had made a pact. The twin biologists, made sisters by the war. Together, they would introduce their crows to the world that came after all of this. A peaceful world, in which the Nazis had been swept away forever. The world all this suffering had earned.

It was dawn. It had been so long since she had seen a dawn from outside the forest. Since she had seen the sky like this—huge, filled with scraps of rain cloud torn apart by enormous, heavy streaks of color that could not be contained by words like *pink* or *yellow*. Color that towered over the lightless pool of trees.

She was in the back of the truck, lumbering over a broken track that was barely a road. The forest was behind her now. She kept looking back at that dark pool of forest.

As if what? As if Neriya would suddenly burst from those

trees, running toward them, waving to them to wait, to take her along?

The shape of a bird was in the sky. It grew larger. Then landed on the gate of the truck.

Buster. Kezia knew his movement, the rhythm of his wings, the canted angle of his flight.

Over the winter, she had learned to identify at least a hundred birds. Some, they had given names to. Others, they had known only by sight.

But Buster was unique among them. He had been with them all from the beginning. But most of all he had been Neriya's crow. Or she had been his person.

He had never come to the camp to see Kezia. During all of that time working among the wounded and the dead, no crows had visited her. They avoided the camp.

But now he was here, his feet clamped on the gate of the truck.

She looked around, at the faces around her. Many of the people on the truck were asleep, their heads between their knees or lolling backward, oblivious to the snarl of the engine and the undulating, jerking motion of the vehicle over the broken road.

Of those who were awake, no one had seen Buster. The eyes were elsewhere.

What were they looking at? At their own deaths at the end of this road. Or at loved ones, not there but more present than anyone around them. Or at nothing at all. They looked without seeing. Doing this—emptying the gaze and taking in nothing—was a trick of war.

Buster dropped something from his beak.

Kezia reached out to him. But her touch came too late. He had already flown away, back toward the forest. Following him with her gaze, she saw again the tower of color that was the sky, and the black forest exhaling crows, like fragments of its own substance, up into it.

She picked up the thing Buster had dropped.

A button.

A particular button. Cracked, a triangle of material missing from the top.

A button from Neriya's coat.

Every time she thought back to this moment, she wondered: How was it that she had known exactly what the button meant? Because she had known it, and known it absolutely, as clear as a spoken sentence.

Whatever boundaries of meaning, of interpretation, of understanding, had to be crossed between crow and human, in that moment they were crossed, and she understood. She understood the same way she understood her horses before the war, the music of their neighing, of their eyes rolling, their hooves scraping the earth, the toss of their heads. Not words but waves of feeling, just as full of meaning as words. Sometimes more meaningful than words.

And to say they were not meaningful would be the same as saying that a gesture was not meaningful. That a hand stroking your cheek was not meaningful. That an embrace, a glance, a grunt, a snap of the fingers, was not meaningful.

It would be the same as saying that a symphony was not meaningful. That the bow drawn across the cello's strings carried no meaning into the air, was without purpose, could communicate nothing.

She understood perfectly. And never doubted it.

Neriya was dead.

Years afterward, she still felt the shape of that button in her fist. The grief of that object. Years later, it was still in her pocket. Decades later.

KEZIA

November 1971

She held it now.

It was before dawn. A dim blue light was scattered among the trees. She walked through the crows' quiet city. Here and there, the crows waddled along the ground in their gait that was like men walking with their hands behind their backs, and had so often made Kezia and Neriya laugh.

She found the place Innokentiy called "the marketplace."

It was just as he had described it. And there were several crows there, pacing around.

One, she saw, was Baba. Baba had stolen a stub of pencil that Kezia recognized from the hut. She placed it carefully down in the marketplace. Proudly? Two other crows walked arcs around the pencil, admiring it.

In Innokentiy's journal she had read:

I make a mistake when I call what they do by the names we use. I am forced to use our human language to describe their actions. I am forced to lend them our feelings, our priorities, our structures.

But I know none of this fits them. What they are doing, what they think of us, the way they see this world—all of it is a mystery that, even after decades among them, I only observe from the outside. They teach, they learn, they live and die in a world that is parallel and akin to our world but is not the world we live in.

Kezia bent down and placed the button on the ground.

The crows fed us during the war. They warned us of danger. They took care of us. But not for the reasons we may have thought they had: it was all for reasons of their own. They had their reasons then, just as they have their reasons for allowing me to be among them now.

One of the crows who had been examining Baba's stolen pencil stub now walked over and stood near the button. It looked at the button, and then up at her.

And Kezia thought of a passage from the writing they had found, the unfinished book written by the man who had known these birds before them, that veteran of the First World War, victim of the pogroms, and doctor to these crows, who had died here among them. The man whose kindness to these crows might be the reason they had protected four children in the forest during the war. A kindness that had been passed from him to them and then came back again, to save their lives.

יעדעס מאָל וואָס איך קוק אויף זיי, פּרובירנדיק צו פֿאַרשטיין וואָס זיי טוען, טרעף איך זיי קוקנדיק אויף מיר, פּרובירנדיק צו פֿאַרשטיין וואָס איך טו.

Yedes mol vos ikh kuk af zey, prubirndik tsu farshteyn vos zey tuen, tref ikh zey kukndik af mir, prubirndik tsu farshteyn vos ikh tu. Every time I watch them, trying to understand what they are doing, I find them watching me, trying to understand what I am doing.

The crow picked the button up in its beak. With a glance at Kezia, it walked to the edge of the circle, then flew to a nearby tree.

She saw the beak with the button through an entrance, a glimmer in the dark of a palace interior. Then it was gone.

The mistake I keep making is thinking that I understand them. I make that mistake, and see their actions as the actions of people. As if they will turn, someday, into people. But they are not turning into people. They are becoming something of their own—something else, so long as they have the time, and the safety, to do so. My job is not to understand them; my job is to keep them safe, so they can become what they are becoming.

She had not noticed Innokentiy's approach, but when she turned, he was there.

He moved to write something on his pad, but Kezia held his wrist.

"I have been holding on to that button every day," she said. "I knew what it meant the moment Buster brought it to me, but I have had it with me for years, clenched it in my fist for years, rolled it between my fingers for years. You can know a thing and refuse to know it, both at once. I knew she was dead, and yet I was waiting for her to come back. Waiting for her to come back and take up the life I convinced myself that I was holding on to for her sake.

"But I wasn't holding on to her life for her. I *stole* her life. I took it for my own. I had nothing of my own. I was no one. An illiterate, angry, half-mad monster. She taught me to read, to see the world, to speak her language. She taught me everything I ever knew that had value.

"And after the war, I was only allowed to enter the university, to study, to learn, because her father had been a partisan hero. The father I stole from her and claimed as my own. So even my education belonged to her.

"Everything is hers. My career, the research I have done. It is all hers. I have been answering to her name for a quarter of a century. Nothing I have belongs to me. Nothing is my own. And so I wrote a book, to give it all back to her. To tell the truth. But even when I was writing it, I could not help but feel that I was stealing from her again. I am a monster."

Innokentiy wrote: *We are all monsters. We are what the war made us.*

He pointed at his own throat, then wrote:

We are what is left over from what the war took from us.

In the hut, Czesław was preparing breakfast. Eggs, yesterday's bread. They were halfway done eating when he said:

"I have been thinking of the part you wrote in your book. About how Neriya died . . ."

"I needed to give her an ending," Kezia said. "Something that would have meaning. Not just . . . disappearing. Not just being *gone* like that, forever, with no trace of her but a button. She had to have an ending. She *had* an ending—we just did not see it. I needed to find out what it was. I wrote to find out. To see it. And to be there with her."

"I think what you wrote is correct. I think it is exactly how she died," Czesław said. "I think it is the truth."

"It cannot be. I wasn't there. I never saw it. The last words she said to me were 'I'm going *now*. Before it is too late.' And she went. She was there with us, and then she was gone. Forever. The war swallowed her up. I know the same thing happened to so many people, but it never seemed possible for it to happen to her. So I just made something up."

"No," Czesław said. "You told the *truth*. The truth isn't something that happened. It is more than that. It is knowing exactly what someone would have done, what they would have said, what they would have cared about, even when you were separated from them. Somewhere, in this forest, she was swallowed up. But however it happened, the truth is that she died trying to help others. To protect you and Innokentiy. She went willingly. She went *now. Before it was too late.*

"You got it all right, just like everything else in the book. My thoughts, hers, your own, Innokentiy's—you are the only one who knows us well enough to tell our story. And it was a story that never made sense to me until you told it."

"All I feel," Kezia said, "is that I've lived my life as someone else."

"After they took my father and my grandfather away," Czesław said, "I lived for them. I did what I thought they would have done, in every situation. And even when I found out my mother had died, I never stopped hearing her voice and following her instructions. If anything, her voice became more insistent when I knew she was gone. I still hear it."

And in the orphanage, Innokentiy wrote, *I did everything the way you would have done it. Or the way Neriya would have done it. Or the way Czesław would have done it. I never made decisions of my own: I never had to. I just did what I imagined you would have done. And that was how I survived.*

"I don't think we live *for* other people," Czesław said. "I think we live *as* other people. We really *are* the people we care about. The people who went before us. We carry on for the dead, we protect the living, and we wait for a better world."

Her own words, words from *The Unnamed Senses*:

> *The biological niche is a concept we most often get wrong. Yes, we are built to survive in the environmental niche to which we are fitted. But the human niche is not the world; it is human society, just as the crow's niche is the flock, and the bee's niche is the hive. Social animals are built to survive only among one another.*

⊡ ⊡ ⊡

They left the hut behind.

The city of birds was quiet again, its daytime activity distributed across the whole forest. Near the cliff, Kezia turned back, and saw Baba limping along sleepily.

Here and there, in the shadow of the palaces, there were other old and injured crows as well, and little blue-eyed gangs of fledglings, left behind by the flock as it foraged for the day.

Here and safe because others took care of them, and because Czesław and Innokentiy took care of this place.

She wondered if Innokentiy understood how important he had been to them. If he knew that he had saved all of them, simply by existing.

It was because he had come to her in the village, she had connected with the others. Had given Innokentiy over to them, to save him, and had been saved by them, when Czesław brought her, fevered and half dead, to live with them, at Innokentiy's and Neriya's insistence.

But that was not all of it. Because Innokentiy had been younger and more vulnerable than them, they had become capable of more than they would have been capable of without him. They had found new capacities in themselves, new reserves of strength to provide for him. He had bound all of them together.

Halfway back to the dacha, she said to Innokentiy, "I never visited the bones of the man from the burned shtetl. The one who was friends with the birds before us. The one who wrote the pages we found."

I buried the bones years ago, Innokentiy wrote. *The crows had taken all the shiny objects out of his skull. He was important to the birds who knew him. But eventually, the flock forgot him.*

By now they have forgotten Neriya too.

Later she caught up to Czesław, in the lead now, as if he were the most eager to leave the forest.

"I thought that after the war we would live in a world where the things we cared about had value. Now I look back at that time, and I think of how naive it all was. To think there could be a place where we would be safe. Where the crows would be safe, and we could speak about them freely, introduce them to a world that would appreciate them, the way we had dreamed of doing. But it has been decades, and this awful world where everything has to be hidden goes on and on and on."

"I thought the same," Czesław said. "I thought the war would end, and with it all the evil in the world. It's what kept me going, during the war. I could not protect everyone I cared about forever, but I could at least keep going for just a few years. And that might be enough. That was all that would be asked of me. Then I could rest. But I realized, eventually, that there would be no good world. And there would be no end to the work. No end to protecting the things I care about."

"You must be so tired. I am tired."

Czesław turned to her. She had been expecting his face to be tired, but it did not show any signs of exhaustion. Instead he seemed alert, alive. A few days ago he had seemed on the cusp of old age. Now she was startled by the realization, after feeling so old, so worn out, for so long, that in fact when she looked at Czesław, she did not see someone who was old. That he looked strong. He was in the middle of his life, with strength left for many things.

"I am not tired, Kezia. I feel even more ready for work than I was when I was young. Keeping the crows safe, keeping Innokentiy safe, keeping you safe—this is my purpose. Just as it is Innokentiy's purpose to keep me safe and the crows safe. And just as it is your purpose. You kept Neriya alive. You kept her safe, with you. And you wrote her book."

"A forgery. I made it all up."

"Not the book about us and the war—though that was no

forgery either. I mean that you wrote *The Unnamed Senses*. It was the book she and you were meant to write together. And you will live to write her other books for her as well."

"I came here to be finished with this part of my life. To give the manuscript to you, to visit the zemlyanka, our bunker on the island, the crows in their palaces, and be done."

Czesław nodded. "And then what? What do you imagine it means to *be done*?"

What *had* she imagined it meant? Standing there, in the forest going silent, readying itself for winter, she could not remember.

She imagined herself on the train, watching the sequence of forest and town that had brought her here reversing itself. She imagined herself in Moscow, in her empty apartment. *Done*. What did that mean?

"Here is something I have never told anyone," Czesław said. "Just after I joined the Red Army, we were out on a training exercise. This was somewhere on the steppe, where the sky goes on and on, forever, over land that goes on forever.

"We had been marching, with heavy packs, all day. We had marched the day before as well. I did not know where we were going, or how far we were from where we had come. I did not know how far we had marched that morning, or how many days we would be marching for. And because none of us knew anything at all about how long it would last, we had to be prepared to march forever.

"At every moment of rest, I took everything I could: I drank every drop of water given to me, ate every scrap of food. I closed my eyes and concentrated on restoring my strength to *keep moving*.

"On one of those rests, I had just drunk from a tin cup of water from a common pail. A dented tin cup on a chain. The ragged line of us was stretched out ahead of me and behind me. Dozens of us, like a snake in the sun. The man with the water bucket had moved down the line. I watched as another soldier drank from it. And then another. All of us doing the same thing. Everyone concentrated on restoring strength.

"The soldier with the bucket was nearly to the end of the column when it happened. One moment I was watching him, listening to the scrape of the cup, the clink of the chain, the coughs and murmurs of the other soldiers . . . And then I was on the ground, with my ears ringing, looking up into the sky. I saw what seemed to be birds, at first. Floating there. But no. Not birds. Scraps of cloth, drifting down. Scraps of uniform.

"Then I saw—there, at the head of the column, where there had been men—a hole. Scattered around it were what had been men, moments before. Now they were nothing more than parts of men.

"When my hearing returned, it was filled with a chaos of yelling, screaming. People running, men with hands over their ears. Wounded men and dead men. Out of an empty sky.

"For weeks, they had been preparing us for war. We had begun, maybe, to even think we were ready. But no one was ready. And I saw, floating over that hole where there had been men, a mist. Pink against the sun.

"And then I heard a rumble, on the horizon, of artillery. Explosions far off.

"We only found out later what had happened. After the long, terrible march back to camp. There had been a long-range artillery exercise, firing at targets kilometers away. One of the shells, among the first they fired, was defective. It fell short. That was all—just a bad shell, malformed in the factory.

"We collected the bodies of five men. But the pink mist I saw was all that remained of the soldier who had been carrying the bucket of water. The shell hit him directly. He *ceased to exist.* They found nothing of him that could be collected at all.

"And when we got back to camp, and we started speaking about all the men who had been killed—whispering about them in the dark, telling their stories to one another—a terrible thing was discovered. You see, the man carrying the bucket had just joined us from another unit—a unit that had already moved on to another camp. And not one of us could remember his name. Our captain, who was also killed, had been carrying his papers in his pocket. They were gone.

"And when the other unit was finally tracked down and contacted, we found out that he had just been transferred *there*, as well, a day before. Nobody could remember his name. *Nobody knew who he was.*

"It seemed like the worst of all possible things—to disappear, unremembered. It still seems that way."

My sister, she wanted to say. *I lost my sister that way: she was there, and then gone, and I never found her.* But she was not yet ready to share that story. Not yet.

Instead she said: "Why tell me this now?"

"Because I have the feeling that you came all this way not to give me a manuscript, or to see the crows again, but for forgiveness, Kezia. But there is nothing to forgive. What happened to that man who gave us water is exactly what you kept from happening to Neriya. You saved her from that. And you keep saving her from that, every moment you are alive."

They know my end is coming. They are gathering to see me on my way.

I would have stayed among them longer, if I could.

—from *The Autobiography of a Burned Village*

27
NERIYA

April 1931

SHE WAS NOT QUITE FIVE, in April of that year. And while there were certainly other memories from before it, this was the first one that stood out whole and clear for her, an island all its own.

The memory was reinforced by constant retelling. For years afterward, in the kitchen with her father, early in the morning while her mother was still asleep, she would say, "Papa, tell me about the flood and how you took me with you to help all the people."

And he would put the newspaper aside and tell the story.

In the spring of that year, 1931, the snow melted quickly. The water in the Neris and Vilnia Rivers began to rise. Both rivers soon broke their banks, flooding the lower town. And the rivers kept rising, drowning thousands of houses along the banks. Drowning the boulevards, the squares, the factories.

In a few days, the floodwaters had risen as far as the corner just beyond their front door. The regular sounds of the city were gone—replaced by the sounds of oars, the calling of people to one another.

One morning Neriya's mother came into her room and said to her, "Get dressed. Put on your coat. We are needed."

Her parents prepared the medical bag. Downstairs a man waited in a long, narrow boat. A boat, floating where there once had been a street! She remembered how they boarded the boat by balancing on a plank. How the man pushed off from the wall of an apartment house that was now submerged up to its bottom windows. How they drifted past the tops of trees just budding for spring, their dark trunks wavering in deep water.

There were other boats in the streets. Boats with police and soldiers aboard, looking along the windows for signs of distress. Barges loaded with boxes, flatboats stacked with furniture around which children chased one another. Rowboats piloted by men in their shirtsleeves, as if out for a day of exercise.

On the grand, drowned boulevard of Arsenalo a bright red rowboat went by. A woman with a parasol ran her fingers through the water. A young man was at the oars, laughing. Neriya remembered how white their teeth were.

On the main square, two boys rowed what looked like a wardrobe past the columns of the cathedral, in the shadow of the bell tower.

People sang. People called to one another from the boats. People who would never have spoken to one another in the street were free to speak to each other, now that the streets were no longer streets. Now that the squares were lakes and the streets had become canals, tributaries of the rivers.

Her father and mother chatted pleasantly with other people as they drifted past, inquiring as to whether there was anyone who needed assistance. And there were people who needed their help: They climbed stairs that emerged from the water, into apartments no Jew had ever set foot in, to take the temperatures of young ladies ensconced in satin bedsheets. To take the pulses of old men in brocade robes who may have owned empires of steel, railroads, but now found themselves trapped in their city apartments by the waters, with a Jewish doctor's fingers at their wrist.

In a drawing room, Neriya and her mother were served tea by a woman so ancient she seemed to be made of the same brittle material as the tea set itself—and spiderwebbed, like it, with the finest cracks. When the woman smiled at Neriya, her mouth flashed with gold. And the sunlight, reflected off the floodwaters below, danced in gold on the ceiling.

The entire city was open to Neriya, and she imagined it would always be this way: that whatever was the reason for the dark coats and closed, masklike faces of the Vilnius before, *this* was the city as it was meant to be. A city where grand marble staircases rose from the water and chandeliers dangled over the drowned furniture of the hotel lobbies. A city where she and her father and mother were welcome everywhere, needed everywhere to take a temperature, stitch a cut hand, bring a child into this magic world. Where people sang at the oars of their boats and waved, and a man balanced on a plank between a boat and a second-floor window, delivering bread.

When the waters receded, it was as if that real city, that real and welcoming Vilnius of blurred and watery edges, was the one submerged. All its wonders flooded by cobblestones and curbs, cornerstones and dark coats, the brass buttons of uniforms. A rising tide of horse manure, suspicious-eyed doormen in blood-colored jackets, the unfriendly stares of the police again on the corners. The inundation of hierarchy and suspicion drowned the Jews and gentiles, the rich and poor, the soldier and the worker, in its choking, unbreathable atmosphere.

The city she had loved lingered awhile in the puddles, and then was gone.

But she could make it appear again over breakfast, return to it again as her father retold it to her.

February 1942

And as they all lay in the dark, she told them the story. The boats drifting along the drowned boulevards. How she looked down into the water and saw fish swimming through the windows of a rich man's carriage beneath her. How a horse swam past, with a young girl riding it. How she saw an entire wooden house floating down the Neris, so complete you expected to see a family seated at the table inside, calmly eating supper.

She told that story until she remembered details she had long forgotten: Her mother trying on a ball gown in a salon, at the insistence of a man in a wheelchair, surrounded by pictures of his dead family. Her father glimpsed through the doorway of a darkened room, holding a man, a stranger until that very hour, as he cried in his arms. And behind the two men, on the bed, white sheets holding the shape of a person.

When Neriya was done telling it, Kezia would ask her questions, find more details to concentrate on. Was there really a man in rubber overalls up to his waist, continuing to staff the half-submerged doors of a grand apartment house? Had there really been a bear in one of the passing rowboats, smartly dressed in a coat and cap, on leave while his master worked the oars? Had there truly been a monkey playing with human children on a balcony so low over the water that it served as a landing stage? A barge from which a string quartet in tailcoats played, drifting past the roof of a drowned gazebo?

Had a man really shown her, in his lightless apartment, how he fed his parrot biscuits from his own mouth, and how the bird then thanked him in three languages?

June 1944

She had fallen from the boat. She had fallen from the boat, that was all. And her father would reach his hand down into the water and save her. Above her, the trees of the boulevard floated past, and she stared past them into the sky.

Papa.

But she had drifted far from the boat. Had drifted and could not move. Had drifted, somehow, out of the city entirely, to a darker place where the current was stronger. Between her and the sky, there was a bird, black and gray, calling to her.

He always makes that same sound when he calls to me. It is the sound I am called in his language. It is my name.

She wanted to reach a hand up to him, but there was no strength left in her.

It was becoming hard for her to think. But she remembered, as she began to sink, and the water closed over her face, the name of her friend.

Buster.

In these last days, my entire life surrounds me. For the first time, my memories of the shtetl have the clarity they had before the war. That fragile world returns, in all its muddy and remote perfection.

I buy chestnuts fresh from the fire on a winter morning, carrying them hot in a cone made from a Yiddish newspaper.

I hurry past the ritual bathhouse and hear the men inside, thwacking each other with birch branches in the steam, laughing.

The crows call overhead. I recognize, among them, the voice of Joseph. I take a chestnut from the cone and set it on a fence post for him.

None of it has happened yet. None of it ever will. The world of my childhood remains unbroken.

And it will remain unbroken forever. Because all times are equally important.

I am there. Exactly as I am here, dying, with the birds

calling all around me. Exactly as I will be, many years from now, a skull no longer carrying worlds inside itself.

These words, carrying worlds, will be found or will be lost forever. But whatever happens to these words, the facts of the shtetl's existence do not change.

What was, is. The past remains whole, in its own eternal moment. The bathhouse remains unburned, somewhere in time.

Somewhere, the seller of chestnuts sings, and is not dead in a ditch from a bayonet blade.

—from *The Autobiography of a Burned Village*

28
KEZIA

November 1971

WHEN NERIYA TOLD HER about Vilnius, and the flood, Kezia had never been to a city. It was hard for her to imagine one.

Would it be like a village, only more compacted, the huts practically on top of one another?

Would it be like a shtetl, only much larger, so that for hours you walked among the low, wooden houses, and where there were two or three tailors there were a hundred? A thousand?

Would the houses be wooden, only many stories high?

No, Neriya had said—though there were wooden houses mixed in, in some neighborhoods, the buildings were mostly of brick and of stone. And they were decorated.

Decorated? Like the sawn-wood decorations of peasant huts?

No, Neriya answered—decorated like temples.

But the temples Kezia had seen were of wood as well. They were the places where the Jews worshipped, that her family had ridden past, or seen across the square as they traded their horses on a bleak market day, as the rabbi held the lips of a mare back and looked at her teeth, before haggling over the price.

So the flood Kezia imagined, when Neriya told the story to them, was far stranger than anything Neriya could have meant. Kezia's flood occurred among crooked wooden houses that towered above the waters. Her flood featured sawn-wood eaves transposed onto dream-towers of stone.

She saw the city for herself in July of 1944. But the city she saw had been smashed by planes and artillery. Its stone walls had been riddled by machine guns. Torn curtains hung in the shattered windows, Red Army tanks ground down its torn streets, piles of broken stone and masonry lay everywhere.

The ruined streets were flooded, but the flood was not of water. It was of soldiers. And of citizens, streaked with dust and grime, shaking the hands of their new "liberators," afraid to look them in the eye.

But because of Neriya, Kezia saw other things here as well, mixed in with the miseries of battle and the crowd.

She saw a boat in which a girl with a parasol trailed her hands in the water. A monkey, playing with children on a balcony. A uniformed bear, drifting in a boat, just above the heads of the soldiers, past the wedding-cake facades of buildings that once were whole and floated in the water like plastered islands.

In the moments when Kezia could raise her head from the wounds that were her work, this was the city she saw.

The city Neriya had gifted her with.

She closed her eyes now and remembered it again. Concentrated, as she often did, on a detail: Neriya's mother, turning in front of a drawing-room mirror in a ball gown.

She knew her face only from a photograph, but she knew more important things about her than that. She knew what kind of person this woman had been. Kezia was there, with Neriya's mother, as surely as Neriya had been there, because it had all been shared with her.

She knew her name: Aderet. And what had happened to Aderet? Kezia did not know. Her husband, Abram, Neriya's father, had told no one anything except that she was "lost."

Lost.

But Kezia had seen, at least, Abram's face as well. Had looked into it, tried to memorize every feature of it, to give it back to Neriya.

Now she found she could remember him too. Could reproduce him, with his arms around another man, comforting him, in a darkened room. Could make Abram flicker into existence.

Even here, in this dacha on the edge of a forest, in a world the man himself had never lived to see, as the day began to fade.

Maybe that was why Kezia was still here: to lend these flickers of existence to the dead. Was that enough?

It might be.

So why did she want, more than anything, it seemed, to put that burden down? And what could it even mean, to put such a thing down?

Innokentiy tapped her on the shoulder and beckoned her to come outside.

They stood together on the porch for several minutes, with their faces turned toward the sky.

At first it was only one or two birds, then several dozen.

It had always amused her and Neriya, the way the crows flew. So awkward, as if they had never been meant to fly. Stumbling through the air, lacking any of the grace of other birds. Lacking, too, the other birds' musicality in their calls. So rudely made and graceless.

There were a dozen of them. Then a hundred. Then the mass of them, loud, hooting and cackling at one another, gossiping and arguing, a city in the air.

Czesław came out as well. The flock grew larger. They darkened the sky, loud and unafraid.

Because they were safe, here. That was it. Generations ago, this flock had given the gift of safety to a few ragged children during the war. Why? Because a little girl was kind to them? Because before her a man on the run, a war veteran looking for a home, had been kind to them?

Or for other reasons, entirely their own?

Whatever the reason, the safety the crows had given to those children was now being returned to them.

Did they even know it? Understand that their world was structured, had been made safe, by this giving and returning? Did they understand why these people here now might care for them?

Not one of these crows had been alive then. Was it passed down to them, somehow?

She did not think so. They were simply here, now. There was a red thread of mutual care, a stitch that ran through it all, but none of them could perceive it.

She thought of what Innokentiy had said about the skull—how eventually the flock forgot its owner, or the purpose of its decoration, and stripped the baubles from its eyes and redistributed them among themselves.

But it wasn't their knowing, or their gratitude, that was important. And it wasn't understanding the crows that was important.

What was important was the fact of their existence. Their thriving. Their safety here, deep in this protected place, where they could nurse their aged and injured, teach their young, make their tools.

Where they could continue to become what they were becoming.

After the last of the straggling crows had wobbled its way through the air above them, Czesław said, "I know that you intend to leave, Kezia. To make an ending here and move on to other things. But . . ."

"I don't intend to leave," Kezia said. "I intend to stay."

ACKNOWLEDGMENTS

When I lived in Ashgabat, Turkmenistan, between the Karakum Desert and the Karakoram mountains, winter was crow season. As the sun set, the crows poured into the city from every direction, in flocks so large they were best measured in the many minutes it took the mass of them to pass overhead. Once the daylight had died, every tree in the city was filled with crows. Their voices were the sound of night's arrival. When I looked out the window of my apartment in a decaying Soviet housing block, the plane trees shuddered and shifted in the dark with their burden of crows.

In Prishtina, Kosovo, crows again dominated the winter city. They took up daytime residence in Arbëria Park, on the hilltop above our house on Ismail Qemali Street. As the sun set, they flew over us, headed to join even larger flocks in the wooded parks of the city center. My daughter, just a toddler when we lived in Kosovo, used to watch with wonder on her face as the crows filled the sky outside our windows.

So much of writing occurs away from the page. Much of the craft is about observance, and I use this word here in all its shifting meanings. It is a constant attentiveness to the world, and to the value of the world. It is the noticing of details. It is an unfailing, active curiosity.

Having spent a lifetime writing, I have also spent a lifetime noticing crows: the crows of Moscow, Bishkek, Kabul, Almaty, Vilnius, and nearly every other place I have lived or traveled. Humans have done an extraordinary amount of damage to the earth, but crows and other corvids have adapted to us, and often thrive within those damaged zones, winding themselves into our lives and into our cultures, fellow travelers in the Anthropocene.

The seeds of what would eventually grow into *Palaces of the Crow* were many. I came across many stories of gift-giving crows leaving trinkets for the humans who fed them. Those stories got me thinking in larger terms about reciprocal behaviors and reciprocal exchanges between animals and humans, and how many mutual ties humans have formed, over the years, with the animals around us—powerful relationships of reciprocity, noticed and unnoticed, in which human society is entangled with the lives of animals.

Soon I was thinking of the constant mentions of crows in our myths and our literature. Of the way they thrive around our conflicts and have for as long as we have been around, hovering eagerly over our battlefields. And so, *Palaces* began its long rhizomatic formation, meshing those early ideas with others until it became a story of crows but also of war, and reciprocity, and the nature of gifts, and our relationships with, and responsibilities to, the animals who live on our damaged peripheries.

In researching the book, I was indebted to many books about crow behavior. As in *The Mountain in the Sea*, I could easily have included footnotes and a bibliography—things that have no real place in a work of fiction. For the study of crows themselves, I read many books, scientific articles, and other accounts, but I was particularly indebted to *Gifts of the Crow: How Perception, Emotion, and Thought Allow Smart Birds to Behave Like Humans*, by John Marzluff and Tony Angell.

I did a good amount of research on the ground in Lithuania itself, in its cities, towns, and forests, but for the history of World War II on the Eastern Front from the point of view of the locals who survived it, I was much indebted as well to Я из огненной деревни (I am from a burned village), an account of survivors of the Nazi occupation of Belarus, by Ales Adamovich, Vladimir Kolesnik, and Yanka Bryl, and to the memoirs of many who survived Nazi occupation in the Baltic and Eastern European forests, in particular *A Partisan's Memoir: Woman of the Holocaust*, by Faye Schulman. In addition to first-person accounts, I read many histories. One that stands out is *"Centuries Will Not Suffice": A History of the Lithuanian Holocaust*, by Prit Buttar, for its clear and uncompromising reporting.

As always, I am deeply grateful to my agent, Seth Fishman, without whom none of my books would have an audience. I am thankful to Sean McDonald, my publisher, for continuing to believe in these stories and help bring them to the world, as well as strengthening them with his editorial suggestions. The assistant editor, Ben Brooks; the production editor, Hannah Goodwin; the designer, Abby Kagan; the managing editor, Debra Helfland; the production manager, Nina Frieman; the jacket designer, Alex Merto; the publicist, Brian Gittis; the copy editor, Dianna Stirpe; and the proofreaders, Chris Peterson and Laura Starrett, were all indispensable to bringing this book into the world. They are a wonderful team. I am very grateful to Dr. Agnieszka Legutko for her review and corrections to the Yiddish text in the book. And once again I feel lucky to have my work graced with a cover by the immensely talented María Jesús Contreras.

My deepest gratitude is to my family: Anya and our daughter, Lydia. Writing is not done in isolation: this kind of extensive, constant work requires an environment of support and community to sustain it. Without their love and caring commitment, none of the books I have written would have been possible. All my books belong to them.

A Note About the Author

Ray Nayler is the author of the novels *Where the Axe Is Buried* and *The Mountain in the Sea*, which won the Locus Award for Best First Novel, and the novella *The Tusks of Extinction*, which won a Hugo Award. Born in Quebec and raised in California, Nayler lived and worked abroad for two decades in Russia, Central Asia, the Caucasus, and the Balkans. He most recently served as international adviser to the Office of National Marine Sanctuaries at the National Oceanic and Atmospheric Administration and was a visiting scholar at the George Washington University's Institute for International Science and Technology Policy. He lives in Washington, DC.